THE LOST TRYST

THE LOST TRYST

A Gothic Supernatural Horror

URSUS ARISTON

Neasperlane Books

ISBN - 13: (978-1-958483-02-2)

ISBN - 13: (978-1-958483-03-9)

Neasperlane Books

https://ursusariston.com

Tule Fog

It happened without warning, not long after the three-vehicle convoy had turned off California Highway 58 and swerved into a dirt road.

Agnes Haskell, who occupied a comfy spot in the Range Rover's back seat, felt a jolt in her chest the moment the lead vehicle plowed into the Central Valley wilderness path enveloped in fog. At once, it turned cold. Into the thick mist, the desert landscapes that would have looked the same across all seasons had disappeared from view. Another truck followed close behind. Up front, a lead work van sped up with caution. Its tail lights oriented her to a road she could barely see. She was no stranger to fogbanks that brings Los Angeles freeway traffic to a crawl. At times, her side hustle required her to take long drives, often alone, as far north as Washington where at certain times of the year zero visibility conditions occur in out-of-the-way places.

Chills happen. This one felt different.

"It's only a weekend and a day," she said to herself, beneath her voice, as the convoy plodded on. With the back of her hand, she wiped the condensation her breath had formed in the window glass. She had been leaning on it for some time while she observed whatever glimpses of the wilderness that the breaks in the fog would allow. The Bureau of Land Management dirt path looked too wide for an off-road track and far too smooth, like it was steamrollered yesterday. No ruts or bumps to wake her employer seated in front of her. At the far end of the bench, across her, the old man's prim-looking executive secretary also had her head pressed against the glass. Dozing, apparently.

Only the driver appeared to be wakeful. The five-hour drive that started before dawn in L.A. had taken its toll on her aging sponsors. Agnes herself struggled to stay awake after the stopover at Bakersfield, the southernmost city in the state's agricultural valley. The city was the closest landmark she had left her neighbor to represent her job's final destination. Tagging it "a relocated house in the middle of nowhere" wouldn't have helped. For insurance, she had texted her neighbor Dr. Caleb Pershing's contact details. Their 72-year-old employer, a Sacramento-based medical supplies tycoon and a regular on Forbes Top 50, wouldn't be difficult to trace in the event of an emergency.

"How far still?" she asked the tall, Middle-Eastern-looking driver whose eyes appeared to be laser-focused on the speeding van ahead.

"No idea, ma'am," he said, after a thoughtful hesitation. "I'm just following the communications van."

"My first time here, too," came Dorothy-Soon Smalls' gruff, early-morning voice. She snapped off her seatbelt and slid to the middle of the bench. Her head craned for a wind-shield view. Agnes figured the dark humps behind the mists that seemed to be drifting from her left to her right must be hill chains that shielded the valley floor from strong winds. Dr. Pershing's aging Korean-American assistant tipped her bifocals. "We can't miss it, I was told. It should be close to the road, on your side."

"This road, how far does it go?"

2

Dorothy flashed a proud grin. "It stops right after where the cleared site is. The BLM never built a road through this pristine valley. We were the first. They gave us permit to build a temporary double-wide path that could accommodate structural house moving rigs."

"Wow. I can just imagine, what a sight it would be, trucking a whole house across highways. Then through this road."

"This is the easy part. Moving the house through city limits, a nightmare. The structural house movers had an engineering team right ahead of them, working the electrical wires, skirting the whole thing through traffic."

"From the house, how far is the nearest town?"

"Our drone surveys showed no other dwellings in the eighteen-square-mile region from the house epicenter. One way in, one way out. After we drop you guys off and we're back on the highway, the BLM rep riding along in the vehicle behind us would set up a barricade at the only entrance to this road."

What difference did a talking head make. The chills diminished. They'd return for sure come séance night. This early, she needed to remind herself that the job would be as strange and personal as any she had consented to for ten of her twenty-eight years on Earth, whenever she allowed spirits gone from earthly life to temporarily inhabit her. Only fellow psychics understood what an intimate contact with the spirit world, at a minimum, entailed.

Fear comes with the territory. An occupational hazard, just like any other.

Nonetheless, she could use a distraction. Chills that drop in without cause would not even hold a candle to the more mundane sort of fear she had experienced just five days ago when Dr. Pershing personally offered her the job and she raised concerns about the arcana that shrouded the project. She recalled how the old man's demeanor fell. Thereafter, he used vague generalizations to dodge issues she brought up.

She thought he would politely escort her out of his office and take his business elsewhere. The eighth-generation Scot-Irish must have ready alternates in his roster. Had she been willing to walk away, she would not just have pressed for more answers. She would also have lobbied for a more balanced upfront fee-to-job completion bonus ratio.

"Where are we?" Dr. Pershing mumbled as if roused from sleep by a speed bump. A tight turn on a hillside slope might have wakened him.

"We're already on our road, sir," Dorothy said.

He removed his circular glasses and wiped his face with a handkerchief. He turned back to Agnes. "How are you doing back there, my dear?" he said, in a gentle, grandfatherly tone. The old man looked dapper and dignified in his white tunic and tan felt hat. His whitened beard was well-trimmed, and his face ruddy and smooth, like an aristocrat who had aged well.

"I'm good, mister Pershing."

"Don't let the Tule fog spook you. Tule, I forgot what it meant. Some Central Valley fog phenomenon. I heard that unlike the Marine layer in L.A., this one could linger. It goes away in its own sweet time. You have the envelope in your purse?"

She nodded and opened her burgundy wallet purse, perfunctorily, as if to check. She obliged Caleb with a glimpse of the green, sealed envelope before she clasped back the wallet close. Besides the envelope, the wallet contained nothing else.

The lead van's brake lights brightened. The sudden rise in the road had forced the lead vehicle to slow down. 8:15 a.m.

To the east, beyond the fog layer, the sun should already be up. The bigger gaps in the mist revealed blips of semi-arid deserts, no different from the familiar chaparral-and-sagebrush counterparts beyond the suburbs of Southern California. Perhaps sunlight had already taken over the valley

4

and it would only be a matter of time before the fog dissipated.

Since they hit the road after the Bakersfield stopover, the tycoon's completion-oriented fee structure intermittently needled in her mind. Building the dirt road and transporting a house from Sacramento to a federally-owned wilderness, must cost a ton of money. She wondered if he had done a background check on her and had subsequently taken advantage of her dire financial situation. In better circumstances, she would have consulted a lawyer first before signing a non-disclosure agreement clipped in a blind assignment where key procedural instructions hid behind a sealed envelope. Yes, the completion bonus he dangled on the contract may be huge. But it could be easily trumped by fine-line conditions in instructions lurking inside the envelope. There has to be a way to even out the deal. Too late. Maybe not.

Up ahead, the silhouette of a tall, boxy structure emerged.

High iron fencing wrapped around what appeared to be a residential compound. An unseen person inside the fence waved an orange-colored torch. The waving light moved outside a front gate and it repeatedly pointed to a spot on the road. As the convoy neared, several incandescent lamps popped up from the structure. Motion sensor lights? Vapory ghost lights streamed through the fog in several directions.

"We're here," Dorothy said. The sports utility vehicle riled up roadside gravel and it stopped a spitting distance from the iron fence.

The house loomed tall from the street, a narrow, two-story one with a high-pitched roof, its long profile obscured by the fog lowering behind it. Spindly wooden supports, like straightened insect legs, buttressed it from two sides. The motion sensor lights died.

The house could be Victorian in design. Its Bristol-blue, wood-cladding appeared to be in various stages of disrepair and the roof leaned forward. She rolled down the window.

The early morning air brought in the scent of moist, dry shrubs and of wet soil.

Agnes realized the on-and-off motion sensor lights has been washing out from the view the façade's true form. As the natural light penetrated the haze, uncanny details emerged.

No part of the house tipped in the conventional sense. She had to stick her head out to make sure an optical illusion wasn't in the mix. The entire façade—from the twin porch posts to the high-pitched roof—was warped in an inward bow shape, the deepest bulge occurring on the second floor, with the attic gable's distortion most pronounced. As if the façade personified a punched-in-the-gut loony toon character. Dim interior lights barely shone from the odd-shaped sash windows. A small dormer window peered out from the gable, a spot it traditionally shouldn't be built into. Could she be staring at an eerie, post-modernist architect's surrealist interpretation of Salvador Dali's art?

Through one of the twin Sash windows on the second level, Agnes could make out shadows, stirring about.

The car doors slammed behind her. The driver and Dorothy rounded the car from opposite directions. Almost at the same time, they opened the right-side doors. The driver helped Caleb with his walking cane and footing, while the surprisingly nimble Dorothy held the door open for her, like a prim VIP usher—chin up, eyes straight ahead, one hand showing the way.

Scooting her way out, Agnes caught sight of two men at a second-floor window, staring straight down into the new arrivals. The gray mists have given way to whiter ones. The creeping fog also hugged the ground low that the people inside the house looked much clearer. She assumed they were her fellow weekenders with whom she had to spend three days and three nights completely off the grid.

On the window, a well-dressed, light-haired Caucasian, old enough to pass off as Caleb's contemporary brother, averted his gaze when they made eye contact. The shorter, stockier man beside him, with a wide face and a prominent jawline, continued to look at her.

It was time to pounce at it before she chickened out. Agnes intentionally held a long gaze at the house's porch before she backed inside the car.

Dorothy must have observed her reaction. She lowered to the door opening and glared at her. "You okay?" She looked quickly toward the house porch's direction, and just as quickly snapped a stare back at her. Agnes made sure she retained the same expression of alarm on her face.

Caleb stuck his face into the vehicle's other window, his bulging eyes a mirror of Dorothy's. "Agnes, anything wrong?"

From that point on, backpedaling was out of the question. Agnes hunched over her clasped hands as she tried to hide her face. She had never wheedled her way to a better deal on an assignment before. She always charged clients a flat fee regardless of how long the séance sessions went. She took tips and never had the nerve to cadge for them. As if an opportunity had presented itself and that she couldn't resist it.

Whatever alarmed Dorothy had surely affected Caleb. Their eyes spoke volumes.

"I understand you've never had an assignment like this one before," Caleb said. "I assure you this. We've spared no expense to guarantee your safety and that of your companions. Your colleagues, above all, are vetted."

Procrastination would only trip her. She went for it and buried her face in her hands. "I'm so sorry mister Pershing, miss Smalls. I'm sure you have other suitable replacements on your list."

"It's daytime. What is it, really?" Dorothy said, a tinge of impatience in her voice.

Too far into the charade to back out now. She realized she need not act at all. Her misgivings about her own impromptu ploy totally consumed her and she didn't need a mirror to know how she came across to her sponsors. With the odd light patterns around her and her onlookers' acute viewing positions, neither Caleb Pershing nor Dorothy Smalls would have been able to glean insincerity in her facial expression. Besides, they shouldn't be able to distinguish someone else's reaction to a spirit presence from the sort of fear that stemmed from an opportunist's self-doubts as she gambled her way to a once-in-a-lifetime payday. What she needed to say next had to be believable: "I don't know. I can't explain it."

"Explain what?" Dr. Pershing asked.

"The feeling, like... like that of dread."

"C'mon, my dear. You do this for a living. You have trustworthy people to see you through the weekend."

It took a while for Agnes to muster the courage and drop the hammer. "I'm sorry, sir, ma'am. I want to go home."

Dr. Pershing gestured something to his secretary and the two stepped away toward the vehicle's hood.

Agnes checked if the two men were still looking out from the house's second-floor window. They haven't moved since she saw them last. They shouldn't be able to hear their conversation from that distance. Both men spoke low and looked at her time and again. None of them must be aware she might have staked not just her gig but theirs as well. Early December and she could use a Christmas bonus. Or pretty much forfeit a chunk of what she already had in the bag. Too late, even for regrets. She had crossed the bridge and had already thrown a hand grenade behind her. Everything was off her hands now.

2

Warped Wood

Ian rubbed his palm on the black oak log post that bent outward, its form following the bashed-in front wall's shape. The wood's patina, texture, and scent suggested he was dealing with a completely organic substance. *Something's not right.* The foreboding afterthought would be an understatement. The meticulous restoration job evident in the second level's front wall alone showed that the house's owners spared no expense in shoehorning wood and glass elements into window frames that had buckled. The sculptural way the log twisted about and the concave shape of the front wall elements, along with the corresponding reshaping of the house façade, could only mean the house itself underwent progressive distortion by some force beyond his layman know-how.

No way corner log posts of that length and shape could have been insinuated into the interior. The four similarly warped posts must have been upright once upon a time. From its ground-floor anchors, the single post he has been examining had shot through a second-floor cavity, and it screwed its way straight through the ceiling and the adjacent attic floor. A cursory check upstairs earlier revealed the missing end segment of the log post. It had broken through the wood planks like a mushroom through a forest floor, with the stem fused to the material around it.

Through a gashed hole on the second floor, the log post shared access with a ground-to-attic iron staircase. Whatever forces threw the façade elements out of whack and had created the scraggly, driftwood-like quality of the log post, totally baffled him.

Just as awestruck was Christopher Castro, the self-confessed all-around handyman and construction hobo and the closest the team could pass off as a residential architecture expert. He has been surveying the ballet dance floor since they had stepped into the second floor. His eyes always held the same stark expression, somewhere in between bewildered and spooked. The man in his early-20s paced aimlessly around the erstwhile dance facility. Faint light started to stream in from three narrow sash windows to the west side of the floor, casting glints through vapor wisps that has been seeping like tentacles through the windows and into the interior.

At the second floor's far south end, an identical iron staircase provided access to all levels. It also rose straight up from a hole in the floor and shared space with a corner post. There were clear signs that one south-side log post, bowed like the one he has been examining, had ripped floor and ceiling sections and that the damage had been repaired.

The wild-haired, clean-shaven third rail in their party, tool bag around his waist, circled about the dance floor center. He intently observed an area of smooth, age-darkened hardwood floor.

"What's your overall impression," Ian said, "about the integrity of the house?"

Christopher regarded him with a glazed, distracted look as if he still processed his question. Finally, he nodded. "Everything looked structurally sound, sir."

"That's comforting to know."

"The repair work is solid. I wouldn't be able to patch this house up even if I had the tools."

Ian couldn't forgo his old habit of assessing every new people he meets. Even before Christopher admitted he knew nothing about residential solar battery repair and maintenance, Ian had already considered the young man's credentials too thin to interest a billionaire like Caleb Pershing. His look, along with the confidence he projected, placed him in the mold of day workers that hang out in *Home Depot* parking lots. Should he ring up a handyman listed at a laundry room cork board, the typical fellow who'd come knocking at his door just might look like him.

Christopher's inclusion into the team also goaded him to look inward. He speculated on the standards by which Dr. Pershing had chosen him for the job. His psychology credentials didn't even have a tangential relation to his special ability as a retro-cognitive dream clairvoyant. Dr. Pershing had explicitly hired him for that gift alone, a gift that should have come across as professionally unimpressive since he hadn't been out there consistently enough to be sought out and vetted by any psychic organization. Not once did he ever collaborate with another psychic on the same project. Was he a substitute for a more stellar candidate who called in sick? Did they peep into his financial records and opted for someone whose cooperation could be easily bought?

"I've never seen anything like this, sir," Christopher continued. "I've done a lot of odd construction work for my uncle. He's unlicensed like me. I've never done any project from foundation laying to the finish. Maybe that's why I can't make sense of the sort of repair work done here."

"I didn't hear a thing or two about what you just said. Your credentials, it's none of my business. You're an associate; you're part of the team. That simple."

"What if she asks me—"

"You won't get asked if you behave like you're one of us.

Everything I know about you, you volunteered. Act like you know more than what you actually do. We know little about your trade anyway."

"Gotcha, sir."

"The sirs and ma'am's, too, drop them."

Christopher showed a coy grin. "Got it, loud and clear, mister Bishop."

"That's what I wanted to hear."

He observed Christopher rubbing the tip of his tennis shoes on the wood floor, at the strange squiggles under the wood surface. The flat, smooth timber grain suggested that whatever forces that structurally deformed the house had spared the dance floor surface. The shiny, dark-brown patina on the wood surface as well as the musty scent the place gave out suggested that most of the materials from the original floor were retained.

Christopher lowered to his knees and rubbed a floor spot with his fingers.

"Anything wrong with the floor?"

"No, mister Bishop. There are lots of warped wood pieces like that one all over. In my other gigs, I've seen old wood warped by heat or damaged by water. They don't remain flat, like the ones on this floor."

Ian paused and canted his ears towards the open window up north, from where the faint rumble of vehicles came from. Soon after, he tipped up his glasses, stooped, and observed the undulating wood lines that formed wave-like patterns. From any angle, it was indeed as flat as any decent dance floor. "Amazing. No cracking. No stains or bumps. My wife once got me hooked on ballroom dancing. I bet this floor is so smooth I can put on dance shoes, turn off the light, and dance my way all over here without tripping."

"The warping must have opened gaps on the floor, sir. New wood was added to the gaps as fillers. Then they were sanded flat and varnished. The warping happened in so many different places and yet none of the wood cracked." He picked something from his tool bag, a laser level, turned it on, and laid it flat on the floor. A red laser dot appeared on a spot at the far south end wall. He turned the tool around one-hundred-eighty degrees and the red dot reappeared on the opposite wall. He stood up and pocketed the laser level. "Yes, sir. Perfectly flat, point-to-point. The house's forward lean didn't even affect it."

"I've lived in six homes before. I've never encountered a household structural problem that both my handyman and I couldn't explain."

The incoming vehicles stopped roadside. The motion-sensor lights lit up, revealing denser mists from the windows licking into the room. Heavy car doors opened and closed. Trucks, he guessed.

"She's here, finally, our meal card," Ian motioned for Christopher to follow him. "It's just a figure of speech. Don't give that idle comment much thought. Though it's kind of true, that without the psychic lady both of us would only be as good as furniture. Please, don't tell her that."

At the north front wall, Ian pushed the half-open, oddly-angled sash window as far up as he could. He pushed hard against the sill. Rock solid, indeed.

Across the front yard's iron fence, he spotted Dr. Pershing outside a Range Rover. A well-dressed Asian woman held the rear door open for someone still inside. The next moment, he was eyeball-to-eyeball with a young woman whose first order of business, it seemed, was to check out her weekend residence. The key member of the team, he heard, juggles two jobs—as a psychic medium on the lesser end, and a boutique bookstore owner on the other.

She poked herself out of the door for a few seconds before she pulled back in.

Despite the distance and given the brief time he was able to look at her, Ian still felt sure of his impression of Agnes

Haskell as a person of above-average beauty. Her lush, well-behaved hair framed a heart-shaped face with such a light complexion the dark of her eyes and her thin-set brows might as well be charcoal drawings on blank white paper. The expression in her large eyes, though, he wasn't sure if they were inquisitive or intimidating. The moment their eyes made contact he blinked first. As he looked away, he caught Christopher's fixed-as-a-bayonet gaze at her, his mouth partly open, his expression mesmerized.

3

Weekenders

Dr. Pershing and company had departed unceremoniously by the time they were called down for the rest of their sign-up fee's official bank funds transfer. The old man and his crew left behind the white van that came with a disc antenna on its roof, along with its driver and an African-American techie guy bearing an active laptop. The psychic medium, after the pre-landing hold-up, must have already signed up ahead of them.

The three-way team member introductions outside the lot got interrupted when Agnes, after requesting and getting handed a pen and notepad by a crew person, rushed back to the relocated residence's porch-shaded door. It was the same spot where Ian had observed her earlier, scrutinizing the numbers scrawled by the door side.

Three hours before, shortly after he arrived at the house, Ian likewise jotted down on his pocket notebook the place's presumed address:

121296.

Had they been allowed to keep a cell phone he would have taken a snapshot of the strange inscription on the cladding. The fuzzily inscribed numbers, each one about two-by-three inches in size, appeared to have been painstakingly etched with the help of some precision-type blowtorch. Burn marks had seared through the old paint and the weather-beaten wood, leaving deep, dark, barely legible lines that could be seen, but couldn't be read, from the road.

"Miss Haskell had already signed up," the jolly-sounding African-American techie guy told him and Christopher. He turned the active laptop around and showed both men the screen. He handed the laptop and a digital pen to Ian. "I need your electronic signatures on the space under your respective names." The man plucked off a satellite phone from a belt clip. "Afterwards, mister Bishop, mister Castro, you may confirm the deposits through your online accounts, either using this phone or that computer."

Ian signed up after a quick read. He re-reads the middle portion of the electronic banking page:

For Direct Deposit, December 10, 2026.
Ian Bishop: 95,000 USD.
Christopher Castro: 65,000 USD.
Agnes Haskell: Wired.

He felt the smile on his face drop. In the ten or fifteen minutes when Agnes, the Asian lady, and Dr. Pershing fell into a huddle around the Range Rover, he overheard talks that sounded like renegotiations, about Agnes Haskell's sign-in fee.

He showed Christopher, who seemed to be unsure how to position himself in the situation, where to sign.

———

AS THE WHITE van roared off into the thinning fog, Ian saw Agnes running through the side of the road, toward the vehicle, her eyes aghast, her long, fluffy, jet-black hair flying behind her.

"What the hell," she said, as she stopped and watched the van's lights disappear. She headed back toward Ian. "Would anyone come back to show us around?"

"That would be my job." Ian approached and reached out. "Ian Bishop."

Agnes pressed his hand, her eyes still in the direction of the vanishing van. "Agnes Haskell. Pleased to meet you."

"Likewise." He grabbed his reticent partner and yanked him close. "Christopher Castro here, the other member of our weekend team."

Agnes, apparently still distracted by the sudden shift in the status quo, pressed Christopher's hand even more briefly. She did have a distant air about her. On closer look, her sullen eyes came off as dark, inaccessible, guarded. She wore a long, gray dress, a dark jacket over it, matching winter beanie on top. They stood on level ground and she wore flats. And yet she stood nearly as tall as he is. Five-foot-ten, he guessed, making poor Christopher inches shorter than her.

"Doctor Pershing handpicked Chris for his all-around expertise on house matters. The whole book. The boy's got it."

"I'm also in charge of the pantry, ma'am," he said, a slight tremor in his voice. He kept his arms behind his back. "I'd be cooking for all of us, too."

Ian blurted a laugh. "It so happened our technical guy can also cook. As far as our employers are concerned, why not."

Agnes regarded them with a full smile, for the first time. She slapped her arms to her sides. "So, this is us."

"Yes. The diminishing tail lights you were chasing after earlier, just made that fact official."

"I was hoping Doctor Pershing would be around during the introductions, to the house. I have questions he didn't answer yet."

"They shipped Chris and me to this place several hours ahead of you. Pershing's people had walked us around inside the house and its vicinity sufficiently enough. We'd be doing the introductions to the entire place for you." He walked into the front gate and held it open. "After you, miss Haskell, mister Castro."

The two filed in. Ian secured the security door with a combination lock the size of a Hockey Puck. He raced after Agnes and Christopher who had already headed to the west side of the house. Agnes, on a good stride, took the lead.

"What are those wooden supports for?" she asked. Her gaze shifted to Chris. "This house, does it have problems?"

"Uh—"

"It's just for insurance," Ian jumped through Christopher's hesitation. "We're in the middle of a valley. High winds, you know."

A cold breeze passed. Agnes pulled down her beanie to cover her ears. She wrapped her arms against herself. Even as the sun rose steadily east and above the distant hills, the fog still hung low and the damp cold of the night lingered.

"Can we head in, now?"

"Let us walk you through the site, first. It won't take long."

Agnes winked a smile and nodded.

"After you," Ian said, showing the way to the shadowy west side of the house. Christopher followed behind her. Ian pointed in the direction of two trucks and a van parked at the far west end of the lot, their rear ends perpendicular to the house. "The film crew props trucks and other vehicles, to the left. To the far corner, a water tank truck."

Barely reacting, Agnes marched on in double steps. He assumed she must have been briefed well during the trip, about their doubling as faux house-sitters for a fake, on-location film set, on the outside chance the site gets a visit from the wildlife office. During his interview with Dr. Pershing, he told him that his corporation's dummy production company named Spiker Incorporated had secured a seven-day documentary shooting permit. He also assured him that with a BLM officer contracted to watch the team's back from the highway, the possibility anyone would come knocking over the weekend is virtually nil.

Agnes ducked under the elevated underfloor space of the house, practically an open utility crawlspace. Air currents liberally flowed through the space, accompanied by faint whistling sounds. She squatted and surveyed the exposed foundations that rested on twelve steel piers.

Christopher, in a cavalier fashion, monkey walked the packed-earth ground, along the way tapping his knuckles on modular plastic cover units that sealed the house's sensitive electrical components. "Solar batteries, cables, and wirings." He pointed at several other spots in the underbelly. "They're all tamper proofed. Though I can remove access panels if they needed service." He then leads her attention to a warren of overhead PVC pipes and other conduits of different sizes. The largest pipes took a diagonal path into the ground before they crept out of the underfloor space and continued to a wheeled service platform a stone's throw from the house. A cluster of large tanks sat atop the platform. Christopher got her attention to the conduit and pipework systems that she didn't seem to notice any of the four log post stumps sticking out of the underfloor corners, as if they were uprooted from a foundation.

She emerged at the house's east side. Ian and Christopher caught up. "Our sewage and water over there. Propane tanks, too."

On the east side of the lot, Agnes stared at two stainless steel water trucks that straddled the length of the house, their rear on the inside.

"Film shoot support equipment," Ian said. "I was told. What else can I say? Our employers did put on some serious show."

"Where are the solar panels?"

"Outside the south side fence. Power lines go on conduits underground and feed the batteries during the day."

"How do they work on foggy conditions as this?"

"I was told they had deployed enough solar arrays to power three homes. Which means, working as a unit, our solar arrays can juice up its batteries even under overcast conditions. Even with fog, I'd presume."

"We do have diesel generator backup," Christopher said. "In case nothing else works."

"Anything else you'd like to show me?"

"That's pretty much it. Oh, one last thing," Ian pointed north and led the march back to the front gate. "We're almost full circle. We have two other fence gates, one in the south, and the other behind the prop truck west of the house. Each service gate opens on the same combination lock number. Both of you, burn the number three-one-seven to memory."

"Three-one-seven," she repeated.

At the gate, Christopher manipulated the combination. A click. The lock opened. He closed it back.

She peered through the narrow gaps in between the vertical fence bars, to a trench outside that runs alongside the fence line. "Drainage?"

"No," Ian said. "They dug a trench all around the property to keep rattlesnakes out from the site."

"Rattlesnakes don't climb," Christopher added.

"It's three feet deep and vertical to our side, and slanted the other way. Any snake that wanders by has no choice but to slither back to where it came from."

"I thought rattlesnakes hibernate this time of the year."

"I know. What else can I say? Our employers overthink every possibility."

Agnes made an emphatic sigh of relief. A smile followed. "It's nice to know they got that one covered. I love to take morning walks."

Ian locked stares with Christopher while Agnes surveyed the house's façade. Ian frowned at him as he made a subtle head shake. After they had stepped into the house, it would be likely three days later before they'd be able to step out into the open again. Dr. Pershing's people must not have clarified to her when the official lockdown would be and what the lockdown parameters exactly were. Or maybe they already did.

He led the way to the front porch.

Ian himself had trouble comprehending why the house itself, not the lot it stood on, would need to be locked down. The interlocked iron bars were high and pointed. Add a high-voltage connection to it and the compound would be a fortress. During his pre-employment interview, he didn't question the lockdown protocols because he had set his heart firmly on the low-hanging prize Dr. Pershing had dangled before him. He simply wrote off his doubts to the cost-of-doing-business ledger. What could go horribly wrong in an allegedly haunted house? He never believed in ghosts anyway. They can dance around him for all he cared. No problem to him double-daring the house's resident spirit. By an order of magnitude, he feared debt collectors and IRS agents more.

He jiggled the doorknob another time before he referred the holdup to Christopher. "Did you lock it from the inside?"

"I swear I didn't, sir."

He looked at Agnes who promptly shook her head.

"The keys?" Agnes said.

"They didn't leave us any," Ian replied, as he wrenched the brass knob harder. "The keyholes don't work and entry doors can only be locked from the inside."

He stepped back for the young man who gave the knob a two-handed push-and-pull. He tried several times, along with clockwise and counter-clockwise motions.

"If nothing works," Ian said. "You can pry the door open, right?"

Christopher backed away. "I left the tools inside, sir."

With their cell phones and personal effects sequestered by their employers, Ian realized the only way to get in is to break one of the two house doors down.

As Christopher pulled back to give the door posts a look, Agnes took over his space. Fists to her waist, she examined the ancient, solid-looking door. She gave it a token kick. "We'd need a battering ram to bring this one down." She jiggled the door knob.

A click.

She laid a blank stare to him and to Christopher as she pushed the door open.

4

Creaks and Skirts

The craftsman bungalow Christopher's parents once owned should have less square footage than the strange house's ground floor. Yet their old home in East L.A. looked more spacious, thanks to its squarish open plan design, the large picture windows for the sun to shine through, and the many common spaces that interconnect so well that whomever you couldn't see, you would sooner or later hear from. Though he had no idea who once lived in the weird house relocated in the middle of nowhere, as soon as he stepped into the foyer early in the morning, it overtook him, a smothering feeling the place's previous inhabitants left unhappy memories there.

At a glance from the front door foyer, everything about the interior looked long and narrow. It didn't help that the living room's pine floorboards were reddened by age and that the cold, blue-green wallpapers reminded him of molds. The two Colonial-era designed furniture sets gave the impression of swap meet finds thrown in there just to make the general area appear properly furnished.

The upgrades didn't look well-planned either. The main entrance door that swings in rightwards blocked the iron spiral staircase step up. Further to the right, flush against the east wall, was a very steep cedar staircase without a half-landing. A store room occupied the under-stairs space, and the entire structure rested on the part of the front wall that bore traces a fireplace was once built into it.

From the living room, three adjacent rooms on the right lined a third of the house's length. Room row just left enough space for a narrow hallway that runs parallel to it. The hallway through view also linked the living space and the kitchenette at the house's far south end. A hallway restroom served as a divider between the first two rooms.

Opposite room row to the west is a plain, structural wall. The tiny casement windows are situated high up the wall that one needed to be up a step ladder to gain a porthole-like view to the outside.

There really wasn't much to introduce Agnes to. Maybe that was how Ian made it to be, given the savory scent of food that has been coming from the kitchen-dining area since they had stepped into the house. Dr. Pershing's people had left them a hot meal packed inside several insulated packages. The short tour, entirely presided over by Ian, ended in the kitchen. He came close to gathering everyone to say grace when Agnes countered him. She insisted they needed to clear the area of waylaid groceries and other supplies, first.

Boxes of fruits and vegetables, fresh-smelling bread in bins, bagged snacks, and beverage crates scattered about. A neat freak. The thought came to mind, regarding Agnes. He didn't mind it at all, both the chores at hand and her house-keeping attitude. Just as her mother would put it, first things first. Putting stuff away before a big, well-deserved lunch, came across to him as the team's first act of cooperation.

"Chris, what do you think?" Ian said as he lined up boxed pears, apples, and bananas on random spots along the L-shaped, tiled countertops. "Do we have enough to last the weekend or not?"

He laughed, as he crushed empty cartons on the floor with

his work boots. "Looks more like two weeks, sir." He collected empty grocery bags and assorted flattened boxes. For the moment he dumped them on the side of the trash chutes at the kitchen's northeastern corner.

"You can start prepping our lunch," Agnes said, coldly, as she pointed at him from over her shoulder without as much as a token glance. She busied herself working at the full-size refrigerator unit. She shoved in egg packages, cold cuts, and packaged vegetables.

He grabbed a table knife and started to cut away the tape seals on a foam-insulated container's lid. As he worked on the rest of the other similar containers at the round, cherry-top dinner table, he observed around him and decided the kitchen-dining area should be the happiest spot in the house. An orange pendant lamp hangs above the foursome dining table. A similar ceiling unit lit up the tiled, rectangular kitchen island. The first-class stainless-steel gas range and a big dishwasher gleamed in the light.

To Agnes' right side stood an open pantry and next to it, a tall, glass, china cabinet. To the remaining wall space to her left, an industrial chest freezer and another open-shelf pantry. The kitchen-dining zone shared a wall with the master bedroom.

Putting away groceries was a chore he grew up on. When his parents arrived from their weekly grocery runs, the kids helped stow away stuff. The goods that came out of the bags were never this much. He saw Ian plop on the shelves expensive-looking boxed chocolates he once saw in boutique magazine ads in the Italian restaurant he once worked for. They were the kind of chocolate he didn't even imagine he would ever receive as a Christmas gift. It must be the reason why he felt light as he rushed through the chores. Plenty, it was new to him.

"All perishables, and the grapes and the berries," Agnes

said, as she continued her fridge handiwork, "bring them here."

Steam rose from the insulated foam. He uncapped one stainless-steel food container. The Seafood Risotto's aroma escaped. He closed the lid back quickly.

Directly across from him, Agnes bent to reach down from inside the fridge. His eyes caught the back of her legs as her skirt pulled up. He glanced at Ian who remained busy emptying boxed fruit near the sink counter. He wouldn't dare check her out in any situation he'd put himself at risk. He indulged himself another look, a quick one, at the pair of long, smooth-looking, well-shaped legs.

During Ian's speedy house tour, Christopher recalled Ian pointing out to Agnes where micro-video cameras were placed, at least one wide-angle lens in every common area in the house. They were tiny cameras hidden somewhere in the ceiling trim. One wouldn't see them without being told where they exactly were. He learned that Pershing's people had already told Ian, even before he got there, that the closed-circuit units record round the clock, purely for documentation purposes. They pick up no sound and the footage heads straight to a master hard drive unit somewhere on the premises. He recalled that the camera at the kitchen dining zone was right up behind him.

For sure, God wouldn't mind him taking another glance.

A crate box struck the floor heavily. His shoulders jumped. Ian had dropped one and apples scattered in every direction.

Two of them rolled under the dining table. "I got these, sir."

He went on all fours under the table. He grabbed one. The other continued to roll toward Agnes' heels. The apple stopped short. He was starting to back out from under the table when the hem of her skirt started to rise, very slowly. At first, he thought his eyes were playing tricks on him. As he looked on, the back of her skirt rose higher. He felt a sudden pressure in his head, like it was getting larger. He froze.

Then her skirt went up fast, all the way up.

Agnes shrieked. Chris hits his head under the table. He backed away and emerged at the far end. On his feet, he saw Agnes' dagger stare locked at him.

"What are you doing? How dare you."

"I was going for the apples. I swear I didn't touch your skirt."

Agnes marched away heavily towards the master bedroom, her eyes hard on him. "You keep away from me, okay?"

The door slammed.

Christopher's hands dropped on the table as if energy had left him at once and he needed to support himself to keep from tipping over.

Creaks crackled from the floor and elsewhere. A serious misunderstanding just occurred and he barely noticed the predictable phenomena.

A your-word-against-mine situation loomed. He looked behind him, up the ceiling trim where a mute witness might eventually absolve him. Then there was Ian, though he was sure he didn't witness the incident.

"My eyes were elsewhere," Ian said, as he surveyed the gap between the dinner table and the fridge. He stood where Agnes once was. "I need a straight answer. Did you touch her skirt?"

"No, sir. I swear on my life. I was under the table and…"

"Stay here. I'll go talk to her."

⊏⊐

CHRISTOPHER HAD the table set up for lunch by the time Ian and Agnes emerged from the master bedroom. Soon after, the two took their places around the table. About ten minutes ago, after some restless pacing, he decided he wouldn't skip the opportunity to make an impression. What had happened couldn't be changed. He must stop sulking. He laid out a three-plate china setting, cutlery on their proper spots in the placemats, and the seven hot dishes on porcelain servers. Even then, the incident continued to bog down his spirits. He couldn't believe how things went south for him that early in the weekend.

Everyone settled on their spots, eyes anywhere but on each other. Ian, a Catholic like him, led a short, before-meal prayer. The utensils tinkled thereafter. Everyone reached for the nearest serving spoon.

"I'm sorry, guys," Agnes said. "I spoke out of turn. Maybe too soon."

Christopher nodded. "Okay, we're cool here. But I need to put it out there, I was too far away to reach your skirt."

"I must be imagining things then," Agnes said, sarcasm in her tone.

"I thought I already made myself clear," Ian told Agnes. "I heard a shriek, followed by a bump under a table. I looked. You spun around, and I saw no Chris retreating back under the table. I'm not taking sides. I'm not sweeping this incident under the rug, either."

"He could have used a stick."

Christopher imagined that this must be how it would feel to have a heart attack. He felt a heavy pressure in his chest, a sudden stiffening in his jaws such that he'd be hard put to say anything even if he had the right words to spit out at that moment.

It happened again, the creaking wood, the vibrating objects. He can tell when one is coming. He was about nine then. People who had observed and who heard of the phenomenon wondered if the home he lived in was haunted. He was the person a visiting psychic once said, who caused things to move.

Belatedly, the empty porcelain coffee cups also clattered. His companions took notice.

Agnes' eyes bulged. "Is that a quake?"

"Winds," Christopher said. "The house is too tall for its width. Then there's the temporary foundation we're sitting on."

Many windows were partly open for ventilation. The cookstove extractor fan system connects to the outside. The pressure created by wind gusts slamming against the back of the house could cause the iron spiral staircase beside the kitchen door to vibrate. Outside disturbances could radiate into the house and be interpreted as tremors. There are many other possibilities.

He couldn't tell them, the same way he couldn't tell people other than his immediate family, about what her mother used to call his "incurable childhood ailment." He survived Typhus when he was eight. From then on, family members observed random objects move, floorboards creak, and glasses vibrate, whenever he got scared. All his life, he tried to make it happen —to deliberately make objects move. He could not. As in everything else, he was a flop, as his older brother puts it. He preferred his mother's version better: it was neither a gift nor a nuisance. Just an ailment, period.

"It's not like I had my back completely turned," Ian was on it again, still on his side, to his great relief. "Stick or no stick, my peripheral vision would have caught Chris's daring feat if he did it." He dabbed a forefinger to Agnes. "You felt it." Then just as swiftly he re-aimed his finger at him. "And you saw it. So, what are we missing?"

"Sir, I'm sure Agnes' hands were both inside the fridge when it happened."

"We can rule it out then, Agnes making this whole thing up."

"How could you even think I had set someone up? What would my motive be?"

Ian closed his eyes tight as he sucked in his breath as if he restrained a comeback. "Behind every crime, there are three things we need to look into—motive, means, and opportunity. Chris neither had the means nor the opportunity. Agnes, no motives. Chris saw both your arms working the fridge, and I saw no Chris, with or without a magician's stick, reaching out or pulling back in. Again, what the hell are we missing?"

Agnes turned to him, just when he was shoveling it in. "Okay, what is the color of my underwear?"

Christopher pretended to be in deep thought as he swallowed hard to clear his airway. "Light blue, I think."

Agnes stared at him for a long second.

"Agnes?" Ian said.

She dropped her utensils. "Again, my apologies. I realized it now. A stick job is plain ridiculous. Chris would have to be right behind me for him to have lifted my skirt that high. But in that theoretical situation, for him to see under my skirt, he needed to squat while still holding up my skirt."

"We have a ghost here?" Christopher said. "What if someone got murdered here? Shouldn't they have told us that?"

"What did Pershing's people really tell you," Ian said, "on the nature of this project?"

"Not much. They said I'd be assisting a psychic who'd try to communicate with someone from the afterlife. They said our team's base had to be as far away from civilization as possible. I wasn't told the house is really haunted." He couldn't admit to them he had ignored Dorothy Small's mention of the otherworldly aspects of the job because he grew up not taking ghosts and spirits seriously. His ailment caused things to move and vibrate. Anywhere he went, he was the ghost.

"Relax," Agnes said.

Christopher could swear he heard a scoff under her breath. She stared at him with her dark, soul-probing eyes, like he was her slave. He wished she simply straightened, folded her arms, and looked elsewhere like some homeowners do to erring household help while they tell them off.

"You know what my profession is and the kind of work expected of me and my assistants. You signed up for it. Ghost or without ghost, we're in this together and we're working for what we got paid for."

Christopher raised both hands shoulder-high, quickly. "Sorry, guys. I didn't give the job description much thought. The good pay must have gotten into my head. Anyway, regardless of what I've missed during my briefing, I'm all in."

"Good."

"Now that we got that skirt-raising controversy and Christopher's misgivings out of the way," Ian told Agnes. "Would you tell us now, what spooked you before you stepped out of Doctor Pershing's truck?"

He could tell, from Ian's posture and his tone, that the subject matter had radically changed. She continued eating, unmindful of the people looking at her.

"You held out until they forked out for you an additional one-hundred grand."

Agnes dropped hammered fists on the table. "How did you know that? Do you guys have a back channel to Doctor Pershing? You guys eavesdropping on—"

"You know where we were then. I have good ears. I can read lips. Regardless, let me rephrase my question. What scared you enough to back out from the deal—presentiments? A presence? Paranormal activity, I believe, occurs only after dark. Apparently, something took an early fancy on your skirt."

"When I arrived, I sensed nothing. I saw nothing. What you saw back there, it was an act."

"Oh, I see. You gambled your gig as well as ours."

"It's called calculated risk. Their project involved enormous logistics. They let me go and their project is toast."

"What about us?" Christopher said. "You got nothing for us?"

"What else can I say. I'm selfish. I should have pushed my luck and negotiated something for people I haven't even met."

"Great. Maybe we should begin the day dividing our food supply."

The chair scraped the floor. Agnes stormed away. He regretted his reaction, all too late.

The pendant lights flickered once.

"Agnes, get back here."

Ian's voice came loud and commanding, his forefinger punching at the tabletop. She stopped dead in her tracks.

"We're all going to finish this meal. We all hit reset. No one apologizes. Come back, sit down."

She returned to her seat. She continued eating, an impatient sigh on her breath. Dead silence thereafter.

"After this meal, we hit the ground running. Work."

"I thought that would be for tonight, sir," Christopher said.

"This whole affair, hodgepodge. Let's all admit it. We took the bait they dangled on us because the rewards are too great for what they required from us. For the first order of business, then, we need to know what they really required from us." He stared at Agnes. "I was told it is in an envelope, with you."

"After you tell me what a lockdown means. I asked you earlier. You brushed it off."

"No, I did not. I just got distracted."

"What is it then?"

"Lockdown is the exact time we lock ourselves in this residence. From that point on, we remain locked in this place, until the pick-up day. It may have a sinister ring to it but it's a simple, security precaution. Come lockdown, doors and windows would be electronically secured. Should anyone from inside or from outside attempt to mess with the barriers or tamper with the locks, a two-way alarm would alert us and

Doctor Pershing's people of the breach. Like I said earlier, worst-case scenario, we have a satellite phone stashed somewhere. Now, on how we activate the lockdown, Christopher would, at a later time, do us the honors."

She said, "Why haven't we gotten there already—the lockdown?"

"We go on lockdown after you had opened the envelope and we all read the official instructions on this project. I was told this morning that the envelope was entrusted to you."

Agnes shook her head while she displayed an enigmatic smirk. "Hodgepodge, you said. I don't think so. Our sponsors know what they're doing."

"It's too early to call them out on anything."

"I was told that I may open the envelope once I had established a connection with the resident spirit. No one told me a lockdown would be tied to that connection. Think about it, a lockdown symbolizes a point of no return. We go on lockdown we're committed to it."

"That's why I thought the first order of business would be to find out what our job entailed and—surprise, surprise. The details are inside a sealed envelope."

She picked up her fork and started to pay attention to her food. She took no bite, like someone distracted by deep thoughts. "We really can't open it, until the resident spirit responds to us, to me in particular, in a significant way. On that, our employers were very clear."

"What if this spirit is not a good one?" Christopher said.

Agnes gave what looked to him like an up-and-down, belittling glare. "I've done this countless times before. I know what I'm doing. The less we know about the spirit at the get-go, the better the chances the spirit would trust us. It must manifest itself, first. Most likely, it would, during our work tonight. Otherwise, we cannot open the envelope."

Quiet again. Not even a clink in the utensils.

"It's my fault," Christopher said. "I didn't even ask if

there'd be a séance or some Ouija board work during our weekend."

"I need to remind everyone," Agnes said, as if she didn't hear the last thing he said. "The instruction inside the letter would most likely be the guide to our work throughout the weekend. Without it, we cannot take this project to the next level."

"I get it," Ian said. "They had collateralized this entire project to one clear proof that you can commune with the spirit. No connection, no go. Thus, no need for a lockdown."

"Exactly. In the latter case, expect an early pickup."

"I can live with that."

"What do we do then," Christopher said. "Between now and tonight's work?"

"For starters, we organize the props we'd need for the séance tomorrow night," Agnes said. "We need prepare for the possibility we'd get the green light. I need to crash train you two on séance rules and traditions. Other than that, we familiarize ourselves with the place. The resident spirit and his residence are entwined. You'd know what this means should we get far into the project."

Ian told Agnes, "Uh, how do you confirm a connection, without a seance?"

"Tonight, we're going to have a candlelight walk-through. We shut down the power, light up candles, and cover all three levels of the house. We play this by ear. Remember, a token sign from the resident spirit won't do."

"What if it doesn't even give us a sign?" Christopher said.

"In that case, we'd have to wait for the next night when we'd perform a second candlelight walk-through. They had scheduled for us a blind two-night séance on the assumption we'd connect on the first night. Should tonight turn into a dud, we'd get another shot at our bonus. Should the second night end up like the first, we try for a third and last one."

"What happens if on the last night we score?" Ian asked.

"Then we'd need to squeeze in a séance session that same night, even if it means we're not getting any sleep."

"Let me get one thing straight. You alone determine whether a connection is established or not."

"Yes and no. It's complicated. As our work day progresses, I'd work out for you guys the details."

"I suppose the spirit had to do something spooky," Christopher said, "for it to count."

She said, "The micro-cams in the house's public areas can verify poltergeist activity, no doubt about that. But visual or aural affirmations are just hints that point to the spirit's willingness to connect with us, and with me, in particular."

"This connection," Ian said, his brows and forehead already crinkled. "How do you validate it? How do you know it wanted to follow through?"

She continued eating. It took a few uncomfortable seconds before she spoke again: "When I feel it, both of you will feel it, too. That's how it works. The resident spirit can manifest itself in ways none of us can predict. We can't second guess what the exact spirit manifestations would be."

"The skirt job, it should count for something."

"It does. It also had nothing to do with the idea of connecting."

"I still don't get it," Ian said. "Feelings, they're subjective. So are our fears and our perceptions of it. Chris had a point. A video record on the skirt job must count for something."

Agnes straightened and placed her hands on the table. "Our employers had hired teams like us, over three hundred times before. I've spoken with a few people who had once worked for them. The upfront fees wired to our bank accounts are peanuts to our employers. We need to score a breakthrough for us to get to the next stage. Extraordinary circumstances should align for us to succeed where everyone before us had failed. Two séance nights would double our chances of succeeding as one séance night would cut our chances by half.

Everything begins with that trigger that authorizes us to open the instructions envelope."

"With that many flunkers, you think we have a shot at it?"

"Every spirit that I had conjured, connected. Every trance medium that I know and have heard of before, all of them had checkered records."

"Then you should have been an alumnus. Pershing and company should have heard about you, eons ago."

Agnes leaned to one side of the table and told Ian, a strange smile on her face: "I have told no one, until now, that as a trance medium I never fail to connect."

"With their resources, I'm pretty sure they know that."

"I'm not sure they did. Psychic work, they're all gigs. No independent entity keeps records of the hits and the misses. Hits are subject to interpretations and corroborations are heavily influenced by the psychic agents themselves. Word-of-mouth always makes a full circle."

"May I ask, why you never told anyone, until now, that you do not fail to connect?"

"I never saw any need for the brag, mister Bishop. Former clients vet me. I don't need to prove anything to anyone."

"That didn't answer why you elected to tell us this little secret of yours."

If it was possible to glare at their eyes at the same time Agnes would have. She spoke in the manner of someone who needed to be sure she was understood: "Because I need you guys to know I mean business."

5

Presentiments

"Here," Agnes said, as she tapped the tip of her slip-on loafers at a spot close to the north-end spiral staircase landing. "Something happened right here." Ian, who had just emerged from the wooden staircase, expected her to elaborate on what sounded like a big reveal. Yet she kept to herself, muttering gibberish while she continued to roam an area of special interest. All that time, she had her hands clasped behind her back, her eyes on the floor, like a supervisor mulling on a problem. She had wandered the dance floor for a half hour before she narrowed down her sensing-like motions to a small area just outside the dance floor proper. During the same period, Ian and Christopher were shuttling up and down the staircase, checking on her intermittently, in between their assigned job of taking an inventory of séance props and other spiritualist paraphernalia tucked away in the under-stairs storage room.

She spotted Christopher emerging from the staircase and she waved him in. "Mark the spot where I'm standing."

Christopher swept in, gaffer tape roll at hand, like a Labrador retriever alert to do his master's bidding. Agnes stepped back and he dropped to his knees and slapped a piece of orange tape on a dance floor border area not far from the cavity the warped log post and the spiral staircase shared.

The boy's un-educable, Ian decided. Despite his efforts to include him in the group as a co-equal member, his servile attitude to their lady associate only engraved his spot in the project's totem pole. Chris's gofer attitude might also be a variant of the obliging behavior men frequently display toward attractive women. Gifted with a statuesque height, a self-assured posture, and what he considered to be a physique endowed with the ideal hip-to-waist ratio, Agnes could be dressed in Medieval sackcloth and the average man would still vie for her attention.

"Bring the séance table up here and center it on that mark."

Christopher turned and was poised to hurry down the staircase when Agnes raised a finger. "Uh, bring up three chairs, too, okay? Ian and I would be at the attic."

He nodded and proceeded downstairs.

Agnes gestured to Ian to follow her lead up the iron staircase. He sensed something was up and he braced for a hard landing any moment.

Midway to the attic, even before Christopher's diminishing footsteps had faded, Agnes opened up: "What are you really here for, mister Bishop, besides taking care of our team?"

The grave tone and the bolt-from-nowhere subject matter stunned Ian. "What do you mean?"

"I've looked up Doctor Pershing and his family. They had put together projects like this countless times before. They would have partnered me up with a certified paranormal agent."

They emerged into the attic floor.

It was as long and as flat as the two lower floors except that the walls and the ceiling came together at a longitudinal ridge beam as a single, high-pitched A-shaped structure. Warm, richly-varnished tongue-in-groove wood cladded the gable's interior. Natural light streamed in from two small dormer windows—one in the north and another in the south. The structural warping and the northward lean looked less exaggerated at the attic than on the lower floor. Light from the windows brightened the interior space while vents allowed fresh air to flow through. Agnes turned on the overhead down-lighters anyway. The high-vaulted attic immediately turned into a bright summer day.

"I see. You must have looked me up, too."

"Chris, I can understand."

"My credentials, not to your standards?"

"I'm not evaluating your professional resume. That is not the point."

"I am a part-time practicing clinical psychologist with neither a doctorate degree nor ivy-league level academic credentials. If that is not the point, then what is?"

"Your name is not listed in any psychic database. There are thousands of people out there with your academic credentials plus a psychic gift or two."

"Doctor Pershing thought you might need a veteran psychologist, as an adviser."

"Adviser for what?"

"I'm still trying to figure that one out." Suck it in, Ian reminded himself. He considered the possibility that he might be the only one in the group that had signed a non-disclosure agreement, as a condition for inclusion in the project. A key legal stipulation in his contract stated that he should not reveal to his colleagues his peculiar paranormal specialty skills set and the assigned duties associated with them.

Agnes traipsed the attic interior's middle aisle. Folding utility tables laid end-to-end, were set flush against both sides of the inclined ceiling. A few tables were bare. Most of them were topped with marked boxes. Under them sprawled plastic crate boxes filled with what appeared to be assorted memorabilia.

She turned on a dime and she was on to his face in a second. "Your credentials or the lack of them means little to me. The resident spirit is very strong and deeply troubled. For my partner in the séance, I need someone with fortitude. In my line of work, that means someone experienced in spirit interrogations. One who has faith that I do not fail without cause. To be frank, you're not the partner I expected."

If only someone, even something could send a diversion their way and take the heat off Agnes' pushback. He knew he had to make something up, fast. "I was hired to provide advice and guidance, in case something goes awry, on a séance's human-spirit communication process. I could interpret or mediate. My lack of qualifications, as you put it bluntly, was very clear to our employers. Should you feel the need to take this matter up with them, I believe it's too late for that."

"That's where my failing was. On the way here, I had the opportunity. I elected to recoup from a sleepless night. Here, I had time to think. I was hoping you have something to tell me."

"Nope. Not much more I can tell you insofar as to how I got vetted for this job is concerned. Sorry to disappoint you." The woman had an edge. Boss material, opinionated, a powder keg tinder. She reminded him of an ex who happened to be a sturdy partner in building a bit of the American dream. In his experience, such women have volatile flip sides. He needed to craft his responses carefully.

She wasn't done yet. "Are you a crony of Doctor Pershing? Are you here to look over my shoulders when I work?"

"No and no. Agnes, frankly, I don't know what's driving these trust issues."

Agnes turned away and raised her head up before she took a long, deep breath. She shook both her hands to her sides. "I'm used to working with open-minded people. I can't work with whiny skeptics."

Even her choice of words. Skepticism, a pillar of good

science. Whiny? A stab in any man's balls. "I don't whine and I'm skeptical only when I needed to be. I'm not here to debunk or prop anything up. To me, this is a pro gig. Nothing more."

When Agnes approached him, he noticed that her facial expression had already softened. Her brows arched, her eyes, less intense. "Do you even know how a séance works, mister Bishop?"

"You channel spirits, make them communicate, through you." It glibly came out of him, almost like a mediumship endorsement. He did some research work on it himself. In an academic setting, he would have as easily pegged his faith in psychic mediums into the same cubbyhole where his belief in ghosts was. Countless con men preyed on people's psychological vulnerabilities. Psychics among them. They have their own TV shows and publishers sign them up for multi-million-dollar book deals. Yet subjected to rigorous scientific testing, many of these celebrity go-betweens between the living and the dead fail when their gifts got tested under controlled scientific testing methods. He believed that most celebrity psychics were quacks and that none them were true trance mediums, in the way Nostradamus or Edgar Cayce were. At least Agnes was one, or so as the official records go.

"I'm unconscious when I go into a trance. I surrender my body, my mind, to the spirit. It's the most effective way to draw them, to our realm. Sometimes, the spirit becomes aware it had the upper hand."

"How do you snap out of it?"

"I can't unless the spirit let go. Or if someone wakes me up. You wake me up, the session is lost. If the spirit remains too long, it would be harder to wake me up and neither of us would have a clue if I'm in danger."

"Are we talking about possession issues, here?"

She made an ambiguous nod. "It depends on the spirit's

strength and his motivation. They don't have the foggiest idea how much mediumship physically taxes us."

"Do you have any presentiments by now, about how strong the resident spirit is?"

"Yes. The warping of this house in itself testifies to the spirit's strength. There's a reason why I take no more than ten séance assignments a year. Here, I'm scheduled to perform two in a row."

"We need to sit down on this one, seriously."

Agnes moved closer. Her eyes remained wide, even as her pupils shrank. "You cannot be intimidated. I need you to field the right questions and to be strong-willed no matter what happens. The integrity of our séance sessions rests on your shoulders."

"What about Chris, in regards to the séance?"

"He's an extra body, a reinforcing presence. He just needs to keep it together."

"Keep it together? The boy's scared shit already."

"He needs to step up. Make sure he does."

"Morale, of course. For starters, you should probably be nicer to him."

Agnes crossed her arms and stared at him. He knew she didn't plan on addressing the issue. He blinked first and looked away.

"Whatever," Agnes said. "We've got a lot of work to do. Even up here."

Ian surveyed the attic contents. The box placements didn't seem to have any pattern in them. Like people had gone over them recently. "Where do we begin?"

"No idea, yet." She started to walk back and forth to an imaginary center aisle.

"I bet all the stuff here belong to the resident spirit."

"I feel a lot of energy here."

"More than that spot downstairs?"

"No. The energy on the spot I had Chris marked is

concentrated on a small area. Here, it is diffused. The energy I feel here is not just weaker but it is also spread out in a much larger space."

"From the little that I know about departed spirits, they're supposed to stick close to places they were attached to when they were still alive. That would include attachments to their most personal belongings. If these were his, then it follows this space should be his haunt."

Agnes closed her eyes for a second, as if holding on to a slipping thought. "Something much more significant had happened down there."

Ian heard a carton box soft land on the floor. She looked over his shoulders briefly, in the same direction the disturbance came from. By the time their eyes meet, her eyes were aghast, possibly just like his. She leaned to him too close for comfort. "Look behind you, to the two empty tables to the right."

A lone CD player sat atop the second table's edge. He felt hair in his neck quaver as if static electricity had excited them. He whispered back, "I'm sure I didn't move anything since we got here."

"The spirit's here."

"It's on then. We can open the envelope."

"Not yet."

6

First Night

One yank at the main fuse-box lever inside the under-stairs store room and it was lights out in the entire house. Each of them already clutched brass candelabras that held three candlesticks apiece. At a glance, in the pitch-black darkness, little flames from the candles appeared to be points of light floating on their own. Ian's vision soon adjusted. Details closest to the three pools of light slowly emerged.

The three of them formed an inverted V formation in the living room's middle zone. He stood behind Agnes, at an angle to her right, while Christopher took on the other flank. A faint glow illumined a side of Christopher's face. At an angle to his front, he could make out the backlit silhouette of the night-time overlord, as well as the afterglow-like incandescence around her hair and her upper body. Beyond the weak light coronas in and around people and the warm glow about the brass candelabras they held, the rest of the room details appeared dark and vague. Black aluminum horizontal blinds shuttered the sash windows from the inside. Even moonlight could not sneak in. To Ian, the void itself was the chief source of the chills that has been steadily creeping up on him even before the first night's candlelit affair had started.

"Is there anyone else here?" Agnes' low yet firm voice almost sounded hollow in the stillness and silence. Besides the padded furniture, the living room was bare of rugs, tapestries, curtains, and other fabrics that would have absorbed sound waves. "Please, show us a sign to acknowledge."

Observing her earlier instructions, Ian and Christopher moved as little as possible. He suspected the flickering light from Christopher's candle might be due to hand tremors. He clutched at the candelabra with two hands, like him. Yet unlike Christopher's, his candle flames behaved.

The young man's inclusion in the project might be a mistake. Ian knew even younger Hispanic Americans live with elders not that far removed from rural cultures where people have more connection to their land, to their progenitors, and to hallowed traditions that involved strong beliefs in the supernatural and the afterlife. He didn't need a degree in anthropology to know for certain that people like Christopher must have grown up exposed to spirit-world tales and haunting folklores.

After this phase, three bedrooms, the kitchen-dining zone, and two whole floors to go. Agnes insisted on one continuous sweep. And they were just out of the gate. He wondered how long the group could keep it together without some kind of a break from the candlelit blackout. For insurance, they all necklaced mini-flashlights. Across the length of the house, brackets also held heavy-duty flashlights.

A clink. Like cutlery lightly striking a porcelain cup.

Agnes tipped an ear in the kitchen's direction. "Why does your soul linger in this place? Please, give us a sign of your presence."

Silence.

"That clink from the kitchen, is that you telling us you are here?"

Silence.

Right after sunset, in anticipation of a possible lockdown,

the team had pulled down all the sash windows and had some of them locked at their lowest increments to allow for natural ventilation. On all three floors, they had adjusted all air vents a third of the way closed. Front and back doors were bolted shut and their electronic locks set a flick away from activation. The two emergency exit doors' levers, pre-rigged with an integrated break-in and break-out alarm system, were also set to standby mode. Four separate yanks on actuator switches beside the living room breaker box and a lockdown would be set beyond recall.

Though the centralized heating system was turned off to keep out ambient noise, the soft whistling produced by wind gusts outside could be easily heard. Air currents should be circulating through the house's passive ventilation system and exhaust ducts.

As the night wore on and the winds weakened, the house seemed much quieter.

A clink. Same sound, same place. A very faint crackling sound also glissaded across the floor. He felt the hair in his nape and shoulders stand as if drawn by static force.

To address her companions, Agnes made a quarter turn, her candle hand still pointed forward. "We have the living room and hallway covered. We move to Christopher's room, now."

"I need to pee, bad."

Even in the candlelight, Agnes' hard stare found its mark. "All right. Keep it down. No flashlights. Use the candle and don't flush."

"Sir, could you stand by the bathroom door, please."

Ian went ahead to the hallway and straightaway opened the bathroom door. Christopher double-stepped. He left the door a tad open.

Agnes caught up and positioned herself to the right of the door. She carefully lowered the candelabra to the floor. Ian followed suit and placed the pitiful light source on the floor on his left side. Two warm pools of light barely illuminated the far flanks. She tipped her head toward him and said, almost in a whisper, "I need to say this again. By sundown, you and Chris are my assistants. I call the shots. Don't argue. I may not have time to explain why things needed to be done a certain way."

Ian nodded. He preferred not to belabor a point that would only lead to a needless argument. "You heard the clink, right?"

"Yes."

"Is that… him?"

"Maybe. I'm not sure. I didn't feel any energy at all coming from back there."

"But did you feel it elsewhere?"

"Yes. Here."

"Uh, where here?"

"Here. Where we are, right now."

"What do you mean—"

"I don't have answers right now, mister Bishop. Something happened in the general area we are standing on right now."

"Like something bad happened right here?"

"Not necessarily so. Leftover energy from someone long gone, I sense that it lingers here. Not much more I can add to that."

Before the lights went out, Ian did an ocular survey of the dreary, nondescript hallway. Not one decorative feature anywhere in the walls to break the monotony. The three small casement-type windows high up the wall across were left a quarter open and cold air seeped in from there. The hallway, to him, seemed to be the coldest spot on the ground floor. He needed to say something, if only to calm his nerves. "Tell me again, why we didn't head straight for it, the seance?"

"Day one, our first night here, that's when visitors and resident spirits make some kind of a connection. It takes time for us to gain the spirit's trust, the right one that is."

"You mean—"

"It does happen."

Ian heard Christopher zipping his pants. The faucet sloshed gently.

"He's with us, now. I need you to have faith."

"Faith in what?"

"The night is my domain. In this project, you must believe in that more than anything else."

7

White Nightgown

After a ten-hour stint at the Los Angeles boutique bookstore she owned, Agnes always dined and relaxed before a favorite TV show. She capped the night with her dental care routines and the obligatory make-up smudge-down. Even in bed, she would end her day before the television screen. Always. The blue screen had always lulled her to sleep. Though she loved books enough to spend six days a week walled by them from all sides, television offered a window view to different sceneries. Such little vices, she believed, had kept occupational burnout at bay. Over time, her nightly pre-slumber habit turned into a fixed routine. She had no cats to care for; no boyfriend to soothe. She was comfortable living alone.

Television. It was the only modern contraption that she missed in the spacious master bedroom that their hosts had set up for her in classic hotel suite fashion. Amenities at her disposal more than compensated for the near-total electronics ban in the house. The weekend job's zero-luggage policy no longer dangled in her grievance list, a list that happened to include the burden of working with two men of questionable competence.

Across the board, the company provided clothing allocation, from brand-name underwear to a signature wool outer-wear coat. The oversized, Baroque-style wood cabinet opens to a wardrobe fit for a real-life princess. She felt a grin forming on her face each time she glanced at the empty luggage bag at the bottom of the cabinet. It reminded her of the sweet side to Dr. Pershing's blanket ban on bringing in personal items: Dorothy Smalls said that at the end of their work week, they can keep anything in the closet that they could fit into the company-provided luggage bag. And it was a big one.

She planned to turn in early, but she couldn't put it off for another time. She pulled back random clothes collars to peruse the haute couture brand names. She window-shopped a lot and she could tell fabrics apart. She could also distinguish high-end textile scents from the smell of clothing that populated bargain store racks. The under-clothes, the robe, the bathroom slippers, even the toiletries, they were all take-home-worthy royal appointments. *You are a paid professional,* she reminded herself. Too early to be in a looting mood. For the project to have a reasonable chance to succeed, she must fortify herself for the rigors of séance sessions. Whatever extra time the circumstances would accord her, she must use them to wind down and relax.

Again, she yielded to whim and for the third time went over her sleepwear options for the night. There hung in the middle of the clothes line-up four white nightgowns, the one set that had grabbed her attention the first time she opened the cabinet doors. A fifth one was encased in a transparent plastic garment bag and it appeared to be shorter in length than the others. The unprotected gowns were plain, shin-length, peasant dress types with fabrics a bit light for the season. All her life, she preferred to sleep on such loose-fitting garments that didn't bind. She could use one the entire weekend and earmark the rest for their final day's grab-and-go. She planned to compensate for the sleepwear's inadequate insulation by slipping into warm comforters and blankets come bedtime.

She wanted to put a gown on, for the heck of it, but she couldn't find any appropriate under-clothing. A quarter past nine. Someone might knock. She decided to wear the silk pajama pair in the meantime, up until she was ready to call it a night. She pinched the nightgown fabric. *"Hang in there, for now."* She pulled down the maroon silk pajama pair from their hangers and slapped it over her shoulders. She grabbed the tooth-care kit from the top of the cabinet and headed for the bathroom.

As she passed by the queen-size bed, she thought she had glimpsed a familiar white nightgown on top of the beige satin bed covers. She stepped back. A nightgown indeed laid out neatly to the left of the bed, with the gown's fabric, from the princess neckline to the embroidered hem, spread flat and taut, as if someone had flat-ironed it somewhere and laid them there for presentation.

"I don't remember putting one there," she whispered, as she looked back at the open closet cabinet. She doubled back. She counted the nightgowns. Four plus one in the garment bag. She counted again. "Four. I'm sure there are only four."

She sat at the edge of the bed and pondered the situation. Even if she had miscounted, she would have remembered laying one out had she been responsible for it. Could this be a sign of the spirit connecting with her? The candlelight walk-through yielded little beyond a few porcelain clinks. Of course, the skirt job and the CD player teleportation feat had without doubt corroborated poltergeist activity. Now, this. But she needed something more than incontrovertible physical evidence. Ghostly mischiefs won't cut it for her. She wanted a connection; and a strong one at that.

AGNES KNOCKED at Ian's bedroom door. She knew she had knocked way too loud when the wide-eyed Christopher's head popped out from the neighboring door. Then came Ian, fittingly bourgeoise in his blue, silk pajamas. He squinted against the hallway lights. She eyed both men. "Let me be clear. I'm not accusing anyone. In the last hour or so, did any one of you enter my room?"

Both men stared at each other first. They both shook their heads.

She waved at both men and turned back towards her room. "Sorry, guys. I'm tired. I'm not above misplacing things. Don't worry about it. See you guys in the morning."

"May I ask why you thought someone went into your room?"

"A nightgown is on my bed. I don't remember taking anything down from the closet. Anyway, it's been a long day. I'm not above forgetting."

"Lock your door. And give me your spare key, just in case."

"Okay. I'll knock again for that."

Agnes slipped back into her room and closed the door behind her.

A few steps inside and she halted. She rounded her bed to be sure. Undulating shivers came and went.

The white nightgown lay neatly in the middle of the bed, right where she would have slept. Who would have known about her peculiar habit? She lets out a brief, nervous laugh. "You're playing games, now."

Years in the trade, poltergeist activities had always stung her with dread. None ever drew a laugh, much less a wise-crack. She was fully aware she'd be spending the night alone in a room where a potentially malicious ghost hangs out. Goosebumps and chills alternated. Yet she felt no urge to bust out the door and whip up a ruckus. She looked behind her at the gown. She trusted Pershing and company wouldn't dare to install cameras in the bedrooms. Yet she still felt like she is being watched. *If you only knew what I've been through, you won't even think about it.* She stifled a laugh another time.

She considered what she drank last after dinner. The strange cannabis-induced levity also struck her as familiar. Drugs consumption, accidental or incidental, resonated with her as a possibility too remote to even consider. She wondered if the true source of her audacious behavior might be the persistent reminders about the lucrative nature of the gig itself all around them. Incentives embolden people. They risk their lives to keep a standard of living. Could be as simple as that. The sign-in bonus alone should give her failing business another shot at survival. On the outside chance they succeed where all the other psychics had failed, a hefty bonus pot awaited them. Then there was the swag in the fat antique cabinet closet an eyeshot away. She glanced another time at the nightgown behind her, beautifully presented, unruffled to the embroidered seams, waiting to be owned.

She dropped the pajama pair on the side table, pivoted, and reclined, her back to the cushioned headboard, her legs straight and relaxed. She and the gown laid together practically side by side. An ironic variation of FDR's wartime remark *There is nothing to fear but fear itself* came to mind. Because what she found most disconcerting about the incident was her lack of fear when the situation clearly called for it. She also found it strange why she considered stripping her clothes there and then to don the nightgown knowing well a presence might be waiting for her to do just that. She felt a smile arcing from her face another time.

A more intoxicating possibility drifted by. The event could be a mile marker in her long process of healing, as her long-time therapist might put it. Agnes visited her monthly for over a decade after a childhood trauma of such magnitude it was only eight years ago when she felt comfortable wearing a skirt outdoors. Her therapist even identified that one positive devel-

opment as a capstone to a long period during which she struggled to gain some measure of proper body image. She clicked
her teeth, grabbed the nightgown, and headed for the bathroom. "The hell I care who's having sexy time. I'll put
you on."

8

Don't Touch Me

Ian had just wedged a second pillow under his head when he heard three dull raps on his door. He groaned, "Coming." Agnes had already entrusted her second room key to him. The knocks also sounded weak and hesitant. Sure enough, when he opened the door it was Christopher. The door was only half open and the young man managed to squeeze himself in, pillow and blanket lugged.

"Say what you want, sir, but I can't sleep in my room alone."

Ian kept the door open. Christopher should have seen the unwelcoming displeasure reflected on his face.

"I'll sleep on the couch, sir. Don't worry, I don't snore bad."

"I do have problems sleeping in a room that isn't mine. Sharing it with someone who's not my wife means I might not be able to sleep at all." He stood his ground and pushed the door wide open. "I'm an old man. I need a good sleep bad. Please, go back to your room."

Christopher clasped his hands together. "I beg you, sir. I can sleep on the floor, or the bathroom, or under the couch. Please."

"No one's ever been killed by a ghost. You're way too young to die from a heart attack should one say hi to you."

"The candle thing we did. I was too embarrassed to admit it…"

He closed the door. "All right, you can take the couch."

"Thank you, sir." He dropped his pillow and blanket on the foam sofa set flush against the wall that separated Ian's hostel-sized accommodation from the master bedroom.

He observed his roommate poke around the forest green wallpaper covering that appeared to have been freshly applied not too long ago. He could tell the young man had a good sense of his surroundings. Despite the dim light, he noticed the depressions on the paper's surface texture. "Don't push against the part where the wallpaper sags. Whatever flimsy thing that's behind the paper, could be rotting wood shot through with holes. That's probably why they laid new wallpaper over the entire thing."

Christopher lightly tapped his knuckle over a solid surface. "Plywood."

"Easy. She could hear us." Ian returned to bed. He tucked himself under his quilted comforters. "Turn the lampshades off when you're settled."

Ian hoped the long day had worn him down enough that he'd be able to slip into dreamland fast. He faced three in-the-shade work nights in a row. As a retro-cognitive dream clairvoyant, he needed to spend, on average, two nights in a single location in order for him to generate enough useable dreamwork. He must be able to re-create for his employer a composite picture of what really happened there, specifically on the ground floor of the house, as per official instructions.

He wished there would be a time in the future when he could admit to his colleagues that he was the one with a backdoor deal with Dr. Pershing. The deal's shady aspects would have impinged on his conscience if not for the separate nondisclosure agreement he had signed that barred him from disclosing to any other soul accounts of his dreamwork sessions. Before accepting the assignment, he recalled having issued one caveat to Dr. Pershing. On paper, he stated that at times, his gift does not yield answers. The doctor must have considered other retro-cognitive dream clairvoyants who didn't append such a remark. He got the job anyway.

Agnes' mention of his lackluster credentials only served to reinforce his nagging doubts as to why he got hired in the first place. He hadn't landed enough dream clairvoyant projects for a paid membership to psychic guilds and associations to make sense. It just so happened that in the eighteen years he did get commissioned to sleep on vacant mansions his clients planned to buy, the elite grapevine accounted for most of the jobs. A satisfied client from upstairs must have recommended him to Dr. Pershing. It had to be the most plausible explanation for his inclusion in the project.

IAN WAKENED to the sound of shuffling beyond the wall he shared with the master bedroom. As if someone in leather-soled shoes dragged his steps about the wooden floor. A sharp metallic click, like that of someone unlocking a door outside, followed. Door hinges creaked with slow, deliberate precision. He threw a pillow at Christopher, smack on his head. He rolled off the couch with such alacrity he might as well have been awake at that very moment.

"Sir, what's—"

"Shssssh. Listen."

The shuffling sounds continued. Christopher's eyes bulged.

"Heard that?"

Christopher nodded.

Ian straightened. The leather-soled steps went on in a back-and-forth pattern. It paused from time to time. "That doesn't sound like someone sleepwalking."

Christopher pressed his ears against the shared wall with Agnes. "It's coming from her room."

Ian pounded the wall. "Agnes, is that you?"

Silence. He grabbed the room keys from the nightstand and used them to poke a thumb-sized hole into the sagging wallpaper section.

His through-the-hole view showed Agnes asleep on her back, both the side table lamp shades on. Then he saw Agnes' comforters being pushed down from her upper torso. He recoiled.

"Sir, what?"

Unsure of what he had just witnessed, he peered through the hole again. This time, the comforters, already bunched down her waist, wormed down past her knees. From the opposite direction, her sleepwear's hem gathered and it accordion folded up her thighs. Ian rushed for the door. "Go grab a weapon. Someone else is here."

CHRISTOPHER BARGED INTO AGNES' room first, brass candelabra at hand, like a warrior spoiling for a fight. Ian rushed from behind him. The next moment, Christopher balked in his tracks. He started to back away. A horrified gasp, more like a rattle, came out of his mouth, a far cry from the war-whoop his grand entry would have made one expect. He looked smaller than he was, as he cringed at Ian's side.

Agnes' comforters piled up on the floor. Her nightgown, its hem at mid-thigh level, rippled up and down her body in a continuous wave pattern. She moaned as someone paralyzed inside a nightmare.

"Agnes, wake up!" Ian cried as he charged towards her.

Christopher, as if emboldened by his move, overtook him, leaped, and landed knee first at the side of her bed. He dropped the candelabra by her side and started to shake her. "Wake up! You have to wake up!"

Ian rounded her bed and turned on the overhead lights. He scoured the place, the cabinets, and the dark corners and all, for possible intruder hiding spots. Clear. When he checked back on her, the wave-like ripples in her nightgown had settled.

From a distance, he saw her eyes open to a rapt gaze. Her eyeballs turned to Christopher before her head did. Agnes rose from the bed, spotted the candelabra at her side and she reached for it with her left hand. Ian witnessed her staid facial expression morph into a scowl.

He should have seen it coming and acted sooner. In one fluid motion, she got to her knees and whacked the side of Christopher's face with the candelabra. He yelped and staggered. Ian failed to close the distance. Agnes, already standing by the bed side, took another swing, a fierce yell behind the force, striking Christopher on the side of his head. He went down.

She leaped in the air, mounted him on the ground, and swung again. Both his hands in the air, Christopher parried both blows.

"I told you not to touch me! I told you not to touch me!"

Ian caught an upward swing and disarmed her. He grabbed her by the armpits and threw her bodily back into the bed.

She bounced back with such speed that she was on his face, fisted right hand poised to strike. Then she froze, like a robotic doll whose battery had run out of juice. The lividness on her face vanished. Her arms went limp on her sides, her chest heaving. She stared around her and at the two men, her eyes incredulous.

With Agnes no longer a threat, Ian helped the groggy victim sit bedside. Christopher bled profusely from somewhere in the right temple region. He started to whimper.

"What happened? Why are you two here?"

"We heard footsteps from your room. Chris was shaking you awake. We're here to help."

Agnes grimaced and shook her head in quick succession. When she opened her eyes, they looked more alert than stunned. She regarded Christopher before she sprinted for the door. "I'll go get the first aid kit."

Ian pulled away Christopher's hand from the gash. "Don't touch it."

"She's crazy; she's fucking crazy."

Agnes ran back in, a white Pelican hard case at hand. She opened it and poured its contents on the bed.

"I have Red Cross training. I know what to do from here." She turned Christopher's head towards the ceiling light. He pressed his hands hard on his lap, closed his eyes, and stifled his whimper. Blood continued to trickle from his wound. "How hard did I hit you?"

"Like two I'm-going-to-kill-you swings. How else can I put it."

She looked at Ian, clearly seeking corroboration.

"Had I been your victim, for sure you would have killed me."

Agnes examined Christopher's ears. "I'm less worried about the wound as I am of a possible concussion. Ian, where's the satellite phone?"

The victim's eyes abruptly widened. He grunted as he tried to stand. "I think I'll be okay." He waddled two steps before he staggered back to bed and sat. During his whole house orientation, Ian mentioned the satellite phone in passing. He didn't expect the matter to stick to anyone's memory. He braced for an embarrassing comeuppance.

Christopher made a steadier back and forth. "I'm okay. Really. I only need a bit of fixing."

She checked his other ear. She leaned close to his face and stared at his eyes awhile.

"I'm fine. You can clean it and close it up. I'm sure I'm going to be fine."

"Ian, line up all the packages marked bandages. Find the trauma shears; any packet marked sutures as well."

"On it."

"Do we have hard liquor in the pantry?"

"Not sure. But I'll look."

"Sir, I'm sure we don't have any."

She grabbed both Christopher's shoulders. "I don't remember doing this to you."

"Well, you freaking did."

"What did you see—"

"Focus on him," Ian said, as he rummaged through the pile of first aid items scattered on the bed. "We'll talk about this later."

9

Fifty-eight Degrees

Ian and Agnes pulled the bedding top and mattress to the floor, exposing to light the padded box springs layer and part of the under-floor space below it. He still had no idea what exactly he should be looking for. He patted the springs and felt his way about the wood surface before he visually checked the headboard and the bedstead. It wasn't the best time to tell Agnes he appreciated her rational approach to the situation. She wanted to turn the room upside down, for any trace of chicanery. The simplest explanation for a phenomenon, paranormal or not, is usually the right one. Every other possibility must be ruled out first, two eyewitnesses notwithstanding. They were on the same page on this one.

Now changed into silk pajamas, Agnes dropped belly first on the floor, flashlights on. She inspected the underfloor space.

Christopher's call on his bludgeon trauma turned out to be the right one. The young man's rebound impressed him. With his cuts well sutured and the wound area heavily bandaged, he managed to shift every piece of furniture in the room from their moorings, save for the hardwood closet cabinet that he claimed could weigh a ton. For the most part,

Ian merely poked his nose at whatever the rest of the crew did.

Fifteen minutes into the inquiry and the team broke real sweat. He reached for the thermostat which needlepoint he expected to line up on the agreed-upon sixty-two-degree default setting. To his surprise, someone had already adjusted the dial to a cool fifty-eight degrees.

He started to pace the room's periphery, eyes on the ceiling and on the decorative cornice that bordered it. If surveillance equipment hid somewhere, it must be ensconced inside intricate chisel-cut woodwork.

"Chris," Agnes called out to him. "You sure you're okay?'

"Better than earlier. Thanks."

"Don't hesitate to tell us, if you feel giddy or if your vision or speech changes."

He waved Christopher in and the three of them replaced the mattress and bedding. "What we saw," Ian started, "how does that stack up with what you have seen or heard before, in your line of work?"

Agnes sat bedside and rubbed her palms on her lap. She shook her head. "Never heard, never seen anything like what you two had described. Believe me, I've heard and seen a lot."

"What do you remember?"

"I felt it, the warm air under the gown. There was this vague sense of someone caressing me. I couldn't move. I wasn't wakeful enough to understand what was happening."

Christopher stepped in. "So, you do believe us."

Once again, Agnes regarded Christopher with that lingering, empathetic look the poor under-appreciated guy surely, sorely craved. "I can't say it enough. I feel so sorry about what happened."

"A wood plank once hit my head on a construction site. I started wearing a helmet after that. Stuff happens. It's okay."

"If something like that happens again, you can slap me in the face. I don't care."

"You went berserk," Ian said. "You went on a bludgeoning frenzy. You screamed, don't touch me, I told you not to touch me."

"Your eyes," Christopher said. "I thought you were possessed."

"Where was that rage coming from?"

Agnes looked away. She pulled out a side table drawer, grabbed her wallet purse, and extracted from it a green envelope. The pensiveness in her eyes lingered and the clench in her jaws hinted at conflicted thought.

Dodge number two. The first one happened before their whole room search when Agnes vanished in the bathroom from where she soon reemerged in pajamas. She returned the nightgown to the cabinet. It joined several similar nightgowns strung up in hangers. He took the opportunity to ask her why she preferred to sleep on one despite the prior conundrum regarding the laid-out gown in her bed. She didn't answer.

"This is it." Agnes displayed the consolation prize to the bloody fright fest, their job description to be unraveled. Now they can make a lockdown official and potentially railroad their employment to some form of completion. "To the dining room, everyone. We'll make this one official."

⸻

"OUR COMBINED ACCOUNTS should have met the standard," Agnes said, as soon as the three of them got seated around the dining table. "Ian, Chris. Your consent?"

The two men nodded. Ian said, "With or without video verification, I concur. Chris?"

"Totally."

Agnes ripped off the envelope from one end and extracted from it what looked like a folded parchment paper. "I'd read it aloud. You two can review it later."

Dear Agnes, Ian, and Christopher:

If the three of you are reading this letter, then my late son, Daniel's spirit, had already manifested himself to you. Please forgive the cryptic setup by which we delivered this information. We saw no point in letting you know the delicate nature of this project if the chance you'd be able to see it through is practically zero.

For the last thirty years, Daniel's soul remained trapped in this house that was once part of the Pershing family estate in the city of Sacramento. Since that period soon after his passing, as some of you may already know, we had employed three-hundred-sixty teams, always led by a master psychic, to help him cross over. Everyone failed. Time and again, he gave hints of his presence. He moved objects, produced scents, and elicited human voices from whispers to whimpers. Fifteen to twenty percent of the time, Daniel did not even respond to psychic intermediation in any observable or recordable way. Each failure, though, added to our knowledge base and helped us re-structure our approach to the next project.

I'm not getting any younger and I know that family members and associates who will continue the project when I'm gone will not be able to see through the effort with the same zeal and doggedness as mine. My people are getting weary, too. A good number had recommended to me an endgame: Burn the house down and force Daniel's soul to cross over. We nearly did just that. Until the word on the endgame got around and feedbacks on the particular solution trickled in from the psychic mediums we've worked with in the past, including from other psychics elsewhere who had learned about our decades-long endeavor. Many psychics had warned us that should we burn this house, Daniel's spirit would most likely migrate to another dwelling. We'd never know where. He'd remain in our realm for eternity.

I can't blame you for assuming after you have read this, that you'd be mere cogs in an endless wheel of paranormal agents presented with an open-ended, seemingly impossible task. I ask, nevertheless, that you perform your duties in accordance with the contract and in good conscience.

In his lifetime, Daniel was a kind soul. Long gone, his manifestations remained benign. Please treat his predicament as you would a good friend whom you would love to guide to his final destination. Feel free to go through Daniel's memorabilia in the attic. They are presented to you in exactly the same way the last psychic team had left it.

Though we have micro-cameras installed in the house's public areas, I don't want you people to think there are eyes looking over your shoulders. We had installed them there for documentation purposes. I assure you we don't have listening devices installed anywhere in the house. Should some kind of emergency arise, I don't want anyone to be anxious about losing your completion bonuses. In the same breath, though, I'd like to remind you that an enormous reward awaits the team that succeeds where all in the past had failed.

Feel free to read the letter again. Then dissolve it in water before you dispose of it in the trash chute. We want you to discard readable outsider messages that the house's resident might pick up on, a possibility that might adversely influence the outcome of your work.

We would be there to pick you all up on Monday, at ten in the morning. At that, I bid you three a good weekend.

P.S. Daniel likes the thermostat set at no higher than fifty-eight degrees Fahrenheit.

Dr. Caleb Pershing.

Agnes passed the letter to Ian. He perused it. She started to pace the floor.

Christopher raised a hand. "I have a question. Uh, is that all? Don't they need to tell us how his son died and stuff like that?"

"I expected more details, especially from a letter that long," Ian said, as he continued to read the letter. He gave the letter to Christopher. "Agnes, you sure this is all there is to that?"

"Yeah. I expected a shorter letter if you ask me." She sought Christopher's attention. "When you're done with that, dunk it in water. Once the ink had dissolved, you may discard it in the trash."

"Will do." He strode off, headed to the kitchen sink.

Agnes transitioned outright to Ian. "The lack of clear-cut instructions, I get it. They want us to work intuitively and objectively. They want a fresh take, unaffected by precedents established by past psychics."

"Of course, a blank slate. But why? Wouldn't it help us to know why the others before us had failed? What if the teams before us were doing something consistently wrong?"

"We don't have the time or the skills to put to good use the past psychics' experiences irrespective of their failures and their successes. Who knows, our team might break new ground and help them get closer to their goals. That would be a big step forward."

"Did it occur to you that we could be the last of them?"

"I don't look that far."

The warping log posts came to mind. "The process of burning releases matter into the atmosphere. It destroys but, by way of extrapolation, I'd assume the process also allows the lingering essence of the spirit to escape. This is his home. A less drastic measure, like a demo job that would break the house into a million unrecognizable pieces, might be enough to force it to cross over."

"I'm pretty sure someone had considered that option. I don't think that would work. Leftover energy from the departed tends to stick to old, natural wood. Burning the place down, not a demo job, that's the textbook remedy for ridding places of persistent spirits. What puzzles me is how doctor Pershing got the idea his son's soul would move to another house if he burns it. Someone, someone he trusts, must have convinced him something like that would happen."

Christopher returned, his eyes stark and inquisitive. He held a tray with a water pitcher and three glasses.

"Maybe someone who would benefit from an eternal racket," Ian said.

Agnes had already left the conversation. She walked toward the countertop section to the east and set her face close to the half-shuttered window. There was nothing outside to see but stagnant mist and cloudy darkness. She said as if talking with herself. "There are no houses for miles around here. Not one tree."

"What if the old man didn't want his son to leave?"

She squinted at him like he said something impertinent.

"Chris," Agnes waved him in. "When you checked the underbelly of the house earlier, what impression did you have?"

"Impression on what?"

"Were the fixtures, the piers the house stood on, did they strike you as recent, or had they been there for a while?"

"Quite new. The seals and plaster certainly were."

Agnes folded her arms and shook her head with deliberate subtlety. "We're probably the first to work in this location."

"So?"

"I mean why us?"

Ian, who has started to pace around the kitchen zone to ward off the cold beelined the wall thermostat. A solid fifty-eight degrees. It must be the default setting set by their employers, the exact one to the spirit's liking. He was about to tweak the dial when he hesitated on his plan of action. "Agnes, did you change the thermostat setting in your room any time since you used it?"

"Of course. We agreed on sixty-two degrees. I had set it at that before I went to bed."

"Did you tinker with the kitchen thermostat since we got here?"

"No."

"Chris, when was the last time you reset the kitchen thermostat to our own standard?"

"Maybe, uh, two hours ago."

"Did you set it at fifty-eight degrees?"

"No. It should be at sixty-two. Unless you or Agnes changed it. Same thing with the thermostats on the two floors upstairs."

10

They Were Here Before

In his notepad, Ian scribbled the ballpoint-pen scrawl on the antique closet cabinet's backboard:

Daniel and Ellie were here—July 12, 1992.

The heavy-set cabinet was turned, from its back-to-the-wall position to a clockwise right angle, to an arc of around forty-five degrees. Mid-morning sunlight streamed from the master bedroom window shutters, delineating the barely discernible faded-blue ink on the dusty, age-worn plywood backboard. From an oblique angle, Ian examined the buckling backboard where dust and grime covered the entire surface evenly.

Soon after breakfast, not long after Agnes had returned to her room to shower, she rushed back out to announce the cabinet's bizarre placement. Ian then asked everyone to step back, as he pondered on the best way to investigate the anomaly.

His two slack-jawed companions stood quietly behind him as he rubbed his forefinger against the date on the note written in cursive. Hardened dust smudged away, revealing a green-gray patina that might have protected the writing from completely fading.

"Ink and wood had completely fused together with age. Take a look. Save for the part that I had disturbed, the surface dust distribution everywhere else is pretty much pristine."

"Dust wouldn't be that thick if a good number of teams had the same privilege as ours."

"I agree. We could be looking at a unique event."

Agnes' eyes gleamed. "We have a complete date. A new name."

"Guys, shouldn't we be concerned about who or what did this?" Christopher said. "The floor didn't even show drag marks."

"Good observation." Ian dropped to his knees and rubbed his hand on the imaginary arc the cabinet's legs had traversed in order for the cabinet to be at its present position. Not a scratch mark anywhere along the putative drag arc. Another poltergeist event had occurred out of camera range.

Everyone had slept in Ian's room the night before and no one had bothered to set the alarm clock. They stayed late and even had a post-midnight snack while they discussed the following day's work schedule.

"Lovers wrote that," Agnes said. "They memorialized an event that happened in this room and they kept it out of everyone else's view."

Ian nodded. "They're supposed to return to this place. No one else is supposed to see this."

"Somebody changed his mind."

"A tryst happened here."

"Isn't a tryst another word for rendezvous?" Christopher asked.

"It's an archaic word—I mean an old, seldom-used word that means a secret meeting place."

"Tryst implies mystery, even something illicit, like a secret meeting place between, say, married lovers."

"Oh, I see."

"In their time, those two lovers must be strong," Ian said.

"They don't make this kind of solid wood cabinet anymore." He looked up and around, as if addressing an invisible presence. "Thanks. We got the message. We're putting it back, right now." He motioned for Christopher's assistance. "Let's go push this back in."

The two men grabbed two points each in a cabinet corner, and then bodily pushed the cabinet toward the wall. They moved it a few inches on the first try. Agnes joined them. Christopher lowered his grab and they tried another time.

Three concerted grunts later, the cabinet rested flush against the wall.

This time, drag marks were etched clearly on the floor. Ian swapped incredulous stares with his assistant.

"Sir, the cabinet wasn't dragged out. It was lifted."

Levitated. Ian nearly spoke it. "Let me play devil's advocate. Maybe the young people used a lever tool or something like that to pull that monster out and to push it back in."

"Sir, we threw our combined muscle against the cabinet to push it back in. Pulling this monster out from its place against the wall, given the available space, that's a different story."

"Maybe if the cabinet is empty, it would have been lighter," Agnes said.

Christopher shook his head. He tapped his knuckle on the wood. "Save for the backboard, this cabinet is made from solid Teakwood, old school thick at that. You know how furniture was long ago. They were meant to last forever."

"Agnes, our trust in our employers notwithstanding, am I speaking too soon if I made a declaration that we do have a very serious poltergeist issue in this house?"

She nodded. "It can go without saying, we'd be doing serious work today."

IAN MADE sure the team hits the ground running by one. Agnes worked the east-side table tops that lined the attic's longitudinal side, spreading out loose photographs, pinning and attaching notes on albums, and scribbling content tags on them.

He and Christopher were on all fours under a table on the west side, picking out every picture frame and any scrap of paper that they could find from Daniel's memorabilia boxes. "With historical timelines as a guide, we need a clear separation between picture groups," Ian told Agnes, straight across. "Don't mix pictures with documents and similar paper stuff."

"Got it."

"Any Ellie or suspected Ellie pics go to the east side table that I had marked seven." He included Christopher. "Paper documents and the like go to table eight, and miscellaneous items of significance, to two. Anything you think needs extra attention put it on one."

Agnes had a ten-minute head-start and he could tell she had covered a lot of ground. Her handiwork had a system to it. She did this sort of investigative work before.

"The situation here is very fluid," Agnes said. "We play it by ear, people. Keep it steady. Things would come to order in due time. Chris…"

The man nearly hit his head on the table, as he crawled out of it. "Yes?"

"All the empty boxes, take them downstairs and dump them in the storage. We could use a little less clutter up here."

The nimble Christopher started grabbing boxes.

Ian sat on the floor and huffed out a sigh of frustration. He surveyed the enormity of the task before them. He checked the time. "We still need to cross-reference pictures to events and dates. The séance interrogatories, when do we squeeze them in?"

"We'd set aside at least two hours for that."

"Two hours?" Ian groaned.

Christopher disappeared through the staircase.

"In a séance, there are no rule books or strategy cheat sheets to fall back on. You have to know the sense behind the interrogatories and have the ability to improvise as we move along. Remember, the spirit speaks through me. You are the one who directly speaks with it."

"Understood." Ian struggled to get back on his feet. He wandered about, stretching his back, suppressing his body-ache sighs as he once again surveyed the general chaos in the attic work zone.

He sat on one of the two chairs at table one, east side, close to the north-end stairwell. Table one is the attic's nerve center. Stationaries, schedule sheets, and a miscellany of office tools littered the tabletop. A pendant light, one of Christopher's hacks, dangled above it. "We don't have enough time. We need to prioritize."

"What do you propose we do?"

Ian approached. "Let's get the interrogatories down, first. Then we come back here and pick up from where we had left off."

"Not a bad idea."

"We can have Chris sift through the memorabilia boxes—"

"No, no, no. He's not touching anything here unsupervised."

Agnes noticed too late Christopher's untimely return. He must have heard her. Ian saw the sudden change in his demeanor as he grabbed more empty boxes.

11

The Cusp of Nightfall

Ian and Agnes hunkered over table one where an 11-by-14 outdoor family portrait was taped flat to the surface. It showed a candid Pershing extended family tableau, where the clan gathered down the slope of a baronial mansion's vast lawn frontage. They dressed formally, down to the little ones, the men in suits, and the women in gowns. The photograph captured the moments before everyone reached their spots in the frame, as if the photographer had accidentally tripped the shutter. It could even be a test shot that got processed and somehow ended up in a do-not-discard bin.

To the left of the family portrait scene stood three tall young men, obviously conversing. All three were already set in their back-end spots. Five women lined up the next layer down, to their right, in various stages of posing. From the right, several others, including one in a power wheelchair, moved into the frame. The young ones appeared to be jockeying for space in the lawn's foreground.

At the lower right of the picture, almost to the edge of the frame, were two women—one middle-aged, the other a lady in her mid-teens—watching the melee, amused smiles on their faces. Bystanders, he assumed, since they stood at an angle away from the camera lens. They also wore plain summer clothes. The bushy-haired, older woman had an apron on, while the pretty young brunette who had a big smile on her face wore a polka-dotted, peasant dress.

Ian dabbed his forefinger to a tall, scrawny young man in the tableau, one of the three already in position. The clean-cut, dark-haired man's eyes turned to the bottom section of the frame, to the direction of the two female bystanders. While going over the photo albums, it didn't take long for him and Agnes to figure out who Daniel was.

"Daniel, of course," Agnes said. She glanced at the dormer window. The filtered light coming from it started to diminish. "It's almost sundown. I'm giving up on Ellie, for now."

"Hold on to that thought." Ian picked up a transparent twelve-inch ruler and laid it diagonally between Daniel's eyes' sightline and the young bystander woman's bashful eyes. He handed Agnes a magnifying glass "Look closely, at those two people's eyes."

Agnes stooped, magnifying glass at hand, as she toggled between the two. "What am I looking at here?"

"People moved about, that was why their eyes often blurred. Not for Daniel and that young lady. Their eyes didn't blur because they were still. They were looking at each other."

She snorted dismissively. "She's like… uh, thirteen or fourteen?"

Agnes scrutinized the two characters again. "He could be looking at another person outside the frame."

"Possible. My hunch is just that. We need more proof. If that's our Ellie, there's got to be more of her stuff here somewhere."

"Where's the actual family portrait? We couldn't have missed an eleven-by-fourteen. Of all the pictures in this formal photo session, why did Daniel or his kin keep this particular one?"

Ian shrugged. "Let me take a wild guess. Whoever retained this picture wanted that young brunette included in the family picture. In the official selection, she wouldn't be."

"If that is indeed Ellie…"

Ian ripped the tape from the picture's corners. He turned it over. "This one is dated May nineteen-ninety-two. Daniel's baby album records showed he was born on August nineteen-seventy-six. Am I right?"

Agnes nodded.

"Which meant he was about sixteen in the picture and two years shy of his eighteenth birthday. Look at this…" He picked from the table to his left a plastic sleeve-protected newspaper clipping. It was part of a binder-clipped group that held obituaries of Pershing scions. He handed to Agnes the obituary page. He pointed at the item circled in red.

Eleonor Martin Hobbes, December 12, 1978, to October 7, 2012.

"If that's our Ellie—"

"Then she was about two years younger than Daniel in the nineteen-ninety-two family picture."

"She'd be eighteen on December twelve, nineteen-ninety-six."

"If this is Ellie's obituary, then there's got to be Daniel's somewhere."

Ian held the same holiday family picture to the light. "Another thing. Look again at the probable Ellie and her possible mom. They're not wearing their Sunday best. If they were household guests in a billionaire estate, they would have been better dressed."

"Could they be… servants?"

"They should have many servants in an estate that big."

"Live-in servants. Most likely."

THE MOMENT the three of them set foot on the second-floor landing, Agnes' eyes glared in the direction of the séance table and the three chairs, now positioned at the center of the dance floor. She confronted the befuddled Christopher. "I told you not to move anything that was already set."

"I swear I didn't move anything." Christopher hastened off to the old spot that he marked with colored gaffer tape. "Look—"

His eyes flashed. The tape marker was gone. "You guys saw it. I marked that very spot." He rubbed a floor surface area. "I can feel the adhesive here."

Creaks. The light flickered once. The vibrations rippled across the floor and through the log post. Ian thought there should have been a steady stream of wind gusts for the house to generate such low-level vibrations for seconds on end.

A tight-lipped Christopher, looking more frustrated than frightened, re-marked the spot, this time with a felt-tip pen. He went straight for the relocated séance furniture at the center of the dance floor.

Ian stood where the pen-marked spot was and observed the ceiling. He recalled Agnes had been gazing up the ceiling, too, soon after she had picked the spot where the séance should be held. There was nothing that stood out from the originally marked spot's surroundings compared to its counterpart zone at the dance floor's center. He stepped toward the spiral staircase and surveyed the immediate vicinity. His interest reverted to the ceiling again. He speculated that sometime in the past, the entire ceiling must have moved forward relative to the house's forward-leaning contortion.

He beckoned Christopher who just arrived at the contested spot, with three chairs hooked in his arms. "Chris, look up and around this area. Use the new marker's spot as a reference point. You see anything that strikes you as unusual?"

Christopher dropped the chairs. He paced about and

bounced glances at the surroundings before he started observing the ceiling.

In the meantime, Agnes traipsed up and down the dance floor, repositioning one of the six candelabras on the dance floor's walk-through borders. Each lined up to a curtained window, about a two-foot distance from them.

A fireplace log bundle, tied together with red ropes and standing in an out-of-place spot by the staircase wall, caught his attention. He told Christopher, "I know this house once hosted a fireplace. Why they have that firewood bundle up here, I don't get it."

"Can you say that again, sir? Sorry, I'm still distracted by the furniture's move."

So was Ian. He wasn't prepared to stir up an argument with Agnes that close to the séance. He could use a subject-matter subterfuge. "If this house once had a chimney, where would it have been exactly located?"

"More to the front side of the house, sir, most likely in between the spiral staircase and the wooden one."

The last time Ian had a peek at Christopher's stitches was an hour ago when Agnes replaced the bandage wrap in his head. Blood had clotted along the wound line and swelling appeared minimal. By far, the aftermath of the attack didn't impede the young man's work performance. He thought it would be wise to conduct a final check.

"How does your head feel?"

"Not bad at all, sir."

"Your state of readiness, from one to ten, ten being tip top."

"Eight, maybe."

"Good. We're down to the wire. I need you to stay focused on your assigned job throughout the séance. Under no circumstances should you freeze. I stay, you stay. I run, you run."

"You're considering the last one as an option, sir?"

"It's just a figure of speech. We take the lead from Agnes."

A few paces from the marker, Christopher gazed up at the ceiling, then across it, laterally. "Extensive repairs had been done up there. There must have once been exposed joists anchored to beams that go from one long end of the ceiling to the other. They may have been damaged and removed. New reinforcements must have been installed behind the plywood layer."

Agnes marched their way, finger pointed down. She smacked her hands once. "It's almost night, guys. Ten-minute-warning. Let's all head down for a briefing. Go to the restroom, whatever you need to do. We're working for our money tonight."

12

Séance Night

She would have dragged the séance table back to its original spot if Christopher hadn't raced to her assistance and carried off the relatively heavy table himself. Moments before, Ian and Christopher were taken aback by the anomaly's reprise. Both of them froze solid where they stood as soon as they stepped onto the second floor and saw the séance furniture set relocated again at the center of the dance floor. To Ian's consternation, she walked past them and plowed ahead to the dance floor's center where the séance furniture set had inexplicably migrated. Agnes' defiant reaction stumped him. No experienced psychic, to his estimation, would have normalized the extraordinary poltergeist activity by challenging a very clear manifestation of the spirit's will. Something was awry— her lack of fear, her stubborn spitefulness, among them. *"The night is my domain."* It played again in his mind, the stark reminder of Agnes' authority arrogation.

Their employers would have nodded at her bravado. He wouldn't, given the circumstances. But in the cusp of nightfall, he must pick his battles. He helped Agnes and Christopher reset pieces of furniture to their old spots. He felt an obligation to say something, at least. "Maybe there's a reason—"

"I know what I'm doing," Agnes snapped, her brows unexpectedly crossed, as she laid down a chair and started rearranging the four, stubby candles lined up at the open right corner of the table. "I channel spirits where I feel their energy strongest."

"You're not concerned at all he had changed the venue, twice?"

"Mister Bishop, while I'm still conscious, I call the shots." She turned to Christopher. "Chris, let's go light up the window candles. Then turn off the light downstairs."

Gas-range lighters at hand, Ian's companions split up and strode the length of the dance floor, along the way lighting up white candelabra candles by the waysides.

At the table, now fully re-established at Agnes' chosen spot, Ian flipped through the blank pages of the spiral bound, 12-by-18 artist notebook. He uncapped one of the four permanent markers and plopped one in his shirt pocket, for backup. He placed his ruled notebook on his side, across Agnes' pre-selected position.

Agnes re-checked the curtains on both the east and the west side windows. Her partner disappeared through the north-side staircase to turn off the light downstairs. Central heating was shut off earlier in keeping with a séance tradition that sought to eliminate all ambient background noise sources. All three of them sported winter wear and used soft-soled shoes. He had gloves and beanies stuffed in his side pockets, just in case.

Ian had no idea how the séance room would look once they had yanked down the switch by the north-end log post. If the venue Agnes insisted on had any advantage, it has to be its proximity to the light switch.

She skipped assigning candle spots at both staircase landings. After the second-floor lights were turned off, the floor's far-end spots—the staircase zones—would be completely in the dark. He wondered if the omission's intention was to allow for the free flow of spirit energy that might come in from else-where in the house. In his book, the darkened staircase zones represented nothing but blind flanks, no different from unlit, open doorways in the dead of night. Too late to ask. As the séance neared, he took a moment to calm his nerves. *This is just a weekend gig*, he told himself another time.

"Everyone to their places," Agnes said. She lit up the five fat candles in a staggered formation on the vacant outer third of the table.

As the murmurs in his chest intensified, he forced out a grin. It did help that Agnes stood tall and exuded unwavering confidence. She dressed in a simple white blouse, a light denim jacket on top, and deep blue jeans to complete the attire. Her long, thick, naturally wavy hair made her bright face seem smaller. No make-up or jewelry adorned her; not even a timepiece. The candle glow gave her pale skin a warm sheen. Christopher, seated at a right angle relative to hers, regarded her with discreet, sheepish glances.

They had rehearsed the séance mechanics once. On paper, the work plan should be straightforward and simple.

Agnes backed away towards the north-end log post. To his relief, she had picked the seat with the back directly to the closer of the two unlit staircase zones.

"Everyone ready?"

He nodded first. Then Christopher.

"I'll turn off the lights and we begin."

Ian took a last sweeping look at the candle placements along the dance floor borders. The candle flames flickered time and again. Each brass candelabra holder on the floor stood a safe distance from the curtained windows. All six of them were shuttered from the inside and to him it made little sense to curtain them off at night. The winds seemed calm the last time he made a window-view check. The fog hung low and moved little. Though the vents still circulated air, they should exert no sufficient strength to disturb or to extinguish the candle flames. He patted the flashlight in his chest like it was a talisman.

The lights went out.

His vision browned out before it turned dark. In a blip, they were basking in an island of weak, warm light enveloped by huge swatches of black. Christopher hasn't spoken a word since they got settled there. He missed getting a good read on him before the overhead lights went out. He looked behind him, at the dance floor reduced to an eerie emptiness defined by two rows of candle lights, like parallel airfield landing beacons that both melded with the black void at the far end staircase zones. Those blind flanks spooked him more than any other aspect of the candlelight setup. If only Agnes had assigned a couple of candles laterally at the far end zones, inner boundaries would have been much more defined.

Footsteps neared. Agnes emerged into the light. She pulled the chair behind her. She gave the materials in front of her a cursory check before she regarded them with a reassuring smile. "Ready?"

Just as quickly as she commenced the séance, her self-assured smile vanished. Her eyes turned ghastly and her mouth lurched in a wry, awkward way Ian had never seen from her before. She must have sensed it first, a mild motion sickness caused by equilibrium-disrupting events such as in a rapid elevator descent. The event caught on to him. He grabbed onto the table's sides. He wasn't sure if all three of them and their props were levitating or if they were moving away or in what direction. He scrounged for visual reference points. Yes, they were gliding, as a unit, at a slow but steady pace, towards the dance floor's center. His eyes shuttled between his two equally terrified companions. Nothing on the table moved. The table candles weren't even perturbed. The air reeked of burnt candle wick and melted wax. Not once did he hear anything scrape the floor.

He barely felt the landing, as if everything and everyone in the séance zone had levitated to just enough height to enable the entire move.

No doubt Daniel had reiterated his point.

A saucer-eyed Christopher chafed at his right arm so hard he might have wakened Agnes from her terrified stupor. She did a token location check of her surroundings. The familiar creaks in the wood escalated to a clacking crescendo before it quickly waned. Ian knew he had to step in. He lets out a forced, though passable laugh: "Goosebumps. It's been a while."

Agnes' color, or whatever he had presumed her face momentarily lost, returned. He thought she could be one of those people who recover fast from high-stress situations. She raised two open hands to the level of her shoulders. A pale smile arced from her face. "Okay, Daniel. If this is where you want it."

The floor vibrated. Ian traced the tremor to a local source. Christopher's legs must be trembling.

"Stay with us," Agnes told him, as she reached over and grabbed his shaky, tightly-balled hand that rested on the table. "He's making his point by manipulating the environment. He's not trying to scare us. Try to stay calm. I know what I'm doing."

"Maybe we should take a break."

She touched the top of his hand. "I'm sorry, Chris, we can't let him slip by. Remember, what we came here for?"

"When Agnes goes into a trance, I field the questions," Ian joined in. "I decide when to end the session should things go south. We all have flashlights hanging on our necks. The light switch is just a few paces away. One north, one south. We have control."

"Chris, look at me. We need to seize the moment. Think of this as a job. I'm pretty sure you have scarier moments in the construction zone."

Christopher took a deep breath. He sniffled and wiped the

sweat off his brows before he nodded. "Okay, okay. I'm in, I'm in."

"Everyone, take a moment to relax. Ian, eyes on me always. Chris, focus on my hands and the goings on at the table level. Keep an extra eye on Ian, for cues."

She took her hands off the table and lowered it out of view. She rubbed her palms on her lap, he assumed. The trembling in his knees started to subside.

"This is it, guys. Good luck." At that, Agnes hands reappeared on the table. She straightened and closed her eyes.

Ian expected Agnes to work herself a good while to get to a meditative state. She got right to it. In less than a minute, her head drooped, and her face disappeared in a jumble of hair.

He couldn't recall another moment in his life where the world was that quiet and still. Not a breath nor tremor from Christopher's camp. He sensed no movement, not from the table nor from the floor.

Agnes slowly straightened. Hair covered half her face and her head gently swayed. A toothless smile grew on her face, as her head movements turned gentler, almost seductive. All the signs that she had asked him to look for were there.

It turned chilly, sans a transitional phase. He chafed his hands hard and fast on his thighs.

On the table, Ian nudged the open writing notebook closer to himself. To his left, he laid his elbow on his reference questionnaire, just in case. He wrote the number one at the top his notebook. Then he straightened his posture, filled his lungs with air, and willed himself to focus on Agnes at the exclusion of the surroundings.

He gave an eye signal to Christopher who then placed a sign pen in between Agnes' right-hand forefinger and thumb.

"Tell me your name," Ian said, with as much voice and confidence as he could muster.

Agnes lurched forward and wrote in the open artist's pad before her in bold, cursive:

"Dan... Daniel."

Ian quickly added Daniel's reply to the lead question he earlier wrote.

Christopher turned the artist pad before her one-hundred-eighty degrees for Ian's perusal. He nodded and his assistant leafed over the next page and returned the pad to its marked spot on the table. He clutched at a backup marker pen. Eyes still closed and her facial expression dreamy, Agnes' pen rested in her relaxed writing hand. Her head continued to sway gently.

"Daniel Pershing, the son of Caleb Pershing, am I right?"

On the blank sheet, Agnes deftly scribbled:

"Yes."

Ian felt it kicking in, how natural the interrogatories came to him. Something unexpected paid off. After so many years of professionally probing people's minds by repeating cookie-cutter questions over and over again. As his confidence grew, so did the volume of his voice. "Daniel, did you die in this house?"

Agnes kept her hands on the table, the pen marker precariously clutched on her right hand. He browsed at the questions he had written and re-checked the item numbering.

"Where did you die, Daniel?"

Agnes leaned back, her head rotating very slowly. Her writing hand remained still.

"Did you ever live in this house?"

This time she slumped forward towards the tabletop with such speed that Ian thought she'd slam her face on it. As her upper torso slowly rose, she wrote:

"No."

"Whose residence is this, then?"

Agnes' hands remained where they were. The pen fell from her fingers. Christopher cautiously replaced them.

"Did Ellie live here?"

She wrote unreadable text on the paper before she abruptly stopped. Ian glossed over his numbered questions and the corresponding answers.

"Did something bad happen to Ellie here?"

On the blank page, she scribbled nonsense again.

The table candles flickered. It made crackling sounds. Gnats that got fried after orbiting the flames too close, he imagined. Sweat beads started to gather on her forehead and strands of her hair rose as if drawn by some static electrical force.

He felt a shudder in his chest, followed by chills that seemed to spiral about his body in a slow, up-and-down pattern. He once saw a news magazine photograph of young people outdoors whose hair were strung out as that of Agnes' right before a bolt of lightning struck, reportedly killing a number of the kids. He wondered what force could generate enough energy to levitate bunches of human hair.

"We know you were here with Ellie, in a room in this house, on July twelve nineteen-ninety-two."

On the blank page that Christopher had just turned, Agnes wrote in bolder strokes:

"Ellie, Ellie, you here... you here."

He saw Christopher stiffen as he showed him the note. He motioned him to flip to the next page.

"Daniel, are you telling us the spirit of Ellie is here with us, now?"

"You here, my... my Ellie."

"If the spirit of Ellie is here with us now, then she must have passed away. Can you tell us when she passed away?"

"Ellie, Ellie, make..."

"Make what?"

"Here... one more... two more..."

Agnes started to sweat profusely. Sooner than later, Ian

knew he had to bring the session to a close. "Did you and Ellie meet in this house, in the master bedroom?"

"One more…"

He reviewed the last set of notes. He couldn't make any sense of it. "Did you die in this house?"

"Ellie… back… in two…"

"Daniel, why does your soul linger in this house?"

"Ellie… make…"

"You must rest in peace, Daniel. My friends and I were hired by your father, Doctor Caleb Pershing, to help you cross over. You must tell us, what is the reason why you remain here?"

"Ellie… make…"

"Make what? Daniel, what are you trying to tell us?"

"Ellie… love… make love to… to me…"

He traded stares with Christopher. Agnes' head still swayed, but her smile had gone and her hair started to behave. Her forehead skin furrowed and her brows crinkled, as that of someone concentrating.

"Make love to me. What do you mean by that?"

"Make love to me… make… make love to me…"

"If Ellie had passed away, then she is on the other side, waiting for you. You have to cross over and be reunited with Ellie, whom you love. Is she here with us, right now?"

"She's here… right there… right there…"

"Ellie is in the afterlife, Daniel. If she's here she only came to see you and she would be back to where she came from. Join her. Cross over. Tell us how we can help you cross over."

"She… Ellie… there."

"Where in this room? Can you give us a sign where Ellie is in this room, right now?"

The two spare pens on the table twirled once. Their caps pointed to Agnes.

Christopher saw it, too, and his chin quivered. His right hand jumped to his mouth. Ian deepened his voice and raised it: "Daniel, are you telling us that the spirit of Ellie is behind the psychic medium?"

"No. Ellie there… right there."

"That woman, across me, is Agnes Haskell. She is a professional medium and you are communicating with me through her. Daniel, did you understand what I just said?"

"Ellie, Ellie, make love to me. Make… love to me."

Agnes' blouse was drenched in sweat. Ian prepared to bring the session to a close. He slammed a fisted hand on the table. "That woman is not Ellie. You must know what Ellie looked like. That woman is not her."

"No, no, no… Ellie… there… Ellie eyes closed."

"That woman whose eyes are closed is Agnes Haskell. She is a trance medium. If you cannot tell Agnes from Ellie, then I'm waking the psychic medium, right now." He motioned to Christopher who pounced on Agnes and started shaking her.

Ian rounded the table and shook her from behind. She tapped at her cheeks repeatedly. "Agnes, wake up, wake up." Agnes' body stiffened, seized. She tipped to one side and Christopher caught her. Her eyes rolled and her eyelids fluttered.

All at once, the candle flames in the room snuffed out on its own.

Ian turned on his flashlight. Christopher likewise. "Hold on to her. I'm turning on the light." He pointed his flashlight toward the direction of the light switch as he made his way north.

Incandescent light soon filled the room.

Dazed, Ian scrounged around for Agnes' gig bag that she had left by the iron staircase. He reached for bottled water inside it.

AGNES HUNCHED over the artist pad on the séance table. She had asked for quiet time, up until she finished reconciling Ian's question notes with the scribbles she made through psychic automatic writing. Immediately after the session, Ian numbered the questions he had fielded and double checked that it matched with the answers on the artist pad.

Ian, her extra blouse and gig bag at hand, waited behind her. With the heater still off, the temperature on the second floor had dropped considerably. Agnes would not let them turn on the heater. Her hair and her clothes dripped with perspiration, yet he didn't sense any shake from her. Her eyes barely blinked as she blistered over the paper references. Christopher reached over and smothered the smoldering candle wicks with his fingers. A burnt candle wick smell lingered in the air. She finished a bottle but refused to change until she was done.

He itched to begin a conversation on the status quo. He waited. As soon as she reached the end of the last of the pages and she closed the pad, he spoke, "I think we have a problem."

"We're done for the day, right?" Christopher said, nervously.

Agnes stood and grabbed her extra blouse from Ian. "Turn around, please."

The two men about faced. Ian heard her swiftly changing. "Agnes, I know this isn't the first time that I've asked but… have you encountered something like this before?"

No answer.

"Have you heard of anything like this before, apart from the movies and from that old lore about the Bell…"

"The Bell Ghost or Witch incident, somewhere in the northeast, sometime in the nineteenth century. You two can turn around now."

Agnes stuffed her discarded clothing into the gig bag. She put on her jacket over the new blouse.

"More than anyone of us, you know best what we're dealing with here. What do we do now?"

She pointed to the ceiling. "The attic. We need to find Ellie's pictures."

"Can we do that tomorrow?" Christopher said.

She shook her head emphatically.

"The family portrait should do," Ian suggested. "I believe she's the one there."

She slung her gig bag and led the way to the staircase. "We need pictures of her with him, in this house."

"Is he still here, now?"

"I feel him no more."

"Are we, uh… safe?"

Mid-staircase, on the way to the attic, she turned on her flashlight. Ian and Christopher followed suit. "We need corroborating evidence," she said, "before we can come to an agreement, as to what really happened."

"You must have some idea—"

"Forget poltergeist paraphysics. Psychokinesis is at work here. Either he had that power during his lifetime or he had a latent one that someone, one of us, has been consciously or subconsciously abetting."

"I don't think I follow."

"I'll explain, later."

Up the darkened attic, Agnes stepped ahead and switched on the lights.

Everyone froze where they stood. Several empty tables barricaded the attic entrance. The portable CD player was at the top of one table.

Ian heard a gasp. He couldn't tell if it was from her or from Christopher. Agnes stepped back and signaled a retreat. "Everyone, to the living room, now."

13

You're in Ghost Country Now

"Fog... fog everywhere," Christopher said, as he peered through the living room's quarter-opened window blinds. He rolled back the blinds shut.

On his knees on the floor, Ian applied another duct tape strip layer to the makeshift bedding's last unsecured corner. King-size comforters, two layers thick, laid flat against the floor in the middle of the living room where everyone had agreed to spend the night together. The compromised master bedroom and the two rooms adjacent to it were designated as alternates of last recourse.

Here, at least, even with just the ceiling pin lights on, they have a commanding view of the hallway, the kitchen-dining zone, and the back door at the far end. Once they retire to bed, the house's front door will be a crawl away above their heads. To their far right, close to the wooden staircase's base is the ground floor's emergency fire door.

Ian met no resistance when he tried to sell the idea of turning the living room into their new camp. Their strategic location lent everyone some comfort that should a true emergency arise, there are two doors rigged with electronically integrated locking mechanisms a short distance off. Just one hard door-handle crank and a distress signal would ring up somewhere in Dr. Pershing's headquarters, wherever it may be.

Agnes has been gone quite a while. Ian heard faucet water rushing from inside the hallway bathroom.

Christopher, garbed in jammies like everybody else, slipped into the left side of the floor bed. He pulled one end of a quilted, cotton blanket to his chin. Ian occupied the far-right flank. They had the middle zone reserved for her. He had the best above-the-head view of the spiral staircase and the wooden staircase near it. Earlier, Christopher replaced the dead incandescent bulb in a pendant lamp hanging at the second-floor ceiling directly above the mouth of the wooden staircase. The faint, incandescent light cone coming from upstairs barely illuminated the stairway steps. Better than nothing, he thought, as he gave his surroundings a cursory check.

"You comfy in there?" Ian asked, from across the gap.

"It's been a while since I slept on the floor. It's quite comfy, as you put it, sir."

Ian had pre-empted the sleeping arrangement to make sure Christopher wouldn't feel left out. At the get-go, he had overtly included Christopher as a co-equal member of the team, only to fail to make that point clear to Agnes each time he had the opportunity to tell her off on it. If there were any side benefit to the hairy experiences doled out to them by the spirit that night, it should be this chance to be physically comfortable together. He had also dialed down the thermostat to fifty-three degrees, a bit lower than Daniel's temperature preference. Sticking close would be a necessity. For sure Christopher would be delighted.

Agnes slipped out of the hallway restroom and joined them. She brought on with her a fresh-smelling minty scent. He admired her nerves, staying in the bathroom awhile, sans a door-side bodyguard. Ian made do with token toothbrushing and speedy gargles. Christopher, no less. He couldn't wait for daylight to come.

"Is this the lowest the lights would go?" Agnes asked as she pulled her blanket's ends up her chin.

"That's pretty much it," Christopher said. "We can turn off the living room pin lights if you want."

"Please."

Christopher rolled away and went for the ground floor master switch on the wall by the hallway entryway.

"Know what, switch it around. Keep the lights here. Turn the rest off."

He turned off the hallway lights.

"On second thought, just leave it all on, at its lowest setting."

In a snap, Christopher obliged. He returned to bed.

Agnes fluffed the pillow behind her head and turned to her side, facing Ian.

Ten past ten.

"Dim the living room lights lower," he told Christopher who was already in a crouching position in his bed space. He couldn't risk another white night. Even for Ian, the night was still young. His companion's eyes reflected the shared situation.

His attempt the previous night to foster a dream clairvoyance event turned out to be a disaster. He had two more nights, this one included, to pay off the score. For the past effort, he remembered just one noteworthy event—that of an assumed Daniel and Ellie whose faces he could barely see. They sat on a floor mat, picnic basket beside them, the attic as the backdrop. Their faces were muddled by dusky light. He couldn't pin the light source, whether it came from the window or from an artificial light source. The particular scene lacked the order, color, and vividness that come with any proper retro-cognitive dreamwork. Without a sustained, Rapid-Eye-Movement level quality sleep, his recollected dreams would eventually fade into jumbled up, phantasmagoric nonsense. Any dream sequence he failed to recall or made any sense of would be as good as gone. The two lovers visited his dream world in an unexpected place in the house and as a fleeting glimmer. They showed up, though. A good sign. He only needed one sustained deep sleep. Then he would still be able to fulfill Doctor Pershing's request.

He checked back on his bedmates. Both looked wakeful. He decided to make use of the downtime at hand. "When you're in a trance and the spirit inhabits you, do you get a peek at the spirit's mind? I mean, do you see what he sees?"

"It's nothing like that. It's more like a dream you could barely recall. I remember very little. If I remember anything, the imageries are a mash-up of meaningless, unrelated events. Just like in most dreams."

"I was hoping you had a glimpse of him and her, together."

"I do better on sense-impression recall, even imagery recall, whenever I perform seances on the place of my choosing. Oh, well."

"When you do better, what do you recall?"

"I get clearer impressions, a better feel on the spirit's motivation, sometimes even messages he is reluctant to reveal."

From her weakening voice, Ian thought she was losing interest in the conversation. Exhaustion must have caught up on her and she has started to drift. "You hear?"

"Like clairaudients do?"

"Do you hear, as part of gleaning sense perceptions?"

"No. I had to figure everything out by feel and by intuition. The question-and-answer review after the séance helps glue everything together. When Daniel responds to your questions and I read the transcript, sensory impressions and spirit messages come together. I fill in the gaps. I gain insight on what he really wants."

"Can you call on Ellie?"

He sensed hesitation.

"There's nothing in our employer's letter that suggested we could. Besides, I wouldn't. Daniel is the resident spirit. I'd be going over his head to do something as radical as that."

"The previous psychics must have tried to conjure Ellie's spirit."

"I wouldn't put anything past anyone in this profession. Three hundred plus alumni. Who knows? Someone must have thrown away the rulebook and experimented."

"Have you tried it before, throwing away the rulebook?"

Agnes shook her head. "Our profession comes with unique risks. We have to be careful about who we bring up."

The floor creaked. He felt sustained vibration coming from the wood floor. Maybe it was the wind seeping under the house's elevated foundation. "You must have experienced it before, an indeterminate spirit sneaking in."

Ian saw Christopher's head, slowly rising, his eyes widening. Another creak. A louder one. The underfloor vibrations originated from different directions. One extended tremor trailed south, toward the kitchen.

"There are really spirits out there," Christopher said, "that are not people's souls."

"People souls or not, through a séance or through Ouija board conjuring, you can't be careful enough."

"Evil spirits?"

"I don't know. No one really knows."

Christopher lets out a sigh of dismay. "You have to know something, about whether a spirit is good or bad."

"All I can assure you is this—I know how to keep the uninvited ones out."

"How?"

"I don't just jump into a séance. I acquaint myself with the resident spirit, first."

"What if a bad spirit tries to—"

"Tries to impersonate?"

"Yes, yes. You're in a trance. How would you be able to keep out impostors?"

"Before I fall into a trance, I had already consented to a specific resident spirit—one that I'd recognize even when I'm unconscious."

"So, the unwanted outsiders, they can't just jump in?"

"They can try. But then I'd likely wake up."

"Sorry that I'm jumpy on this subject. We grew up with grandparents who didn't mind telling kids ghost and evil spirit stories."

"Too bad. You're neck deep in ghost country, now."

"Between ghosts and evil spirits, I'd choose ghosts anytime."

"I'm hungry. What do you have in the pantry that's quick?"

Christopher, as if spring-loaded, sat up. "What do you feel like—"

"I don't care."

"I could use something warm, like coffee," Ian said. "I'm in a nibbling mood, too."

"We have coconut cookies, pineapple-carrot cake, cheese bread, and from-the-pot leftovers in the fridge. Oh, we have empanadas. I can heat up some."

Agnes slipped out of her blanket, got up, and stepped into her night slippers. "Warm cheese bread sounds good right now."

Christopher sped ahead, overtook her, and turned on the hallway lights to full.

"On second thought, I shouldn't be drinking anything stronger than green tea tonight," Ian said, as he caught up with the two. "But I wouldn't mind being wakened in the morning by the aroma of freshly-brewed coffee."

"I'll set one up for brewing, sir. Just show me how to set the automatic timer."

"Let me take care of that."

"Tea for you, sir?"

Ian nodded.

"Agnes?"

"Same for me."

A full smile went with it; perhaps, just an appreciative grin exaggerated by a downlighter.

Ian found the lilt in their mood a welcome respite from events that turned out to be stormier than anyone could have anticipated. It was a breath of fresh air, their springy walk together to the dining-kitchen area. He wished such collective spirit would last.

IAN OVERHEARD AGNES, while she helped herself with a slice of pineapple-carrot pie, mumbling in a such low tone he couldn't decide if she was asking a question or making a statement. To whom, he could only guess. The only distinct word he made out was "psychokinesis."

Then from across the dining table, she gazed at him. "Do you have that gift, mister Bishop?"

This late in the night and she had the temerity to bring up an issue laced with suspicious context. Ian noticed a change in the tone of her voice. Hesitation would send a far worse impression. He replied outright. "Psychokinesis? An unequivocal no on that."

"You, Chris?"

"Is that the same as telekinesis?"

"Yes. Do you have the ability to move objects by thinking about them moving?"

He made a nod of recognition. "Wish I had that power. I mean the power to make things move at will."

"I'll ask both of you again; is there anyone among you who can make things move by mind power alone?"

Ian traded empty stares with Christopher. They shook their heads at the same time.

"Why would you ask us something that outlandish?"

"I needed to be sure."

"I may have no training on the subject of the paranormal, but I can extrapolate. Let me turn the wheel the other way. If a usual suspect needed some rounding up, why not you? We're not the person who went ballistic that fright night in the master bedroom. None of us butted heads with the spirit during the pre-séance table reset. Shouldn't we be the ones asking outlandish questions?"

Her rapt, unwavering eyes shuttled between Christopher and him, as if she was tracking them and seeking out meanings in their facial expressions. "One of you is holding back. I can feel it. That person has to come clean."

"Agnes, wherever this inquiry is going, let's keep this friendly, okay?"

"You are prevaricating. Are you hiding something?"

"Again, no."

She turned to Christopher. "Are you?"

Christopher looked away reflexively as if he needed time to process the question. "Uh, no."

Agnes folded her arms, and gazed at the two men's eyes alternately, as if testing them, on who would blink first. Her eyes were laser-focused. The dark in them seemed bigger and opaque.

"I saw your eyes that night," Ian said. "I heard your voice. You could have killed Christopher. Again, if there's anyone hiding something here, why not you?"

Her defiant eyes welled before they simmered down. She appeared shaken up, from the inside, as someone working up a will to keep her composure. The wind had shifted. He pounced on the opportunity. "We are a team. You can't talk down to us like that."

"I'm being direct."

"You are demanding, not asking."

"Take it the way you want it. Let me ask again. I need to know if anyone of you is gifted with telekinetic powers."

"How many times do we need to answer in the negative? If these were a police interrogation, I would have already asked for a lawyer."

The moisture in her beset eyes remained as steadfast as when Ian first noticed it emerge. It clung there with just enough consistency to keep it from accruing into a teardrop.

Agnes planted both her elbows on the table and she gripped both sides of her face with such force it smacked. She lets off a deep sigh of frustration. Her hands slipped into her hair and she grasped at them like she wanted to tear it off. Her closed eyes tightened. Still no tears.

If she had prior knowledge of his psychic specialty background, Ian knew she would have pushed the confrontation to a different trajectory. This wasn't the first time she had broached the subject matter up. At his age, he should be a hundred-percent sure what psychic powers he could lay claim to and what he couldn't. He ruled out Christopher. Ian considered himself competent in detecting guilt. Besides, he believed the young man could be cornered easily if he was nursing a lie. He couldn't say the same about her. He'd take Christopher's side in any circular blame game.

He should have had scoured the internet for anything about Agnes' past. Thanks to Dorothy Small's gossip talk, he had learned that Agnes, orphaned at birth, was a foster care basketball until she had turned eighteen. If he were to make a bet on anyone in the team who could be binned as a paranoid-schizoid specimen, it would be her, hands down.

Agnes straightened, took in a lungful of air, and lowered herself again, elbows to the table, tense hands clasped tightly together. "I need to know why this spirit is exhibiting psychokinetic powers," she elocuted the words for emphasis. "I will find out, sooner or later. So, I'd ask you two one last time. A billionaire wouldn't hire laymen to support a séance. Please, lay it out on the table, right now."

Ian saw nothing in Christopher's eyes but question marks. They shook their heads again, almost at the same time. Had it been early in the day, Ian would have put on a fight. He leaned back on his chair and mulled over his alternative plan of drawing as much heat as he can from the conversation. "You'd ask that question one last time, your own words. I'll hold you to it."

"For tonight, that is."

"Fair enough. Can we finish what we started here and transition our way to bed in peace?"

He took her blink as a tacit nod. He gulped down his lukewarm tea. She forked in another morsel from her plate as she motioned Christopher to pour her cup a fill.

"Your gift, you weren't born with it." Ian threw it in, at the risk of sounding impertinent, to derail the possibility of her relapsing to another paranoid line of inquiry.

"How did you know?"

"It's an educated guess," Ian said, even more determined to preserve the still shaky status quo. "Sometimes mind gifts emerge after a physical or psychological trauma, such as concussions suffered in car accidents, or extreme emotional anguish, most especially if such traumatic incidents happened during childhood."

Agnes' fiery eyes simmered. She resumed her work on the last fragments of her broken-up cake. Christopher picked one from the untouched empanada pile. The surface of Agnes' plate squeaked. He knew that if she were using plastic utensils, one of them would have surely snapped. He resumed his diversionary talk.

"There are numerous studies on savants—children born with developmental deficiencies—exhibiting extraordinary skills in art, math, and other disciplines. We can correlate savants with people who suffered from traumatic brain injuries. The undamaged part of the brain compensates for the damaged one and as a result of the brain's re-wiring effort, new regions of the brain become enhanced in a way evolution never intended it to. It's a game of numbers. Of the eight billion people on the planet, how many had suffered from brain-related trauma. Say, for mathematical expediency that the number is one percent. Very few in that one percent range would have their brains rewired in a way that would produce a savant or people with unexplained abilities such as psychics. But a fraction of that number would. This fraction would translate to tens of thousands of extraordinarily gifted individuals."

"Sir, would an illness like, say Typhus, do the same?"

As Christopher's voice trailed, Ian saw Agnes' eyes turn sharply to him.

"Did you nearly die from Typhus, when you were a child?"

"Uh, it wasn't me. It's just an example."

Agnes' sharp stare hounded Christopher. Something about her eyes, their juxtaposition of unsettling starkness and youthful brightness at the same time, made Ian wonder what lay behind them. He suspected they might be hiding a cold, calculating character.

"Daniel could have had such a gift, in life," Ian jumped in. "We might have witnessed psychokinetic manifestations in the form of enhanced hauntings."

"Believe me, if there was a single case out there with this much directed energy, I would have heard of it."

Ian desperately sought to further his diversionary talk. "Forget poltergeist phenomena. Nothing else bugged me more than the fact he mistook you for Ellie."

Agnes, after a lag, shook her head. Her eyes took on a weary, tired look. "I don't know what that glitch actually meant."

"In the many other seances that you had officiated, were you ever mistaken for a long-lost love by a spirit?"

She frowned before she shook her head.

"He mistook you for Ellie. You're not worried about that incident?"

"First thing tomorrow, we dig. We have to find an older picture of her."

"Any particular reason for that search?"

She didn't answer.

"In retrospect, other words through the automatic writing texts struck me as really odd."

"What words?"

"Make love to me. He had said that through you, several times."

"Departed spirits are not above manifesting incoherence. Daniel turned eighteen in nineteen-ninety-four. By then Ellie would still be about two years younger than him. A minor. He probably practiced abstinence and hadn't gone over it."

"What a bad time for a man to turn eighteen," Christopher said. "Had he made love to her then, he would have been a child molester."

A hollow thud came from somewhere in the living room.

Everyone stilled. Agnes gazed up. "Heard that?"

"It came from upstairs," Christopher said.

"The front door, I think," Ian said.

The floor creaked. The porcelain and the glassware on the table tinkled.

Agnes pulled back from the chair and stood. "Would everyone stand up, please."

The two men obliged. Agnes stared at the tabletop, then to the china cabinet.

Another thud.

From upstairs, Ian decided. The glissading floor-level creaks and the tinkles from the tabletop soon followed. The two incidents could be related.

Ian tracked Agnes' eyes. She appeared to be observing his teacup vibrating from its porcelain base. He felt no tremors coming from the floor. Yet the tea cup appeared to be vibrating.

Her brows crossed. A malevolent gaze swung in Christopher's direction. "It's you causing this."

"What? The sound came from upstairs."

Agnes slammed both her palms on the table. "I'm not talking about what's going on upstairs. The creaks on the wood, the vibrations from small glassware. I've been putting two and two together. These disturbances in the surroundings happen every time you get scared."

Christopher blanched. His eyes started to wander reflexively; his mouth opened before it collapsed and tightened. He looked cornered and he sought him for succor.

A thud.

A second later the tea cup vibrated again.

"Agnes, let's take a step back and not rush to conclusions."

She was still at it, a decibel louder, her eyes coruscating: "It all makes sense now. Doctor Pershing hired someone with psychokinetic abilities to whose energy fields a resident spirit could tap into." She pointed at Christopher's face. "I've asked you more than once and you said nothing."

"Don't point at me like that," Christopher shot back. "Where I'm from it's insulting to point to people like that."

"I went into a trance not knowing I was walking into a trap. You had so much chance to warn me."

"Maybe if you didn't treat me like I'm your slave I would have been more open. You treat me like I'm your slave. Slaves don't talk. They only go along."

"What the hell are you talking about."

"Agnes, take a step back and calm down. Let Chris explain."

Ian heard porcelain tinkles amid the bedlam. He could swear two more thumps occurred since the start of the squabble. His two irate companions didn't even seem to notice.

Arms to her waist and her chin high, Agnes showed no sign of relenting. "Okay, go ahead, tell us what your deal was with Doctor Pershing."

"What deal? I don't do deals. Just like you I came here to make some money."

"You two sit down right now," Ian took the lead. He pulled his chair and sat. "Go on, sit. We became professionals the moment we got paid to do a job. You two better stop bickering like kids in a playground. Sit down and let's discuss this like adults."

"Kids in a playground? Do you not understand the gravity of this—"

"All right, wrong choice of words. I know it's still dark and this is your domain. Now, would you two please, sit."

"I prefer to stand."

Ian slammed a fisted hand on the table. "If I don't see any teamwork, right now, I swear I'd pull down that door lever and we'd all be going home."

Agnes wrapped her arms around herself and looked away. Christopher's eyes fell. He knew he got them thinking. He waited.

Christopher pulled the chair first.

She got herself seated ahead of him.

Ian stared at Christopher "I know you have something to tell us."

A thud.

Everyone's eyes roamed the ceiling. It definitely came from the second level's far north end.

"Whatever might be causing that sound, we have bigger issues here, among ourselves." He remained on Christopher whose eyes reflected unambiguous guilt. "Chris?"

Shoulders drooped and his hands between his knees, Christopher closed his eyes and kept still for a few seconds. He let go a deep sigh before he re-established eye contact with him and Agnes. "Okay, okay. Everyone, please, hear me out."

Agnes pulled back against the chair, crossed her arms tighter, and waited. The fire in her eyes had gone. Perhaps it was a deliberate façade, as in situations when a police interrogator shuts up the moment the perp indicated he was about to confess. She said, in a milder tone, "When did you first become aware you can move things?"

"Since I was a boy. Little things, like these cups. They move and make noise for no reason. I was a kid. How would I know I was causing them? Ghosts, we grew up being told. We move to another place, and the same thing happens. Unlike you guys, me and my folks, we know nothing about psychic stuff and all that. It's just ghosts doing their thing."

"Something more spectacular must have happened," Agnes said in a much calmer tone. "Or else, Pershing and company wouldn't have found you."

Another thump from upstairs.

Everyone froze for a moment.

"I don't know how stories about the ghost activity got around. When I was fifteen, the family got a visit from a lady psychic. I forgot whom she worked for but I remember she asked me lots of questions. She came back with two others, three more times. They put videos around our house. They slept there, once. We never heard from them ever again."

"They never came back? Really?"

"I swear—"

"Are you able to move objects, at will?"

Christopher shook his head emphatically. "As I said, I wish I could. I'm a superhero comics fan. It would be cool to have that power, you know. Believe me, I tried to a lot of times. I couldn't even make an egg roll off a counter. My siblings saw me try. I'm a flop. What else can I say."

"When was the last time you tried, making something move?"

"Three or four years ago, maybe. You people need to understand. Those strangers who asked me questions regarding my so-called ability, I know shit about those things they were asking me. When you asked me if I can move things, how do I answer the question? Technically, I can't anyway. I have every reason to hold back on it."

Christopher barely finished his spiel and Agnes had already left her seat. She rounded the table. She placed a porcelain cup at a far edge between her spot and that of Christopher's directly across. She backed away towards the hallway. She sidled towards the cabinet and leaned her shoulder on it. "Chris, put your hands together. Then I want you to focus on the cup. Make it fall off the edge."

Another solid thump from upstairs. The phenomenon must have gone the way of finicky car alarms. It didn't seem to bother anyone anymore.

He shook his head. "I've tried many times—"

"I want you to try again. Point your hands into the cup. Eyes on it. Concentrate on the intention. You want to push the cup off the table."

Christopher held his hands together in prayer fashion and stared at the cup. He lined up his middle fingers on it. Seconds pass.

"Try it with your eyes closed."

Ian noticed Agnes backing away stealthily. She stepped past the cabinet and reached for the wall switch. "Keep your eyes closed. Try again."

Lights out.

A crash.

By the time she turned the lights back on, Christopher was already scrounging for the dustpan.

"Fear, that's it," Agnes said, dryly.

"Whoa," Ian said. "There might be another explanation."

"If we only have time, we can replicate this experiment many times over. You bet we'd get the same results."

"Okay, you had crafted the experiment expertly. I concede. But here's my point. Consider our team's magic furniture ride to Daniel's preferred séance spot. The coordination and control of the entire movement, no way Chris could have, inadvertently or otherwise, helped facilitate even a smidgen of that feat. It took a perfect configuration of circumstances to enable him to cause a cup to fall off the edge. Think. How can a long-departed spirit, no matter how much psychic power he had during his lifetime, exploit the latent powers of a living, fully conscious human being and then elevate the manifestation of its own power by several orders of magnitude? You're the psychic phenomena expert. What are we really dealing with, here?"

A thud, at the tail of the last one, mere seconds apart. For a second or so, everyone's eyes turned to the source of the strange sound, surely north to the living room's direction. He could make out a glint of terror in his companion's eyes.

Agnes shut her eyes tight and shook her head wearily. "Energy fields."

"Say that again?"

"Energy fields. That's all I can think of. It's like specific bandwidths that certain radio waves can use as lines of transmission."

"Frequencies."

"Something like that."

"Can you elucidate on that, for our layman sensibilities."

"I can't. Not right now. The power this spirit had manifested, it's totally beyond me."

He would have called it a night then and there. But the next thud landed heavier, perhaps a tad closer. He forestalled on it. "I'm sure you've heard about Maglev or magnetic levitation trains. Electrified rails induce magnetic effects to raise multi-ton trains to just enough height to circumvent friction and thus enable it to reach speeds of hundreds of miles an hour. Magnetic levitation techniques would explain our magic furniture ride better than generalizations such as frequencies or energy fields. Even then, none of us are made of metals. And even if we were, the furniture isn't. Therefore, the whole ensemble, us and the furniture, couldn't have been magnetized to levitate and be propelled to the center of the dance floor. Some other force, related to magnets and electricity or not, made that happen."

"Mister Bishop, I appreciate your bringing science into the conversation. From my end, let me say this. Everything I know about paranormal phenomena didn't square with the controlled power the resident spirit had demonstrated to us. I might be out of line, the way I tried to squeeze answers from both of you. But you and Christopher need to understand why I got desperate for answers."

"Let's look back on this energy fields-frequencies conundrum. If we earthlings attempt to communicate with alien civilizations elsewhere in the universe and intelligent life out there did the same, both sides would likely tap into similar cosmic frequencies. If the distance between the two alien civilizations is too far, contact may not even be possible in a single human lifespan. The celestial speed limit is fixed. Okay, to circumvent that limit, we can throw in principles of quantum entanglements and apply it to the mystery at hand. But by doing so, we stretch the limits of what is possible. I'm not prepared to take this conversation that far."

"Same here. Although, someone once told me that if one day the physics behind psychic mediumship were to be established, that it's likely quantum entanglements would offer an explanation." Agnes closed her eyes and shook her head. "Forget what I just said. I'm just blabbing, now."

Three more heavy thuds had come to pass by then, as if an entity was deliberately trying to intrude. It seemed to him everyone was returning the favor by ignoring it. No one showed interest in addressing the matter, either. Perhaps, like him, his companions preferred to stay put until the poltergeist activity had run itself out. "On the contrary, what you said offered another angle to this conundrum. Imagine two psychics from two different places in the universe attempting to communicate with each other. What frequencies would they use? Would these mutually alien psychics be bound by the same rules such as the universal speed limit of light? Quantum entanglements is about the reality that such laws can be circumvented. It is at the far edge of what could make the impossible and unthinkable possible in a blip of future scientific discovery. By far, everything we've talked about on this subject matter involved phenomena that science can't explain yet. Agnes, you communicate with the dead and gone. Not a second of time lag. It takes about eight minutes for sunlight to reach Earth, three minutes for a radio message from Mars to get to a receiver here. How in God's universe do you explain that? A physicist would rather dismiss you as a fraud. A cosmologist wouldn't know how to explain you. But you should. At least you can try."

Agnes, looking tired, slouched and closed her eyes tight for a long second. "Clairvoyants see, clairaudients hear. It's true. Trance mediums like me relay communications between people and souls. The common thread that binds all psychics is the ability to connect to or with something, across time and space. Maybe even to a completely unknown realm. We don't require extraordinary brain power to achieve the connections the way satellites with tiny batteries can ping around signals from one end of the Earth to another." She pointed to her head. "Extra sensory perception and its power source comes from here. It's called paranormal because nothing about it is normal in both the physical and the metaphysical sense. Machine inventions exploit radio waves in the cosmos. Theoretical physicists try to explain the unthinkable. What do you think psychics exploit to communicate with souls in the afterlife in real time?"

"This is your trade. You must have some idea."

"No, I don't. It frustrates me that I do this for a living and I'm stumped every time I try to make sense of all of it."

The heavy thuds would not stop. It has been creeping into his nerves for a good while he was tempted to bring the conversation to it. He still clung to hope that waiting it out was the best option. "What about psychokinesis?"

"Much more so. Every psychic I know struggled to understand psychokinesis because we have no idea how its agents harness certain energy fields to make physical objects defy the laws of gravity. Imagine a magnetic levitation train running on people's mind power. That is the kind of force that's on the table here."

He checked the time. Sooner or later, they have to migrate to the living room. For sure his companions were waiting for him to address the issue. "The CIA had a decades-long program that enlisted psychic agents skilled in a psychic specialty called remote viewing. During the Carter administration, a Soviet bomber crashed in a jungle in Africa and neither the American nor the Soviet military, with all their satellite surveillance capabilities could locate it. Enter an American clairvoyant who gave the U.S. military the exact coordinates of the crash site. Lo and behold, she was right on the money. Remote viewing is an ability akin to clairvoyance. It is clairvoyance, in fact, and the phenomena is backed by science and have real world applications. If psychokinesis is exploitable, national intelligence organizations would have used it to some degree. To my knowledge, none did. And yet here we are, witnesses to it. A live specimen is even among us. Again, what are we missing here."

"Mister Bishop, locating hidden objects is one thing, levitating objects by agents living or gone is another. I've been around this business awhile. I'm telling you now, the psychic community have very little anecdotal evidence on psychokinesis."

"Your verdict then, on our magic furniture ride."

"It's not possible."

"If it's not, then again, what are we really dealing with here?"

"I don't know. I don't really know."

"We've all heard this one before. Another long day awaits us tomorrow."

Ian glanced at the wall clock. Nearly midnight. Ready or not, he decided to go for it. He stood and smacked his hands. "Five-minute warning, people, and I'm calling it a night."

"Wait," Agnes said.

He found himself settling back on his chair. So did Christopher.

"Yes, it's not possible. But unless the three of us are under some kind of mass delusion—unless our employers did us a number—unless Daniel who has psychokinetic power is still alive and is just nearby and doing magic tricks on us. Unless some sleight of hand had been foisted on us, we need to acknowledge what we had experienced did happen."

"A double affirmative on that."

"Since what happened is not a miracle, there has to be an explanation behind it. Had our project already ended, I wouldn't be this adamant about answers."

Ian raised both hands in a mock surrender pose. "It's my turn to declare, without reservation, that I can't wrap my head around this one."

"This is way beyond my pay grade," Christopher said. "I just want this whole thing to be over."

"We still have a séance session left and I need to understand."

"The afterlife is your domain. Try. Tell us."

"If Daniel had replicated his feat to other psychics before us, the story would have leaked. The psychic community is small."

"You do believe the incidents here are unique to our team then."

She closed her eyes before she nodded. "Exactly my point. We must have introduced something unique to this place, something that enabled Daniel to magnify and exert control over his new-found power. Chris' latent telekinetic abilities can't be enough."

Her gaze predictably landed on him. "You have something to tell us?"

"For the hundredth time, I have nothing to declare."

"What if we have summoned a different spirit?" Christopher said.

"Do not say that again," Agnes said.

"You're the one who told us about that possibility."

"I've been doing this for most of my life. I know it's Daniel."

"What if you're wrong this time," Ian said.

"I didn't just feel him. I saw him with Ellie."

"How—"

"I saw them in my dreams, the previous night. I didn't tell you guys because I'm not sure about what I really dreamt. I'm pretty sure I do not have that gift. I think they call it dream-work. Retro-cognitive dream clairvoyance, to be precise. This is a clear sign Daniel is entrusting to me an identity signature. I felt him and I have seen him. That's more than enough assurance for me that entities cannot slip into our shared realm."

14

Nowhere to Run

The hollow thud from upstairs went on intermittently, its tempo more random than clockwork precise. Ian had asked his bundled-up bedside companions once, for them to check it out. Neither of the two responded. Not a stir. During the thumps earliest manifestations, he suspected the disturbance might be no more otherworldly than a utility door window outside the house that Dr. Pershing's people had missed latching up during their one once around during the day. Then a sobering thought swiftly nullified the assumption. The house's insulation layer and the metal jalousie-type shutters that protected all windows but for the attic dormers would have muffled noise from the outside even if a battering ram is pummeling the house. The deep, heavy thumping sound could only have come from the inside. Then they had settled down in the living room and an onset of icy coldness sets in. The temperature must have plummeted a couple of degrees more in less than a minute. Blankets and comforters tightened up.

He gave up on his hope the thumping noise would cease on its own.

He could place it now. The thud mimicked the sound that

would have been produced by a log dropped into a solid wood floor. This time it came from the direction of the wooden staircase landing. Even closer. From a fetal position, Agnes straightened. Her eyes bulged. Christopher stiffened; his eyes roamed the ceiling. He should be aware as he was as to where the last thump emanated from. Like him, he just couldn't get himself to investigate.

A heavier thud, this time, coming from somewhere mid-staircase. Its neighboring iron spiral counterpart would have produced a solid, yet tinny sound.

Ian flipped to his belly. He observed a faint light pool on the wall that illumined the wooden staircase. Not a blip of a shadow.

Another thud, from a stairstep or so, down way. He flipped to his back. "Agnes, what do we do?"

"What do you expect me to do."

Christopher pulled a section of a blanket over his face.

The next thud landed at the staircase base.

A second later, another one fell right at his side. Ian's shoulders jumped. His two companions cringed and squished against each other. Someone whimpered, and in the ensuing melee, he couldn't tell who it was.

The log thump reoccurred above his head, with the succeeding one, closely following. As soon as it migrated to their camp, the thump intervals narrowed.

The next one landed somewhere above Christopher's head. The man gave out a child-like shriek, as the thump continued clockwise to his side—then in the wood below his feet—then back to his side again, as if was attempting to complete a loop.

All at once, the lights fizzled out.

In the darkness, Ian couldn't tell who cried, who moaned, or who bucked around under the comforters. He turned on his necklaced flashlight. He couldn't tell if his companions had turned on theirs because they had buried themselves under the cover. He yanked down Agnes' covers and a light pool emerged.

Ian sat up and shone lights in every direction. Somebody's got to do it, he reminded himself. "Keep it tight. I go turn the lights back on."

Flashlight pointed straight ahead, he made his way into the hallway corner where the living room and hallway light switches are.

He flicked the switch repeatedly. Nothing.

A hard thud landed somewhere above his companions' heads.

Blankets flailed. Agnes sat, cupped her ears, and let off a piercing scream.

The wood tamping sound intensified and it landed in quicker succession over a small area. Ground zero seemed to be above Christopher's head, as if the spirit had identified its target. He repeatedly worked the rocker switch controls.

Ian heard it first before he saw it coming. Agnes and Christopher turned into blurs as they stampeded toward the narrow hallway, screaming their lungs out.

Likely fueled by adrenaline than fear, he chased after the two as soon as they zipped by him. He grabbed his panic-stricken companions by the collar. Both yelped as he bodily yanked them back. He pivoted and pushed them to the structural wall and pinned them there. "There's nowhere to run! There's nowhere to run!"

He realized he had his hands on their chests, pushing hard at them. He lets go. Their necklaced flashlights lit up the floor on their immediate area. Christopher used his to send shaky flashlight beams up and down the dark hallway. Ian sought the wall-mounted emergency flashlights in the hallway. Not one was there.

"Chris, do you know where the other flashlights are?"

"In my room, sir," came Christopher's tremulous voice.

Ian shook his head. "For all we know, those flashlights are

gone, too." He backed into the structural wall and squeezed himself in between his two companions who were so badly shaken they stood like statues, their arms to their sides, their eyes straight ahead to the restroom door.

The thumps had already ceased.

Apart from the sound of ragged breathing, dead silence.

Seconds later, he sank into the floor. The other two followed his lead. They sat close together. With the necklaced lights hanging, the light beam constricted. The void had completely enveloped their flanks. He could only make out one distinct feature in the vicinity—the hallway restroom door in front of them. His companions shivered as if they had just escaped a wintry spell.

"Guys, I need to tell you," Ian said. "Our power system is redundant."

"What does that mean?" Agnes asked.

"If a complete power failure occurs, a fresh battery backup power source takes over. We can experience power fluctuations. Not a total power outage."

"That's true," Christopher said. "I've checked the power backup system this morning. They're brand new."

"There's got to be another way to restore power," Agnes said.

"The diesel generator. I can't set that one up without going out of the house."

Agnes pulled back hard, letting off a sigh of frustration. She wrapped her arms around herself and curled her toes hard that Ian heard them crackle.

He gazed up the hallway's two high-mounted ventilation windows, partially opened. The ambient light allowed him to see fog-borne wisps sneaking in. They had their backs on a structural wall, the elements behind it. Where they were, with or without ghostly presence, it would only get colder.

Christopher wrapped his arms around his folded legs, his face nuzzling against his knees.

"There's a box of candles inside the storage," Agnes said. "In case we ran out of batteries."

"No way I'm going back there," Christopher shot back.

"It stopped," Agnes said. "Maybe this is a safe zone."

"Yeah. I'm staying here till daylight."

Ian shone a light into his wristwatch dial. "Two-twenty. Three to four hours to daylight."

"I agree with Chris," Agnes said. "Let's wait it out, right here."

Ian went on all fours. "Without blankets, we'd freeze out here. I'll go get them. Agnes, shine a light over there."

"Oh my god," Agnes' small voice faded, the moment she directed her light to the darkened living room: their beddings, blankets, and pillows, all gone.

He backtracked and squeezed himself beside Agnes who had also backed into Christopher who must have also witnessed the anomaly in the living room.

"I need to pee really bad," Agnes said.

Ian rose. He opened the restroom door. "Go. We'll be right by the door."

"Leave the door partly open." Agnes rushed in. Christopher backed against the right side of the door. Ian took on the other. He shimmied and jigged about for a while to stave off the creeping cold. No one spoke for a while.

"We need to assess our situation," Ian told Christopher. He kept his voice low, to hide the tremor in his throat.

"Sir, what if this is some kind of a game, you know, a practical joke by bored billionaires."

"Unlikely," Ian said. "Him and his clan. Good record. They take care of their employees, and their customers…"

"Go on, sir. Nice to hear… some talk, you know."

"They take care of their old multi-generational properties, like the one this house came from. Doctor Pershing, to my view, is not even eccentric."

A flush. The faucet water ran briefly. Agnes emerged,

rubbing her hands on her pajamas. She grasped both men by the elbows and led them back to the same wall corner they originated from. "Mister Bishop, our options."

"We yank a door lever. Hopefully, it sends a distress signal."

"Then we forfeit."

Back to their old spot, Agnes seated on the floor in between the two men. She rubbed her arms and legs. Christopher seemed unusually preoccupied with the void in his flank that led to the kitchen.

"Even if help comes," Agnes continued, "rescue probably wouldn't happen till past daylight."

"What about the BLM guy at the highway gate?" Christopher said.

"They were vague about him being posted at a gate," Ian said.

"The way I heard it," Agnes said, "he'd only check the gate to the road time and again."

"He's probably a moonlighting employee keeping an eye on the private road. He won't risk his job for us. That is even if there was a way to send a distress signal to him without the risk of forfeiting."

"It's quiet now," Agnes said. "Let's stay where we are. We'll figure things out tomorrow."

"We need to find blankets, soon," Christopher said.

"We'll get to that in due time," Agnes said. "We're not done assessing our situation yet."

"There's heavy fog out there," Ian said. "Rule out an airlift. They assured us they have a geostationary satellite fix on our compound. We can't be approached by outside forces without their knowing. It's just us and him, here."

"I'm good waiting it out, here, sir."

"Me, too," Ian said. "Chris, speaking of blankets, do you—"

His eyes to his flank, Christopher crossed his lips with his forefinger.

In the calm and silence, Ian heard a barely audible click, like a door latch being carefully disengaged.

Then came a continuous creak from old door hinges.

The master bedroom.

Ian sprang up. Should there be a threat, he thought they'd be in a better position on their feet than otherwise. He considered alternate places of refuge. The rooms, even the restroom in front of them. Agnes and Christopher rose up slowly, their flashlights necklaced and pointed to the ground. "People, no matter what, do not run."

The creaking sound ceased.

Everyone leaned out and gazed in the same direction the creaking sound had come from. Ian couldn't get himself to point his flashlight into the void. His muscles stiffened to the point of paralysis. He couldn't even swallow because his throat had dried. None of his other companions shined flashlights into the void.

It turned much colder quickly and they found themselves pressing against each other. Ian could no longer tell where the shudders came from. He changed his mind on his plan to call for calm because he knew his tone, by then, would only betray his terror. They were trapped. It struck him, a fleeting wish they would black out at the same time where they stood and wake up later with daylight on their faces.

Their necklaced flashlights reflected enough light throughout the immediate vicinity that Ian noticed the patch of opaque white fabric, emerging from the master bedroom's direction. His companions noticed it, too. They backed hard into the wall and scrunched into each other.

The floating white manifestation neared them.

A white nightgown, as if strung on a hanger, hovered towards them, the gown midriff to the level of their eyes. His companions pushed against him, in the direction of the living room. Ian held his ground and the sidelong retreat stalled. There was no point in sidling further away. They weren't in control anymore. It had to come to a head, whatever their fate in that night might be. Sure enough, the floating gown overtook them.

It stopped in front of Agnes. It turned and faced her.

"What does it want," Christopher squeaked.

"He wanted me to wear it."

The gown moved closer to her. Agnes wrapped her arms around herself, shaking. A supernatural force had them cornered. Standing their ground while acceding to the spirit's wish was the only option left.

"Wear it," Ian said. "There's nothing we can do. We cannot fight or run. We must survive this night. Go wear it, now."

Agnes reached for the gown. Mid-way, she flinched. She reached out again, with two hands this time. Her pajama top was unbuttoned in one rippling motion. A low whoosh and her pajama pants pulled down to her ankles in one, smooth stroke. She wriggled out of her top and stepped out of her fallen pants. She grabbed the nightgown and slipped into it. The change was over in a few hectic seconds.

"Talk to him," Ian said.

"I don't know what to say."

"Just talk to him."

"Daniel, we're all scared to death. Please, I've done what you want. I'm tired, we're all tired. Let us all rest for the night."

A succession of shuffling steps rippled through the hallway's floor and headed toward the kitchen. The old, neglected hinges squeaked. The master bedroom door closed. A click.

The household lights turned on at the same time.

Ian shielded his eyes from the glare. He felt cold sweat lining down his back. It was only then that he fully saw his companions' tortured faces, their confused eyes, the ashen paleness that reflected the unnerving experience. Agnes squatted and folded the pajama pair gathered on the floor in front of her.

In the living room, their beddings—comforters, blankets, and pillows—were all restored to its layout prior to the big scare. Even the missing wall-mounted flashlights were back in their holders. It remained cold, but no longer beastly cold.

"Sir," Christopher said, as he pointed at the three bottled water bottles on the floor beside him. "He brought them here." Ian motioned him to bring one up. He took and drank half a bottle. Christopher followed suit. Then Agnes.

"Maybe we should use the satellite phone," Agnes said, after a few gulps. "We're not forfeiting. We don't know if the cameras are working or how they are working. We need to let them know what's going on."

"I agree, sir. He might not be done with us, yet."

Ian leaned on the wall and shook his head. He wished the question was asked to him under more favorable circumstances. "There is no satellite phone."

"What?" Agnes said.

"I made that one up during the orientation I gave you. Doctor Pershing's people were adamant about limiting communication electronics in the household. I wanted everyone to feel relaxed. I've never dealt with spirit phenomena before. I never thought anything could go this wrong. I'm sorry."

"What if none of the safeguards in place actually works?" Agnes said. "What if they had no idea what just happened to us?"

"Past three," Ian said, after glancing at his wristwatch. "You asked him for reprieve and he acquiesced. The lights are back and our bed's ready. The message couldn't be any clearer. Here's my suggestion. We all head back to bed. No one's talking about this until the morning. I know this would be hard but we need to empty our minds of the events that happened this night. It would be daylight in a few. Sleep in as much as you like. Do we understand each other?"

Agnes and Christopher nodded.

———

IAN HAD TURNED the lights way low and he still couldn't sleep. From his companion's flopping under the comforters and their strained sighs and frequent fidgets, he knew both his companions were also struggling to fall asleep. Not one soft snore from their camp. The restless movements continued. Agnes.

It might be her stirrings that had kept him from falling asleep. In an hour or so, shafts of sunlight would slip through the blinds, no matter how tightly they had closed them. He needed to dream. He must deliver enough dreamwork material to Doctor Pershing in an appointed time that would inevitably come. He could either deliver or he could make things up. Those were his choices. He saw no third option worth considering.

Agnes stopped moving. Ian turned to his side, away from her, and tucked himself in. A cold spell had descended. Temperatures typically drop near dawn this time of the year. Yet it seemed the cold seeped in from under the covers. The lights flickered a millisecond. He checked on Agnes. She appeared to be asleep, on her back, both hands clutched on the blanket that covered half her face to the level of her cheeks.

He sat up and glanced at the fully shuttered window. It has to be still pitch-black outside. The lights continued to behave. All he could hear were the low, whirring sound from the refrigerator's ice maker. He looked up and down the blanket that covered her. The fabric looked undisturbed.

Half past four.

Ian almost slumped back to bed when he heard a faint

moan from Agnes. Night terrors. Perhaps the harried, frenzied, frightening night had caught up on her. He listened close.

She couldn't have fallen into a state of deep sleep that fast.

"No... no... please... no..."

He leaned closer. Her half-shut eyes looked glassy. Though the part of the blanket that covered her mouth had muffled her voice, the words' meaning was undoubtedly clear.

"Agnes," He nudged her repeatedly. Her shoulder muscles felt hard and rigid to touch. He gazed across the length of her blanket-covered body. Her hands weren't holding on to the blanket to protect herself from the cold. She clutched hard at it because something was pulling it down. Her toes appeared to be anchored on at the blanket's end, causing the fabric to remain taut and flat.

"No, no, no." Her breathing increased at a staccato pace, with the word "no" coming in between shallow breaths as if she was starting to suffocate.

Ian raised her blanket up from her side and shone his flashlight under. He gasped. He saw her nightgown fabric rippling up and down her body. The waves looked more exaggerated than the one they had witnessed at the master bedroom. One wild undulation came at the tail of another, in a continuous up and down motion.

Christopher had just started to snore. No one else could be abetting the spirit in some psychokinetic realm. Here was proof of it.

He slammed a pillow at Christopher who sat up, startled. He snatched Agnes' blanket away and flung it to his side. Her clothes' rhythmic undulations went on in a steady cycle. Her toes pointed straight and stiff. Her hands remained petrified in the grabbing position as if the blanket was still there.

The next moment, her body squirmed and her legs crossed in a spasmodic reaction to something intrusive in her lower torso. Ian noticed her underwear trapped between her scrunched-together knees.

Christopher jumped out and turned the lights to full.

Ian grabbed Agnes by the shoulders and rocked her about. "Agnes, you have to wake up. Wake up."

Her eyes opened. She sprang up and screamed towards the hallway: "I told you not to touch me! I told you not to touch me!"

The lights flickered. A glissading, shuffling sound on the floor traveled the length of the hallway before it dissipated somewhere in between the master bedroom and the kitchen.

On her knees, she slipped up her underwear before she pressed her ruffled clothes straight. Her harried eyes shuttled between Ian's and Christopher's. She patted around her waist as if checking if her undergarment ended up in the right place.

Ian wasn't sure if she was fully awake. "Do you recall what just happened?"

She nodded. "I was dreaming. I woke up and I couldn't move. I couldn't talk. Like I was paralyzed."

"Him?"

She nodded and sat back. Ian took a place by her side, though Christopher slid back to his territory. He looked the other way like the recent event barely affected him.

"It would be daylight, soon," Ian announced.

Boiling water hissed from the kitchen. Precise mechanical clicks from expensive coffee-machine components followed. Metal and plastic parts clicked and clacked. A strong scent of fresh-brewed coffee wafted their way. The salubrious aroma made Ian pine for the morning when they were right at the throes of it.

Before they turned in, Christopher had filled the coffee maker glass with water and ground the coffee beans. But he was sure he forgot to set the timer for daybreak. Daniel.

It was a peace offering from him.

15

The Morning After

"It's your call," Ian told Agnes, not long into their breakfast at ten.

"The burden is on me like I'm the only one with money problems."

Ian laid a long, hard stare on her, unsure whether he was dealing with a fatigue flare-up, or just with someone's increasingly familiar nasty attitude. Christopher continued cutting up fruits at the kitchen counter, oblivious to them. "I was beside myself when I agreed to call off the dogs until the morning. I had time to think. The only thing that stops me from opening that door is one vote. I may be as cash-strapped as everyone here, but if you want to put this on us, then I'm willing to walk away."

Christopher raised a hand, without looking back. He has been wearing a glum, numb expression since they regrouped in the kitchen. His sheepish glances at her and his cavalier attitude whenever an opportunity to serve her arose was gone.

"After last night, I'm willing to walk away, too, sir."

He never heard Christopher voice a statement that flat and that dispassionate. Agnes took notice. In an unexpected turnabout, her eyes morphed from totally confrontational to one that was defensive and embattled.

"We're that close. Let's finish the job."

"We can't protect you," Ian said.

"Both of you witnessed it. He leaves when I tell him to. Whether he thinks I'm Ellie or not, he wouldn't hurt me."

"He might hurt me," Christopher said. "Like anybody cares."

Ian pulled back from his chair and weighed his approach on the matter that he knew could irreversibly end their project then and there. He has been thinking about his companions for some time—about Agnes' incorrigibly precipitate temperament, as well as Christopher's latent telekinetic powers potentially evolving. Then there was the needling enigma on the resident spirit mimicking some form of human consciousness in a realm different from his.

He recalled his conversation with Agnes on the energy fields Daniel might have exploited to harness extraordinarily precise psychokinetic powers. He wondered if there were some metaphysical transference issues at work that included energy fields common to the human species. What if all this time Daniel's spirit was channeling their respective psyches and was feeding off their weaknesses and their compulsions? What if he has been probing the subtle interrelationships between their different psychic abilities, even underdeveloped abilities as that of Christopher's, and had found ways to manipulate them? Ian didn't even have the chance to process his own take on last night's pivotal events, particularly on the log-like thumps that he believed occurred shortly after Christopher commented that Daniel would be a child molester if he had turned eighteen and had made love to Ellie. Clear as daylight by now, ghosts can manifest themselves to people. That they can manifest reactions to people conversations like they were actually there was the emergent reality Ian wasn't prepared to accept yet.

Be it in the theoretical world of the academe or in his psychotherapy practice, Ian never considered parapsychology and paraphysics as serious subject matters. He had to make an exception. They were knee-deep in uncharted territory and they have very little time to understand what they were really dealing with. He believed that none of the psychic agents that had once worked for Doctor Pershing had experienced the level of haunting as they did. Otherwise, as Agnes once suggested, word on it should have spread in the psychic community. Indeed, there must be something truly unique in their team, or to one or more of them who had access to a psychic frequency or some cosmic quantum conduit in time and space that the resident spirit had stumbled into and has been utilizing with incredible success.

He glanced at the wall clock. "It's past ten. Where's the cavalry? If there was real-time video surveillance in this place, we should have at least already heard from them. They have to show up. It's called liability."

"Unlike you people, I know shit," Christopher said, as he placed an oval plate filled with cut-up fruits on the table. He probably dropped it an inch from above the table and it clattered. Agnes, once again, took notice. "I know that what happened last night was stuff from horror movies. We deserve our bonus, you know, being put through all that. Forget the big prize. I don't mind them or us calling off the project."

Ian tried a middle way. "Even if video recording in this house is totally passive, our beyond-strange ordeal last night should still be in a hard drive somewhere. That means we have the right to take precautions as we see fit without forfeiting our contract obligations. It was never made clear to us what makes our job done and what doesn't."

"Do we even need to do a séance tonight?" Christopher threw it out there, without making eye contact with the séance leader.

"Without a séance, we might as well pack up," Agnes said.

128

Ian went to the kitchen door and fiddled with the lever lock. He didn't need a show of hands. He saw his companion's faces darken like they were calculating the probability that he might unilaterally set off the alarm. "If we unlock this door, two things can happen: the cavalry arrives before sundown or they do not. The first case is as good as the second one. We forfeit. The difference is that in the second case, we'd be hanging around here doing nothing, and wondering all that time if we should have done something and not forfeited in the first place. Of course, there's a third choice. We don't give them the satisfaction of us giving up."

"Let's carry on," Agnes said. Christopher, behind her, nodded rather reluctantly. "Of course, if the cavalry shows up without us tripping the alarm, then they had decided the fate of the project for us. If they don't show up, it's a sign we must persist."

"Very well, when we're done here, let's plan our day."

Agnes gulped down the rest of her coffee. "Skip the shower. When we're done here, let's get right to work. Let's not think about tonight until it's night."

16

Missing Pictures

Agnes dropped the last of the ten-volume Pershing Heritage Album atop the heap of other leather-bound ones piled over a table on the attic's west side. She scanned the three other tables to her left where a miscellany of loose photographs occupied taped-up spots. She wore the same denim jacket, over a maroon shirt this time. Blue jeans, always well-suited for day work, completed her attire.

Ian sat before table one at the far end, near the north staircase. Incandescent light shone over an aerial photograph of the sprawling Pershing estate in Sacramento. He has been scrutinizing the photograph for some time, magnifying glass at hand. All around the table and under it were other estate-related pictures he had set aside for use as references. He saw Agnes, shuffling the albums without any discernible purpose, growing frustration scribbled all over her face.

"Know what," she said after a disconcerting sigh. "I'll start all over again."

"Maybe the Pershing family didn't approve of the young lover's affair. After Daniel passed away, they could have discarded her pictures."

"That's not what I'd do if I cared about putting my son's soul to rest."

"What if the two lover's relationship didn't end well? I'm just thinking out loud."

Agnes continued her way back to the album pile, mumbling to herself. "The collection ended in the nineteen-ninety-six volume... we have her obituary, not his. We have his pictures, not hers." She looked back at Ian. Her eyes narrowed. "Her pictures have to be somewhere in this house, if not here."

"Presented with the same data set as ours, I'm sure previous psychics who had worked on this case would have brought up the same contradiction to the attention of their employers."

"What if the contradiction is distinctly ours?"

"Either way, him or them, someone's playing games with us."

Ian beckoned her to his desk. "I need to show you some-thing," He stood up and offered her his seat. She obliged.

He pointed at the black-and-white Pershing mansion aerial photograph, at a heavily-wooded middle quadrant of the estate. He tapped his forefinger at the slate roof of a narrow dwelling partially hidden in between tree canopies in the back corner of the estate. Other small, residential-type structures are tucked in between canopies in the surrounding area. "Look at the eaves, the house's long, narrow design. This place, this might have once been a servant's house."

"A servant's house with a streamlined folk Victorian façade and a dedicated dance floor? None of those narrow houses had ornate crests you only find in Victorian houses."

She made sense. Ian diverted her attention to a cluster of similar-looking, townhouse-type structures at the opposite corner of the property, closer to the mansion. "Given the size and the uniformity of these buildings, these are guesthouses." He pointed back at the picture's opposite end, where the narrower houses were. He tapped his knuckle on the scattering of smaller dwellings on the corner across the narrow house. "The size of these homes, and their remote location relative to the mansion, indicate they could be servant houses. Ellie and her family must have lived somewhere here. See those coops in that clearing?"

"What are they?"

"Chicken houses. Fresh eggs for the highborn."

Agnes nodded agreeably. "Another possibility is that this place might have been a late addition to the estate, maybe even a conversion."

"A place reserved for a Pershing scion who is a dancer."

"Daniel?"

"Why not?"

"What if this place and the dance floor were built for a live entertainment troupe composed of servant family members?"

He might have scoffed. It nearly slipped from his lips, that he did see those lovers in the second floor landing, very briefly, during that one heartening segment in his recent dreamwork when he spied on the young lady's backpack pocket stuffed with faux ballet shoes.

The previous night, the last time they had returned to bed to shore up more sleep time, Ian gained at least two hours of deep sleep. Slivers of sunlight on his face wakened him prematurely. He spent another half hour in bed, re-playing his dreams over and over again so they'd stick to memory. This time his dreamwork had yielded a higher volume of quality, recollected imageries.

Very briefly, he saw the two lovers romp about the dance floor and he heard the suppressed glee in their young voices. One time they sat by a still-standing chimney, leaning on each other; in another, they raced the spiral staircase to get to the attic. In between the colorful imageries was a maelstrom of phantasmagoric, nonsensical scenes. In the latter segment of his dreamwork, he could barely recall or recognize the subject's faces. At one point, he identified another of the lover's many haunts compressed to one dark place, the vacuous second floor, at a single point which background he could barely see. When he tried to recollect the scene, he could glean nothing but black-and-white imageries of people so close together they appeared to be fused as a single entity that swirled about in place, like a spinning top that occasionally plopped arms and limbs.

He pondered on the possibility that outside influences could be diluting the quality of his dreamwork. In all his past projects as a dream clairvoyant, he either fails or succeeds. Checkered results only happened during his dreamwork attempts in the house.

"I fell into some kind of a trance last night," Agnes said. "I had visions."

She might as well have fallen into a trance that very moment as her eyes turned dreamy and her elocution sounded soporific.

"You dreamt something, you mean."

"They were visions, not dreams."

"You said you fell into a trance."

"It's complicated. Let me explain. I didn't experience dreams. Only visions. A trance state must have midwifed the event."

"Okay, all ears here."

"When I was with you guys and he was touching me, I wasn't asleep. I was in a trance. I knew what was happening but I can't move. I believe I had visions of the two lovers then."

"I thought you have to be awake first, to work yourself to fall into a trance. And only in a séance at that."

"True. The peculiar trance I experienced last night was the first."

"You think he induced you into a trance, while you were asleep?"

"I don't know. I was half awake much of the time. The dream sequences streamed in so fast, I could swear, it all happened in a blip."

"To have visions, generally speaking, you need to be awake. You can be in between states of consciousness in a trance, but not in one or the other, right?"

"Correct. But I'm sure I was more awake than unconscious when it happened."

"A wakeful trance?"

"No. That's why I suspected I had visions."

"Let's back up a bit. How much did you actually recall?"

"As much as an amnesiac recovering lost memory wholesale for the first time. I saw Daniel and Ellie, on all fours, peering through the living room window to see if the coast is clear outside. Hands together, they ran into the master bedroom, giggling, as kids about to do mischief." Agnes stepped into the middle of the attic floor, went on tiptoes, and dropped her heels on it. "Right here, I also saw them roll out a gray wool blanket. They sat together, straw picnic basket by their side."

He might as well be listening to his future report to Dr. Pershing. Matters their employer would love to hear, she had laid it out there, ready to be pilfered. The gaiety and the enthusiasm by which she delivered the story, he could filch, too. He could embellish them and make them his own. His claims would be beyond anyone's ability to corroborate. Unless she beats him to it. Then he would have his pride on his hands when he gets debriefed by Dr. Pershing, regarding his post-project reporting obligations. "The second level, the dance floor, did you see them there?"

"No. I had no visions of them there."

"They should have passed by it on their way to the attic."

"They must. Not a glimpse of it."

"Then you have seen her, in her more mature stage."

Before he reached mid-sentence, Agnes had already shaken her head. "Her face. At times they were like the Ellie in the Pershing family portrait. At times it was me." She walked back to the family album table.

"Like your face was superimposed on Ellie's?"

"I recalled it that way. I knew for sure it was Ellie, even as I saw a younger version of myself in her person. This may sound weird, but in the vision, whatever they actually were, I deliberately went into Ellie's body and in that brief moment I was there, I searched for a mirror. I found one. There was no face there."

"I heard somewhere that inside a dream, people can't look into the mirror and see themselves."

She nodded. "That's where I started to wonder what my visions meant."

"They could be dreams."

"I can tell the difference."

"The power of suggestion manifesting into your subconscious. It could be as simple as that. You knew Daniel mistook you for Ellie. He insisted on it many times over. The power of repetition. Confirmation bias. I'm sure you've heard of them."

"Visions. I'm sure of it."

"Dreams, clairvoyant ones or not, are easier to explain. They happen when you sleep. Visions, though no one really knows how that works, happen when a person is conscious."

Agnes returned to her old work zone. Her jaws clenched and her steps sounded heavy. "I know how I dream. They weren't dreams that came to my head that night."

Heavy footsteps ascended from the iron staircase.

"What if..." Agnes said. "What if Daniel hid Ellie's pictures."

"What would be the motive?"

She shook her head a bit. "I don't know. Maybe he didn't

want to be reminded of her, of the past. I'm just rattling random possibilities."

"Now you got me thinking. He might have a motive for it. We just don't know it, yet."

Christopher emerged from the staircase, his face deadpan, his eyes unsteady. "What time would you like our lunch to be?"

"Around two," Agnes said. "Make it good. Should we fall behind schedule, we may need to make do with microwaveable dinner by the end of the day."

Christopher nodded. He started to backtrack. He stopped. "Uh, regarding the CD player. I checked the batteries. They're all fresh. Do you want me to bring it up so you can—"

"No. Leave it on the dance floor side, and in the exact operational condition we found it."

"Will do." He turned and disappeared down the staircase.

Agnes drew close to Ian. She waited for the staircase footfalls to diminish. Up until the steps had hit the ground floor. She said, to a hush, "What's his problem?"

"You mean why he's glum—why he seemed to be just going through the motions—why it seemed he had already tuned you out?"

Agnes' brows arched. "No, no, no. This can't be about the night before when I caught him holding back and I freaked out. How long do people hold grudges?"

"Well, some people are sensitive," Ian folded his arms and leaned back on the office chair. "Don't worry about it. As you once said, all of us are just strangers passing through, trying to make a quick buck. Why should anyone care? We live on a Darwinian planet."

"You are the most senior member of this team. You should have told me—"

"You've been treating him like an underling from the very start. It came to a head that night. It was inevitable."

136

Ian waited. He followed her averted eyes, as she turned away. He had seen them so many times before, no matter how they tried to hide it, guilt reflecting in people's eyes. "Did anything else happen that I didn't know about? Did you butt heads with him again?"

As he tracked her, he felt sure Agnes was rummaging through the albums rather perfunctorily. He waited.

"Sometime last night, before the paranormal event, Chris backed to me."

"Like in a snuggle move?"

"Something like that."

"Then?"

"I elbowed him. Twice, I think."

"It was a cold night. I might have backed into you, too. I know you did, to me."

"Yours. It's like a fatherly move to me."

"Really? You can tell the difference?"

"No. I'm just making excuses."

"Any other moves that he did?"

"No. I don't know why I did it. I can't justify my reaction."

"At least you're sure now, where he's coming from."

"I want to apologize."

"Don't, if you're not sincere."

Agnes marched heavily towards the staircase. "That's on me."

"Whatever. Just make it quick. I need you here."

17

Cold Fish

Christopher has been working the busy kitchen countertop when from the corner of his eyes, he thought she spotted Agnes, turning the kitchen corner. He shuddered and nearly yelped. The colander, filled with thawed lobster tails, nearly slipped from his hand. He turned and there she really was, right shoulder leaning on the fridge, arms folded, her large, unblinking eyes at him as if she was sizing him up. As always, he found her cold fish stare disturbing. For sure, she was there because she needed something from him. What other possibilities could there be?

She had sneaked in light-footed, despite her wearing loafers. A sorry-you-got-spooked apology would have been appreciated. A cold fish. The impression didn't stay around long enough. How she looked to him at that moment did: one beautiful face framed by luxuriant hair and defined by a set of deep-set eyes and a sensuous pair of curvy brows. Her shirt was as form-fitting as her pants, the kind of outfit that would bring out the best in any woman at her prime. He wondered what sort of scare she would have delivered to him had she appeared in a white nightgown instead. In fact, he desired that she did. Even if the trade-off involved him yelping like a woman and her consequently mocking him for it.

"I've been squatting too long up there," she said. "My back's hurting." She unfolded her arms and approached him. She surveyed the long countertop, crowded with colanders and strainers of different sizes, all of them brimming with vegetables and seafood. "I figured I might be of better use here."

"I can manage. You've worked hardest. You deserve a break."

"The last time I checked your wound, it had healed remarkably fast. You have a good immune system."

"Thanks for taking care of it."

She laughed. "I beat you up with a brass candelabra. That's the least I could do."

She squinted at the large bin that overflowed with lobster tails. "Wow. Lobsters. It's been a while. What are you making?"

"Paella."

No yum. Not a twitch on her lips. A cold fish.

"Do they typically put lobsters in Paellas?"

"No."

She shook the rectangular plastic bin containing Alaskan crab legs. "Crab legs, too?"

"You told me to make it good. There are lots of expensive seafood in the large freezer. It wouldn't hurt to go all out."

She found a colander full of tomatoes, vines still on. "Yeah, why not."

Agnes started plucking off the deep-red tomatoes from their vines. "Let me work on this one. How small would you like me to dice them?"

He passed on to her a plastic cutting board and a curve-tipped, ceramic knife. "Pick four of the larger ones. Peel off their skin first, then you cut them so you can remove their seeds. Then cube them all; really small cubes." He slipped on surgical gloves and started extracting lobster meat from their cracked shells. He couldn't shrug the tension off. He wanted to sidle a step from her but he knew such an avoidance move would be obvious.

"I can be mean. But I'm not evil."

Out of the blue. He was sure he never told Ian something that might suggest she was mean or evil.

"I said I can be mean. But I know I'm not evil."

"I don't know you enough to say that you were even mean. Though you're kind of, sometimes. To me at least."

Agnes lets off a chuckle. "Mean. I can live with that."

Christopher grinned. He noticed she worked on the tomatoes very well.

"You cook great. Where did you learn?"

"Part-time jobs in Italian, Spanish, and Chinese restaurants. I'm a gig guy. I don't have a solid resume to show for my tidbits of work experience. My family's not even lower middle class, you know. I did lots of things since I was fourteen, from selling Tamales to working on building projects."

"Your work experience, not bad for someone as young as you. What do you plan to do with your money from this gig? I overheard you saying you plan on going back to school."

"Maybe it's not too late for that. Though it's not what I had in mind when I think of a really good bonus. I want to buy a house. I'll take my mother there, so she can be in a house we own before she passes away."

"Your mom never owned a house before?"

"She did. Though we lost it during the housing crash."

"If we get more money than we expected, you should probably aim for both—a house and a college education."

"Many years ago, I was already preparing myself for college when things went south for us, financially. I had to work gigs, full time. I'm thinking of re-applying again. Maybe take a few courses in junior colleges and work my way elsewhere from there."

"Smart. Fate gives you a chance, go for it. Go get a degree. Uh, what degree do you want to pursue?"

"Literature."

"I expected something like architecture or engineering."

"I hate math or anything that has it. I ended up in construction out of necessity."

"You own a library?"

"A little one, yes."

"You must have heard I own a used book store. Had you been living in my neighborhood you would have already walked into my store sometime."

"With my budget, I only buy books in library book sales and thrift stores."

"We get this one down, your buying habits would change. You'd have a book collection that can fit in a small public library. You might even become a regular in my store."

"How about you? After this gig, you'd probably be famous in your community. You plan on doing this psychic thing full-time?"

"Oh no. I don't know anyone who does this full-time."

"Your book business must be doing good."

"My L.A. bookshop, it's a small business. Just me, one employee, and a temp. I'm drowning in debt and am four bad months away from laying off my people, myself included."

"That's tough. Do you have backup plans, in case?"

Agnes shrugged.

"Anyone helping you? Family, friends, a boyfriend?"

"Nope. Just me and myself."

"I really hope we can pull this one through, without, you know, the scary stuff—like that from last night."

"We'll pull this one through, together. For all we know, the worst had already passed." She plopped the last of the diced tomatoes into the colander. "Done. What else can I do?"

"I got this, really. If you want, you can prep our table. Check out the desserts."

She looked over her shoulder. "Know what, you started this no-holds-barred paella. Why not indulge ourselves to the max and use the best porcelain ware and cutlery. Let me take care of the table setup. Do you have a white tablecloth any—"

"In the pantry, beside the china cabinet."

When Agnes went for it, Christopher's eyes followed her, almost reflexively. He couldn't help it. He imagined her in the white nightgown, its soft fabric hugging her shape, its edges just below her knees. He started to think about her again, despite his promise to himself, the night before, to avoid regarding her with any measure of affection. In fact, he had gone as far as vowing not to give her the satisfaction, even in his own mind. It got to that point. As always, whenever it got to a boiling point, his sexual fantasies about her ramped up in dark ways that he ended up regretting.

She worked her chores fast. The cabinet doors slammed; the porcelain wares clinkered. The next time he looked back, gleaming plates were being laid out on a white tablecloth cover.

"If the weather turns gloomy, we can make good use of the long, lovely candles over there," Agnes said, a teasing smile on her lips. "I'm nearly done here. I can set one up, too."

"Maybe we can skip the candlelight part."

"You sure? We're all going to dress up. It will be romantic."

"Some other time. What do you call that thing when you put something off…"

"Rain check."

"Yeah. Rain check on the candlelight thing."

Not long after he had returned to his countertop chores, Christopher heard her shuffling fast toward him. This time she landed closer to him.

"I'm still trying to understand Daniel and the many strange things that have been going on in this place."

Christopher slipped off the gloves and washed his hands.

He needed to feel the harvested lobster meat, for shell shards that slipped past quality control.

As he suspected earlier, she might have an agenda for her visit.

"What I'm about to tell you, this is between you and me. Don't think too much about my question. Just answer it as you would to a confidant or a doctor that you trust. Have you been fantasizing about me, like, for example, of you touching me?"

"Can I pass on this one?"

"I won't judge you. Tell me, please. It is important, for our upcoming work."

Reluctantly, he nodded. "It's just regular male fantasies, you know."

"Do you have a girlfriend?"

He shook his head.

"Did you have one before?"

"Uh, yes. Just one."

"Can you tell me something about her?"

"I'll be working on the crabs, now."

He put back his gloves on. He could tell Agnes hadn't backed an inch and that she had locked on to him what he assumed to be a scrutinizing gaze. It puzzled him, whatever her angle was. He was fourteen then. She was thirteen. They were too young to be intimate, sexually. Only years later, when they had broken up when memories of her started to haunt him.

"You didn't make love to her, didn't you?"

How could she have guessed? It could be as simple as an educated guess; maybe a case of woman intuition at work. "Can we talk about something else?"

"I'm waiting for your answer."

"Okay. We didn't do it."

"Do you know how I guessed it?"

"No."

"Our backgrounds. Yours and mine. Certain aspects of

our lives seem to have some significance to Daniel's in his life-time. I don't know if it's just fate or if there's some design to it."

"How about mister Bishop? Do you—"

"If time allows it, I'd probe into his background, too."

"You had already busted me on that telekinesis thing. Maybe you should pay more attention to the old man. Not that I'm suggesting he's hiding something like I once did. I mean, you two speak the same language. I'm just a regular dude, you know, trying to make a living, trying to stay out of trouble."

"What a scare we had last night. The thumps on the floor and all that. Yet, since this morning, I didn't hear a creak, or saw an object move."

"Maybe—"

"Your latent psychokinetic abilities. It had changed. You got spooked when I sneaked up on you on purpose, earlier. I didn't hear a tinkle. What a striking difference from last night, when I asked you to focus on the cup on the table and I turned off the lights. Fear." She linked her two hand's finger-tips together. A connection, of course. "Our first day in, when I mistakenly accused you of lifting my skirt, you had caused it."

"Who wouldn't get scared, seeing a skirt float like that."

"Fear came after the fact. Your fantasies enabled it to happen."

"My fantasies, what does it really have to do with anything?"

"Chris, listen to me. I understand why my back-and-forth on fear and fantasies might be confusing you. Even pros like me and Ian, we had encountered anomalies here that were so new to us that we have trouble wrapping our heads around them. Keep an open mind. Listen to what I have to say."

"All right. I'm listening."

"I think our terrifying experience last night proved to be

too traumatic for you. Your fears had crossed a threshold. Trauma had severed the link between the part of your brain that processes fear and the unknown part there that nurtures your undeveloped telekinetic ability."

"Are you saying I don't have that ability anymore?"

"No, that's not what I'm saying. You may recall, this morning, you got startled when I accidentally sneaked up on you on my way to the restroom. Ian dropped glassware that broke. I suspected then that your fears didn't cause things to move anymore. That led me to look back at the skirt-raising poltergeist activity. Then the incident in the master bedroom. There were many other related incidents and I missed the clues. After the falling cup experiment, I got embroiled in the fear response links to telekinesis that the subject distracted me from another possible backdoor, an alternate path Daniel might be using in order for him to operate in our realm."

"The last thing you said, kind of sounded creepy. Can you elaborate more on that? I'm behind on both the supernatural and the science stuff in this project that I'd need more than a point in the right direction."

"Okay," Agnes drew closer. "When my skirt rose that morning, you had stray fantasies that something like that would happen, am I right?"

"What if it's just him? That I have nothing to do with it at all."

"Be straight with me. I won't judge you. I promise."

"All right. I saw your legs. It might have crossed my mind, what it would be like, to see more."

"My legs?"

"Yeah. They're very nice-looking. You should know that."

Agnes tried to hide her smile. For all he knew it might have been an embarrassed smile, even a sarcastic one. The next moment, her smile widened before it opened to let out a suppressed glee. She pointed to her right temple. "It all comes from here. Your repressed sexual desires, your problems with them in the past. As you become more mature, those primal drives affected your accidental gift much more."

"I'm still not sure I understand."

"That night, before you and Ian broke into my room, you were still awake then, thinking about me, right?"

"I might be."

"Can I take that as a yes?"

Christopher nodded.

"Last night, before you and Ian woke me up, were you awake then?"

"No. Mister Bishop woke me up."

"Are you sure?"

"Very sure."

Agnes' eyes lowered. Her forehead crinkled, like someone immersed in deep thought.

"Anything wrong?"

Whatever the distraction was, she quickly snapped out of it and smiled, probably just to herself.

"How would sexual fantasies, mine or anyone else's, have anything to do with Daniel's power to move stuff."

"Human sexuality is much more complicated than human fear. Yet both come from the same ancient place in the brain." She pointed at the back of her head. "I think they call it the amygdala. The telekinetic power you have, whatever part of your brain it comes from, I have no idea. When I asked you to push the cup off the table using mind power alone and I turned off the light, that test showed you had the potential to harness the gift. I succeeded with this little experiment because it was as easy to manipulate fear as to observe them. When fear overwhelmed you and traumatized you, only fear's connection to the part of your psyche that caused things to move had parted ways. The other one, wherever fantasies come from, likely remained intact."

"You sure the trauma didn't snuff that other one out, too?"

"I don't believe it can. Fear is linked to your psychokinetic ability as a reaction or a reflex. Sexual fantasies that you create are not. Both may come from the same place but their paths are very different."

"If they go to different paths, then my fantasies may have nothing to do with the telekinesis part at all."

"That's my point. We have established a connection between fear and your telekinetic ability. Yet Daniel's extraordinary power to move things is way more sophisticated than yours. How did that come about? I think that right from the start, the resident spirit had figured out a way to harness your earthly telekinetic power by piggybacking with your fantasies, using it as some kind of a vehicle, even a power source."

"Are you saying that my fantasies, and the fantasies of this spirit, that they kind of collaborate in some way?"

Agnes nodded.

"Sexual desire is a powerful motivator in itself. It can make things very real in your head."

"What should I do? I don't want to put you in harm's way. I mean what do I need to do about it? These fantasies. They come without warning. It's not that easy to make them go away."

"Let me take you back, again, to our team's first morning together. You didn't have the power then to lift my skirt remotely, no matter how much you willed it. Then how did that happen? In your own words, fear came after the fact."

"He made it happen?"

"You two did. Daniel and you." She clasped her hands and tapped her forefingers together. "You really think that during our team's first few hours here, that the first impulse of the resident spirit was to lift my skirt?"

"Again, please tell me what I must do to make you safer, during a séance."

"What about not fantasizing about me, for starters."

"Done. I mean, I'll do my best. It's not that easy, you know."

"C'mon, is it really that hard?"

"It might have been better if you didn't come here to help. Maybe you should treat me like a slave again. Do stuff to make me dislike you."

She slapped at his biceps playfully. "Do we need to go that far? Think about something else. Someone else."

"I feel so embarrassed. I don't think there are other men out there who admitted they had fantasies about you."

"For god's sake, Chris, if not for our work, we wouldn't be having this conversation."

"I'm not always like this. It just happened... you are my type. You really look good. There I said it. I hope that doesn't make you feel uncomfortable."

She cupped her mouth to muffle a burst of girlish laughter. She patted her chest. "I'm flattered. Really. Anyway, regardless of how you do it, think less of me for the rest of our time together. Okay?"

"No problem. That's not exactly true. But like I said I'll try my best."

Agnes, struggling to wipe the smile from her face, waved a warm goodbye at him and backed away. "I'll see you soon."

18

A Spring in Her Steps

Ian pushed out of table one and swiveled his high-backed chair one-hundred-eighty degrees. He planted his feet atop a stack of plastic crates and tossed into a stationery box the bread knife that he had used to poke at gaps between floorboards and at any crevice on the attic's timber frame. Assorted memorabilia that he suspected might serve as a hiding niche littered around the table's vicinity. He couldn't even get himself to kick them away to the sides. The chore took its toll on his back. He also had sleep debts waiting to be paid.

The longer-than-normal late lunch they shared had pushed their schedule closer to sundown. They were staring at another long night. He declared his efforts to find Ellie's pictures futile and granted himself a break from the effort.

On the sly, he has been observing Agnes who had taken an unusual interest in the sculptural nub of one log post since she got there. She must have also given up on her nook-and-cranny search at the second level. Up there, she has been circling about the log post end section northwest of the front gable, the one that had penetrated the floor and bowed outwards, to the general direction of the house's warpage. The two-foot long, eerily deformed log tip reminded Ian of a pier piling if it was made of driftwood. Agnes knelt beside it and rubbed her hand on gnarly wood grain, her eyes reflecting wonder and curiosity. Its counterpart on the northeast side had likewise torn through the floor and had projected out of it for just half a foot or so. Unlike its more aggressive neighbor, the log's end was smooth and well-rounded such that Agnes once sat on it while observing the world outside through the dormer window. At the back gable zone, the remaining log post pair had already deformed entire floor sections, indicating those log posts would over time break through.

Though Christopher never used the word 'evolution' to describe how the logs figured into the house's architecture, he had alluded to it. He recalled him saying that a helicopter couldn't have lowered a single log post to its present state. With the house as it was, it would be next to impossible for people to work its scraggly length through two floors, down into a foundation anchor. By inference, Ian concluded the four log posts were at the house's construction plumb-line straight, weight-bearing supports. Up until Agnes gave the log post special attention, their mystery no longer occupied a spot in Ian's roster of unsettling paranormal concerns. Not with all the stunts hitherto thrown at them by the resident spirit.

"What are the odds," Agnes said, as she continued to circle around the log post tip, "that Daniel really possessed telekinetic abilities?"

"Possible. Though I wouldn't consider it likely."

"What made you think that?"

"If you take away the frauds, I don't think there are that many people on Earth who have that gift."

"Chris has it."

"A bit of it, to be sure. And we know that only because you had proved it. If you didn't, everyone and Chris would have, for their lifetime, attributed the disturbances he causes as generic poltergeist phenomena."

"Over time, people should be able to distinguish the difference between the two."

"Your people, not people in the general sense. I've read somewhere that poltergeist activity may not be caused by spirits but by people, often children. Once the children are removed from the household, poltergeist activity ceases. The problem is, how do we tell them apart? Where do we draw the line between psychokinetic action and poltergeist activity?"

"The more I think about it, the more I'm inclined to believe Daniel had the gift when he was alive."

Ian shook his head emphatically. "C'mon, living corporeal bodies and the disembodied dead, the gulf between the two, its heaven and earth. Powers we have in life, we lose them all in death."

"Did you always believe spirits can haunt a place?"

"Until recently, no."

"Then you must also believe that whatever you consider now as improbable might actually be plausible."

Time and again, Agnes reached down to caress the wood surface. "What is this wood telling us?"

"Beats me."

"A tortured soul in this place wants something and can't let go of it. Its upward and outward bend tells me its inclination is to go somewhere else. There's got to be a way to convince him Ellie won't come back."

"If Daniel hid her pictures and those pictures were once a regular fixture in his memorabilia, then he must have hidden it from the other visitor psychics, too."

Agnes regarded him with a puzzled gaze. "But why?"

"No idea. I lean more on the possibility Ellie's pictures were never here in the first place."

"You think so?"

"This is a small place. We would have found it if it was here."

"It could still turn up. I think they're here."

"Did that come from intuition or from psychic presentiments?"

"Both."

Agnes stepped away from the log post area. She lowered herself to a well-traveled aisle floor area first, before she laid flat on her back. She propped her arms under her head, legs splayed, her eyes on the dormer window that lent a view to the darkening skies. She could have used the blanket nearby that she had once rolled out on the floor when she sorted through memorabilia. Like him, she must be too tired to care.

"Ian…"

"Yes?"

"When this is over, do you think the three of us will see each other again?"

"Yeah. We can have regular reunions. Why not. The digital record of our experiences here, I doubt we'd be given access to it. Hence, we'd forever be keeping to ourselves fantastic stories such as our magic furniture ride. We need to meet again, just for the sake of keeping our sanity."

Agnes burst into laughter. The high pitch and the boisterous edge of it took Ian aback that he joined her in laughter even if his timing was a bit too late. She said, "We do need to meet and start our three-person community of believers. You're right, relieving the terror, as a shared experience, might help keep us sane."

"For our first meet, remind me to bring a video camera, tripod, and the day's newspaper. I'm not getting any younger. Record my testimony, about our extraordinary experiences here."

"For posterity. I like the idea."

On the floor, Agnes rolled over her belly, wrapped her arms together, and then laid her left cheek on them. With the table lamp light on her, Ian made out a rare gleam in her eyes, right when her bright smile emerged. That once, her icy, forbidding beauty took on a warm, gentle sheen. Her eyes didn't look tired. He would have smelled alcohol had she sneaked up a chug or two.

"Know what, I have never asked you. I presumed gray-haired men have a wife and kids."

"My wife Joan and I, we've been married thirty-one years."

"Wow. Your kids must be grown up. Got grandkids?"

Ian hesitated. "How about you? How—"

She waved him down, dismissively. "Forget me. Rain check on my life. C'mon, you must have it in your wallet, a picture of you, your wife, the little ones, together."

"My only child, my son Trent. He died in an auto accident, nineteen years ago."

Agnes sat up. She flipped around on all fours and reached for him. She grasped the top of his right hand before she gently chafed at it. "I'm sorry. I'm so sorry to hear that."

"He was born from an affair I had with an ex-student of mine. I ended the affair to save my marriage. He just turned seventeen when I met him for the last time. I happened to be in Colorado and I invited him for a weekend of trout fishing. During a road trip on the way back, we had quite a time. He really liked my Benz and I gave it to him. Three weeks later it happened. I procrastinated on apologizing to him for lost time. He was young and there was so much time to catch up. Or so I thought."

Agnes, now seated in a lotus position, kept her attentive gaze on him. Ian regretted allowing Agnes to coax out from him a capsule version of an old wound that he wouldn't even confide to a professional psychoanalyst. From whatever part of her soul that her new-found warmth and sensitivity came from, he got reeled in. He should have known better and held back. He leaned further back in his chair and wrapped his arms tight around himself. He wanted to continue but he feared he may not be able to keep his emotions in check. "I'd need a few winks before the séance. If you don't mind."

She rose to her feet quickly. She patted around her pants. "Go ahead. Chris and I got this. I'll be down. He might need help."

"Relax. Her pictures would have been here by now if it was meant to be found."

She reached out and briskly rubbed the top of his hand another time. "Take it easy." She smiled and winked at him before she headed for the staircase.

Ian tracked her as she scurried down the staircase. He couldn't decide whether she double-stepped her way or whether she skipped while she double-stepped. Maybe he was just imagining it—the unusual spring in her steps.

19

The Big Favor

Christopher kept the trash chute cover flap inward with one hand, and with the other hand poked a lit-up flashlight into the opening. From his awkward kneeling position, he saw nothing but piles of black trash bags. He straightened to rest his stiff muscles. He tried another time from a different angle. He had searched every possible hiding place on the ground floor. The three chutes at the kitchen's southeast corner were the last items in his assigned search list. He dropped the chute cover, stepped aside to his right, and started probing the recycling chute.

"Chris."

His shoulders jerked. His flashlight fell into the chute, and his arm scraped against the metal edge of the flap as he pulled out. To his relief, the accident didn't cost him a blister.

Agnes cupped her mouth to stifle a laugh. "Sorry. Though I did mean to startle you."

"Oh, I get it. You needed to be sure."

"I'm sure, now."

"Next time, please make a fake cough or something. You walk like a... never mind."

"Note to self. When approaching Chris from behind, I

need to drag my steps. A fake cough might also startle you. So, scratch that one. Anyway, what are you looking for in the trash?"

"Been crossing out places mister Bishop had asked me to search. I've looked everywhere. These chutes are the last on my list."

She pushed in the recycling chute flap and peered in. "Your flashlight's a goner."

Christopher looked away while she stooped and observed the recycling chute interior. *Knock it off; she's wearing pants.* The more he avoided the thoughts, the more they wiggled their way in. Without TV, radio, or even books to occupy his mind, unwelcome thoughts, most especially the ones he wanted to avoid, find their way in with ease. All the more now that he had spent considerable face-to-face time with her.

Some time ago, he tried a different strategy. He traded sexual fantasies for plainer fantasies of her fully clothed. He focused on the wholesomeness of her clear, clean face and her tight body form clothed in anything but a white nightgown. He would slap the side of his face whenever stray images go beyond the purely aesthetic. Barely half an hour after he started the exercise and he stopped slapping his face. There has to be another way.

He never really understood Agnes' prescription, regarding his flyby fantasies. Does it apply at all times, or is it necessary only during a séance? He was embarrassed to ask for clarification.

Agnes straightened. "Ian's right. This is a good hide. Even if we find it here, the only way to get to it is to go out. Smart ghost."

Without leave-taking, she turned around and walked away. When he looked back at her, she had flipped a dining chair around. Then she back-stepped until she pressed her back against the refrigerator, arms crossed, her eyes on him. She pointed at the chair. "Sit, over here."

Christopher's felt his heart race and his throat tighten. He could do little else but comply. When he sat, he found himself setting his sights elsewhere, as she gazed down at him from such a close distance. He felt uncomfortable, rolling his eyes up to meet hers, as she continued to gaze down at him from what seemed to him like an intimidating height.

"I need to ask you a favor. A big, big one."

"Okay…"

"Daniel would touch me again tonight. I have to control my fears, my fear of being touched, or else I'd be starting off from a disadvantaged position. The less fear I have before I have induced a trance, the deeper I'd get into it. The deeper the trance, the less I become vulnerable to the spirit inhabiting me. I'd also emerge from a session less drained."

He wasn't sure he understood the point. He gripped his knees as hard as he could to suppress his fidgeting tendencies. He lifted his eyes only to acknowledge her to a bare minimum. He tried to distract his mind away from anticipating what the favor would be. He rubbed his hands on his pants like they were covered in sweat.

"Is there another way to tell, if you really need to be wakened?" He just needed to say something.

Agnes shook her head. "Other than what we have already practiced, not much else. The point is, I need to hold on to the séance longer without the need to be wakened prematurely. I'm a strong medium. I don't normally return from a trance that exhausted. They were the old fears, deep in my subconscious that punishes me from the inside even before I reach a trance state. When I'm in it, my conscious mind is out of range to help. I have no idea how my subconscious mind is coping with the spirit's takeover. Much more so in this case when I already have complete awareness the spirit is taking special interest in me."

"This problem, how much does it really have to do with my fantasies?"

"A lot. But that is not the issue here. There is a remedy that might work to my advantage. On this, I need your help. I know this favor would be very awkward for you. I need you to touch me like you would your lover."

"I'm sorry. I need to hear that again."

"I said I need you to touch me like you would touch your lover."

It was the first time he experienced it—when fear and excitement overwhelmed him at the same time. He stood up and locked his arms behind his back, to hide their trembling. "Mister Bishop, does he know?"

Agnes shook her head. "All three of us can discuss anything about a lot of things. This one is very personal. It's just between you and me."

"It's not that it would be a hard thing for me to do. It's so easy to do—in my fantasies. But… can you say it again, what you want me to do?"

"I need you to help me overcome my fear—my fear of being touched by Daniel during the séance. I've learned something from that terrifying experience that had short-circuited the connection between your fears and your telekinetic abilities. The same idea might work for my particular problem. I'm not talking about touching like you want to check if someone had a fever. It's much more than that."

By then, he knew his face looked totally flushed. He rubbed his hands briskly to the sides of his hip. "Whatever crossed my mind, from the time I first saw you till now. It's just hormones. I need to let you know first that I respect—"

"Will you cut the crap. We don't have time. You're not helping anyone by being squeamish. I gave my consent. Now, give me yours."

"Okay. Whatever you say."

"I need your consent. Your explicit consent."

"You have my consent."

She turned her back and motioned him to follow her as

she strode towards the master bedroom. All that time he watched her, wondering how more worked up he would have been if she wore a white nightgown instead. She must have been too embarrassed to flesh out the details of her request that she had deferred it. He couldn't calm his feverish anticipation of the favor because he was certain it would involve some variation of heavy petting. Otherwise, there would have been no need to move to a more private place. Things were already set in motion and he still wasn't sure what the exact boundaries of her request were. Whatever they were, he knew boundaries between fantasy and reality would be somewhat crossed. He needed to stay calm.

Like an obedient consort, he followed her quietly into the master bedroom.

She paused as soon as she stepped in as if she surveyed the place for a suitable venue where it would happen. He looked around the ceiling instead, distracting his mind from the excitement of anticipation. Immediately, an overpowering sense that he just entered a hotel room with a lover took over. He pinched himself in the arm discreetly.

It didn't work.

AGNES LOCKED the bedroom door and faced the wall next to it. She dropped her hands to her sides before she rested them awkwardly, by her hips. Christopher milled restless right behind her. He rubbed his clammy hands on his pants while he prayed the fluttering in his chest would come to a stop. Agnes trembled in a way that would make a joke out of the worst tremors he exhibited during a séance session. Her body's violent involuntary spasms seemed to him like a helpless victim's reaction to predator threat when the escape routes had all been blocked. He could feel vibrations from the floor. He started to wonder, with Agnes' repulsion to the intimate touching that she herself had encouraged, if something horrible had happened to her in the past.

She glanced once over her shoulder as if checking his state of readiness. He rehearsed in his head a list of moves he recently planned on. He could touch her gently by the hips—or grab her by the shoulders—or take her by way of a full, locking embrace. The way Agnes behaved, he had to scrounge for a subtler fourth option.

"This might help." The tremor in her voice sounded as genuine as her body's shakes. She crossed her hands over her forehead and pressed against the wall, in a hide-and-seek pose. She started to perspire. "C'mon, we don't have much time."

She took long, deep breaths. The body-shaking lessened. Emboldened, Christopher moved closer and surveyed her waist, along the perfect slope by which it rounded her hips. He must have grabbed her waist too hard because he felt her shoulders shudder with such force that she could have busted his teeth if he had kissed her there at the exact moment.

He could scarcely believe how natural the moves came to him. His two-handed grip slipped and moved down to her hips. He wished there was time to convince her to switch clothes so that his hands would be caressing a softer, single-piece fabric. She lets go a frightened gasp when his hands probed further out, to the front of her. He dropped back. He weighed the risks between taking it slow and getting her piqued and his cutting himself loose and potentially ending the affair on a bad note. As he sought a middle way, Agnes sighed, a hint of impatience behind it. She placed her hands higher on the wall like someone consenting to a frisk.

"I asked you for a favor. Just do it. Got that?"

"Got it."

That instant, Christopher let himself go. He bear-hugged her and buried his face in her back. He pressed against her hard that her supporting arms folded and collapsed. The wall thumped and crackled. He reached up and down her upper body, caressing where he could, up until Agnes grabbed both his arms. He couldn't tell if she gasped or sighed, or if the sound she made implied disappointment for her own failings rather than an expression of disgust over what was being done to her. Christopher tried to disengage, but Agnes held on to his arms. He felt her fingernails dig into his skin. He groaned. Only then did she let go. When he checked on his right arm, he noticed deep-set, scalloped bruises.

"Don't stop until I ask you to," she said, her tone more frustrated than impatient.

He jumped in and embraced her by the midsection, lightly this time, caressing his way up to her bosom. He avoided the lower abdominal regions where she reacted most adversely. Her sighs sounded more relaxed. He resolved to abandon caution and to stop only if she asked him to. He pressed his body hard against hers and pinned her against the wall. He reached down the sides of her pants and pulled out her tucked blouse. The moment he unbuttoned her pants and worked on the zippers, Agnes backed against him so hard he flung and staggered back a few steps.

Agnes hammered her fisted hands on the wall.

"I'm sorry. I thought—"

"Don't be sorry," she snapped back, as she recovered her hands-in-the-wall position. "Don't think I'm mad at you. Ignore what I'm saying. Don't stop."

"I need to know if I'm hurting you."

"I mistreated you, didn't I? Look at this as payback."

"That was settled the last time when you reached out to me in the kitchen."

"Forget payback then. We don't have time. Let me put it this way. If I tell you to stop, if I make you stop, don't stop. Got that?"

"Okay, okay."

If only he could only tell her that fantasies do not have boundaries—that more than once he had played in his head the two of them making love—that he wasn't sure how he himself would react if for any reason she insisted that he stops. It wafted to his mind, to take things as far as he can, to go for broke. Agnes took deep breaths before she crossed her arms on the wall and rested her forehead on them. He understood by then Agnes had the last word and that the level of consent at the moment no longer left any room for interpretation. She was right. On the first day when he saw her skirt rise, it has to be his mind, not Daniel's, that made it happen. He would have wanted to be in this situation if by some magic he could wish it to be. It was happening right now. He had every reason to let go.

He pressed close again, scooped his hands up under her blouse, and cupped her bosom. He felt her stiffen before her legs started to tremble. He pressed against her until his face nuzzled over her left shoulder. He carefully reached down with both his hands, grabbing at her waist side belt line, pulling them apart to make sure he had the pulled zippers all the way down. He whispered close to her left ear: "This is how I really want to touch you." Her trembling intensified. He expected her to say something back but she did not. Nor did she make any move that he could interpret as rejection. In that moment of calm, he made a decision. She shrieked when he lifted her off the ground and took her to the bed. She was in his world now. He went for broke.

20

The Final Night

Right before sundown, Ian and company regrouped on the second floor to give their workplace a pre-séance once over. He paced about the dance floor periphery, double-checking the window candle placements and shutting the curtains tight. He made sure they had backups to every séance essential, from extra writing pads to a nightgown change for Agnes. The portable CD player was the lone artifact from the attic that Agnes had insisted on relocating to the second floor.

The lead-up to the séance bore none of the forebodings that came with the last one. Battlefield experience? More than likely, the level of terror the team had collectively experienced the previous night had inured them to whatever else they anticipated this night might have in store for them. One other oddity preoccupied his downtime musings. His companions carried over their lighthearted disposition during dinner to the dance floor. As if they were newly-acquainted people checking out a place of common interest to them.

Agnes, dressed in a white-as-white can-be nightgown circled about the north-end log post and occasionally pressed her ears against it. A less chores-oriented Christopher hovered around her without reserve. Gone were the dagger stares she flung every chance she got to the team's self-abnegating gofer. More than once he overheard the two laughing over something known only to them.

He did recall, while he drifted on and off in his chair in the attic, that he heard a rash of moving day noise coming from the ground floor. What sounded like bangs on the wall and scrapings on the floor came and went.

The disturbances all came from somewhere at the far end of the ground floor, possibly the master bedroom. His companions might have moved stuff around in a last-minute flurry to find Ellie's missing pictures. He'd only consider the alternate possibility in a bizarro universe. Not quite possible. Agnes was neither naughty nor nice.

Ian pulled back the curtains of a west-side mid-room window and rolled down the shutters. He watched the sun's yellow-red afterglow through a break in the thin, persistent fog. Five-fifteen on the clock. He shuttered back the window blinds and closed the curtains.

When he approached Agnes and Christopher, both of them had their hands on the wood, whispering gibberish to each other. "Would any of you care to share with the old man any vibes you had gathered from the log posts?"

"So much energy locked in this old wood," Agnes said. "That much I can tell you."

"How about you, Chris? Any feedback you'd want to share?"

"None, sir. I'm just copying what Agnes is doing."

Agnes closed her eyes tightly as if trying to remember something. "The word, it kept slipping. One word that defines the exact feeling, of that locked-up energy coming from the wood."

"Sadness—heartache—pain—sentiments?"

"No." Then her eyes brightened. A eureka expression formed on her face. "Yearning, perhaps? Yes, that's it. Though longing sounds more like it." She tapped her fingers on the wood and smiled at it. "The wood. That must be why it's been bending, warping, and deforming across the years. It cannot let go. It's pining for something, in an endless cycle."

"Why can't he just go," Christopher said. "Like other ghosts do?"

"He might let us know," Agnes said. "I haven't given up on it yet."

"Sooner or later, somebody's got to burn this place down," Ian said. "We don't even know how the default assumption that burning the place up would only relocate the spirit to another haunt came about." He touched Agnes' left shoulder to head off an apology. "No offense, but psychics are not above pulling stuff out of their asses."

Agnes said, "The extraordinary efforts that doctor Pershing and his people made to relocate this house in the middle of nowhere, they have to be part of a plan to bring finality to the problem. We could be at the tip or at the tail of an endgame. Perhaps in between."

"The endgame team, if we get lucky."

"What if they burn the house and it follows us home?" Christopher said. "Like in the movies."

Agnes lifted her hand to the level of her hip, a more polite forefinger at Christopher's direction. "Expunge that from your mind. This is not the time for that kind of joke."

"It's not a joke. If he can move to another place once his place is burned down, it must be easier for him to follow home visitors, like us. He can pick and choose which of our homes he'd like to haunt."

She clicked her teeth and grinned at him. "Zip it, Chris."

Hands inside his pockets, Christopher made a coy nod.

Ian couldn't get over his companions' mutually complaisant attitude. Christopher's less vulnerable body language, her off-character behavior, and their fretful eye contact. Until recently, he had gotten used to Agnes' standard facial expression—deadpan and grim, with exceptions to the rule being a rarity. He wondered if something happened downstairs. People do change. Though not that quickly. "Agnes, it's night. As always, do us the honors."

She checked the time. "We've been through this before, guys. Let's keep it tight and together."

⸻

HER DROOPY EYES opened briefly at intervals, as her head gently gyrated. A faint smile grew from her lips. Ian focused on Agnes at the exclusion of everything else. Warm candlelight made it easier for him to narrow his field of vision, and for him to ignore the exaggerated shadows cast by the lit candles that bordered the dance floor. He imagined a solid wall of black immediately behind Agnes, to keep his thoughts from probing the void's depths that melded with the unseen passages at the floor's far end. As always, the icy cold descended. The tabletop candle flames made their familiar flicker. Christopher could manage, he reminded himself. He should know by now that somber backdrops could only harbor ghosts, not goblins. For sure, her grandparents had told him worse tales that most likely included horned soul-takers and fanged bloodsuckers.

They had signed up for it, as Agnes would have put it in the plainest of terms. While he waited for a clear sign she had fallen into a trance, he pondered on the promise he made to himself the night before—that he would give his one hundred percent to his team and to the official record.

He and his team had stepped into the séance without a clear-cut plan of action or even an end goal that would define a fulfillment of their contractual obligations. He didn't even have the slightest idea who would drop the curtains on the project and how paranormal events in the house would be verified by their employers. Agnes still held most of the cards.

Commitment issues aside, all that he looked forward to was the night's end.

Finally, her eyes turned from dreamy to glassy, and her full, toothless smile arced on her face. Christopher acted on cue. He planted the open spiral artist sketchbook on the table and carefully reached out and placed a sign pen on her right hand.

"Daniel, are you here?"

Agnes scrunched over the table. She scribbled on paper: *"Yes."*

Christopher flashed the page to him. Ian nodded and his partner turned over a new page.

"What is your last name?"

"Daniel, Daniel Pershing."

"How do we know it is you?"

Agnes held the sign pen up. Ian tried a new tack.

"Daniel, thank you for letting us sleep last night. We apologize if something we said offended you."

"For... forget."

"I have to ask you again. Why do you remain in this house, in this world of the living?"

"Waiting."

"Waiting for?"

"She's here... my Ellie, my Ellie."

"How many times do I need to repeat it to you. That woman writing down your messages is Agnes Haskell. She's not a spirit, like you. Ellie is. And she's waiting for you on the other side. You want to be with her, you must cross over. Do you know what crossing over means?"

Agnes scribbled scrawls.

"You've imprisoned yourself in an empty house for thirty years. All that time why didn't you cross over? Can you please tell us why?"

"Ellie, Ellie, right there. Make love to me... Ellie... make..."

Ian paused, as he reviewed in his head follow-through

questions. He patted his back pocket to make sure his trump card, Ellie's presumed obituary—should he need a foolproof way to verify the spirit's identity—was there.

"Daniel, when did you die?"

Agnes' right hand rested on the table.

"We know that you had passed away and that you and Ellie parted ways. Ellie had two children from a man whose last name was Hobbes. Your Ellie passed away on—"

"No, no. Ellie, there."

Christopher's eyes drew attention to Agnes' upper torso, around the princess's neckline that rippled as if a hand probed down her clothes. Ian filled his lungs with air before he said in a hard tone: "You know Agnes doesn't want to be touched. She's in a trance. She's unconscious. She cannot give consent. Stop touching her."

The ripples in her clothes waned. It surprised him that Agnes' complexion appeared to be pristine; not a glisten of sweat.

"You must know where Ellie's pictures are in this house. We want to see her. Share her pictures with us. Show us where they are."

Agnes' hands rested on the table. Ian decided to toughen up the interrogatories.

"Who are you again?"

"Daniel, Daniel, Daniel, Daniel, Daniel…"

For the most part, he was able to read the automatic writings even if they were upside down. "All right, stop."

Her writing hand lowered.

"Daniel should be able to tell Agnes and Ellie apart. You cannot. Are you really Daniel?"

"I… I… I…"

From his diaphragm, he dredged up the loudest, most commanding voice that he could muster, "Prove to us that you are Daniel. Show us Ellie's pictures."

Shuffling footsteps glissaded across the floor, towards the south-end staircase. The pall of coldness ended.

Agnes remained in a trance state. Her tamed hair no longer let out strands made to sway by some invisible force. More than in any of their past seances, her face reflected more calm, even an aura of innocence he'd associate with youth. He could swear she looked a decade younger. Maybe the candlelight merely washed out any trace of harshness in her face.

The globe-eyed Christopher pointed out to him the anomalies in the candle flames around them.

The candle flames—from the stubby tabletop ones to the tall, narrower ones plugged into the candelabras in the dance floor periphery—licked to the direction of the southern stairwell, as if following the wake of a wind tunnel. Yet none of the drapery layers over the shuttered windows moved. Maybe they were signs Daniel's at it. His ploy might actually work. He waited.

A metallic thump came from downstairs, south. He listened close. The trash chute covers? Nothing else in the house makes such a distinct sound. Christopher's eyes bugged out; he stiffened. He saw something ahead of him and he pointed his thumb to the void—toward the south.

Ian turned around and scanned the darkness around him before he turned his chair at an angle and he faced the direction of the south-end staircase. He thought he had a glimpse of something floating in the void directly ahead.

Another second and he saw a flat object, floating at eye-level, toward them.

A gift-box carton the size of a cigar box emerged. It coasted in a straight line until it floated above the table, directly above the point in the table surface where Ian rested his arms. The upper box cover separated and the bottom part flipped over. No garbage bin scent came with it. He couldn't imagine another spot where Daniel would have hidden it all along.

Photographs of various sizes fell towards the tabletop, twirling as if in slow motion. They all landed face up. The two parts of the box dropped, back first, into the table. He noticed that one of the box's parts harbored more pictures that seemed to have been stuck in place.

It was pure, controlled magic. As if an invisible force was with them, deftly shuffling the pictures like it was a deck of cards on a poker table. Fear took a backseat to the sense of wonder and indescribable awe.

He stood up. He lined the six pictures in a semi-circle, angled to share viewing with Christopher. He tapped a fore-finger to one picture in the middle, to a candid portrait of Daniel and Ellie where the two lovers smiled at the camera—likely on tripod and self-timer—their cheeks pressed together, arms forward and clasped as if poised to dance. The master bedroom, for sure. He locked incredulous stares with Christopher.

Ellie, in full bloom, looked much more mature than in the Pershing family picture taken in 1992. Even in her ponytailed hair, Ellie resembled Agnes.

Ian turned the picture over. The handwritten note on the back read:

Ellie and Daniel
September 7, 1994.

The two parts of the boxes levitated at the same time. They joined as one. It floated away, back through the void, toward the south.

Almost immediately, the ripples in Agnes' clothing intensi-fied. Light beads of sweat gathered in her face and perspira-tion seeped out of her hairline.

"Daniel. I really appreciate your opening yourself to us. But if you don't stop touching Agnes, I have no choice but to wake her up."

The ripples died down.

He picked a picture and pointed at Ellie's image in it. Then he displayed it in four general directions. "This is Ellie. That is Agnes. Your Ellie, our Agnes, two different people who just happened to look alike."

When he looked back, the disturbances in her clothing continued. Unseen hands worked around her chest. Her breasts moved, like someone invisible is actually kneading them. She wore no brassier precisely to protect herself from bruising in the event the fondling goes out of control.

Christopher stared at him as if waiting for a cue.

"Stop. Stop right now. Agnes doesn't want to be touched. The way you are touching her right now, Daniel, it's totally inappropriate."

Agnes grabbed a pen and wrote in large letters:

"No."

"What do you mean no?"

"No."

"You stop touching her right now or I'll wake her up."

"No. Ellie... like touch."

21

Doppelganger

"Not one picture, taken on the second floor," Ian muttered to himself as he shuffled through the six-picture set he had coaxed Daniel into delivering. Agnes, at the other end of the kitchen dining table, pored through the automatic writing notes, swiftly leafing from one page to the next. Christopher, who had repacked her change bag with a fresh nightgown, plopped her moist clothes into the laundry.

"What you're wearing is the last unused one," Christopher said, as he turned on the machine.

"I thought she had several of them."

"I don't know where the rest went, sir. I've gone through her closet."

Agnes hasn't spoken a word since she started reviewing Daniel's messages. She appeared laser-focused on analyzing the notes, returning over certain pages, staying on one page awhile, as if searching for nuance in the language. The woman must have a tough constitution. As in the previous séance sessions, she had recovered from the taxing possession rather quickly.

"The next séance, should Daniel touch you again and he refuses to take no from me, I'd wake you up."

Without taking her eye off the page, she picked up another cookie from the plate. Not even an inadvertent glance, or a knowing squint.

"I can't risk it, the possibility he'd accidentally harm you when he goes for it. You should understand by now why I'm putting my foot down on this matter."

Ian lowered himself as he sought her eyes that looked increasingly annoyed by his persistent intrusions. He picked up a belated nod from her while she continued to read. She munched on a cookie, her last bite harder than the previous one.

"You understand me? We're dealing here with a spirit who can levitate our combined weight, whose control over its own strength we know nothing about. The harm that even violent people could do to another, we can see it coming. We can run or put up a fight."

Her fisted hands hammered at the table. Her eyes flashed at him. "What the hell do you know, about what harm people can do to another." The unexpected outburst shook him more than the jolt on the table.

Stunned speechless, Ian could barely hold a stare at her.

She buried her remorse-stricken face in her hands. "I'm sorry. I'm so sorry. I'm just so tired."

"You need to get some rest," Christopher said. "Where do you want me to make your bed?"

"I only need ten or fifteen minutes. The hallway. No, the living room would be fine. Lay some comforters there."

Christopher took off into the hallway.

Agnes squeezed the top of Ian's arm. "Sorry again, for my outburst."

"No worry. At this age, a man had experienced more than his fair share of getting dressed down. I was once assaulted by an ex-patient of mine whom I refused to see because she had gone too far off the rails."

"Did she hurt you?"

"No. It's just my pride. It happened in public. She got me by the hair; left me shaken."

As she resumed her work, Agnes curtailed a laugh.

"You may not remember it, but the intense way he had touched you was beyond worrisome."

"I wasn't bruised or anything like that."

"I witnessed it. It was borderline sexual assault. I can't stress this one enough: when you're in a trance, you must trust my judgment. I decide when it could go on and when it should end."

"The bed's ready," Christopher's voice piped in from the living room.

"Coming."

Agnes waved Ian goodbye and disappeared into the hallway.

He followed and turkey-peeped from the hallway corner. He saw Agnes slump into the comforter-layered bed. Christopher covered her with a blanket to her shoulders. She pulled up the edges to the level of her chin. The young man watched her awhile until she had flipped to her side.

Ian waved at Christopher to hurry back.

As soon as Christopher turned into the kitchen, he yanked him toward the far end corner, by trash chute row. He whispered close to his ears, as low as he could. "I need you to be truthful to me. During the séance, did you have fantasies about her, about you touching her?"

Christopher blushed. He glanced wearily towards the hallway. He whispered back with equal caution. "Sir, believe me. I resist like crazy. Agnes told me not to think about her that way."

"I know."

"I tried closing my eyes. I thought about the dream house I'd like to buy for my mother. The more I try to think about something else, the more it slips in."

"Is that normal to you? Do you fantasize a lot about every attractive woman you get to hang out with?"

"No, sir. It just so happened. That everything about her, they're what I want in a woman."

"Like snotty women who behave like you're beneath them?"

"We're cooler now, sir. Like I said, everything about her… I mean, just between you and me, sir. I have the hots for her like I couldn't explain."

"I'm sure you had the hots for other women before. Have you gone this overboard, in your head, as you have with Agnes?"

Christopher's brows narrowed as if something he just said connected.

"It's hard to describe it, sir. But…"

"Unusual? Extraordinary? What?"

"Somewhere between the two, sir."

"I'm trying to gauge here, the cards held by the opposing side. I suspect Daniel is channeling not just your psychokinetic talent. Let me take you back to the first time you saw Agnes. I saw it in your eyes then. I have no idea if his influence on you then was already at work. How you regarded her, from that time, till now, was there a natural, point-a-to-point-b progression?"

"I don't think I get the question, sir."

"Were your feelings about her consistent from the first time you saw her till now, or did the feelings become more intense as our work progressed? To put it in another perspective, did those feelings reach such level you suspect outside forces might be responsible for your irrepressible desire for her?"

"Honestly, sir, I can't tell the difference."

Ian pondered on the conundrum for a long second. "Agnes and I had a long discussion about your fantasies' possible role in enhancing the resident ghost's power. Our little talk right now had corroborated my suspicions. The rest of the séance, I want you to stay here."

"Sir, please." His hands clasped in a supplicating manner. "At night, I can't even pee without you outside the door. If the lights go out, I could drop dead where I stand."

"All right. Can you at least try? Practice it. Once the fantasies come knocking in, distract your mind with something very specific. Think about, for example, a naked man."

"I'm straight, sir."

"That's my point. Think about the image of a person you couldn't relate to sexually."

"I'll do that, sir. If that doesn't work, I'll think of something gross, really gross."

"I may be a psychologist, but I have no power to tweak your mind. Only you can. Practice."

"You have other tips for me, sir?"

"As you had already suggested, once a fantasy blows in, you auto-rewind to that repugnant imagery."

"Whatever it takes, I'll do it, sir."

"You better. Here's something to motivate you: if you fail, you get left alone in the kitchen."

Christopher's unusual fixation on Agnes also goaded him to consider the possibility that moments of sheer terror in the project had exacerbated the young man's sexual infatuation. He had heard of this phenomenon way back in his college days, though he had never observed one in action. The Capilano Bridge Experiment, that was it. Somewhere in Vancouver, Canada, was supposed to be this scary, hanging bridge spanning two hills and running through towering treetops. Over a hundred feet below it, a small bridge across a stream. A volunteer psychology student of average look would intercept men crossing the small bridge for a brief, fake survey. The same woman would repeat the same experiment, this time, at the hanging bridge. She alternates her survey ambuscades over the low bridge and the hanging bridge over a period of time. She notes the encounters. Over the years, psychology students repeated the original experiment, and each time the same results emerged: volunteers get hit on by their subjects in the hanging bridge by an overwhelming factor vis-a-vis identical survey encounters at the low bridge below it. The experiment corroborated what psychology pundits knew all along: that fear and sexual attraction run along the same lines in the limbic system of the brain. Stimulation of one system affects the other system. People in scary situations, as well as those who emerged from a hairy experience, find the opposite sex more attractive than in safer circumstances.

Nonetheless, he couldn't pin it, where fear and sexual attraction actually fit in the scheme of things in the project. He suspected that psychics in the past must have exploited fear, a common denominator in séance sessions, to squeeze out stronger reactions from the resident spirit. The pattern in Daniel's behavior also suggested Agnes wasn't far off the mark to attribute Daniel's unusual power to his ability to exploit novel energy fields present on his turf.

The new developments in the status quo continued to puzzle him. More than once he had observed his companions flirting. Had she apologized to him, then Christopher might have seen her in a totally different light. They start over and it wouldn't be far-fetched if he had found her more desirable. But the clean slate wouldn't explain Agnes' responsiveness to the minion figure she had, for the good part of their project, accorded minimal respect.

As he pondered on an ideal endgame strategy, he decided to ask Christopher one last question, a very sensitive one that he wouldn't foist on him under normal circumstances. He motioned him for a huddle.

"You and Agnes, did you two do something intimate in the master bedroom?"

Christopher's face soured. "Can I take the fifth on that one, sir?"

"No. But I'll take a nod for a yes."

Reluctantly, Christopher nodded.

"Thank you."

"Anything else, sir?"

"No, that's it."

He couldn't tell him yet, his final decision on the matter: Christopher and Agnes should be as far away from each other as possible for the remainder of the project.

22

Psychokinesis

Eight new photographs lined the séance table in a pattern that resembled a professional card dealer's handiwork. The first four were oriented right side up while the rest faced down. Ian had placed the previous six photographs behind the table-top candles. The two empty sections of the picture box rested near the table-top candle cluster. Ian oriented the table to get the right-side-up pictures illuminated. He motioned Agnes to keep off the upside-down photographs. At the moment, it made little sense to speculate on Daniel's motive for presenting the way he did the rest of the once-missing pictures.

Agnes picked a right-side-up 5x7 colored photograph. Yellowed and faded with age, the picture depicted Daniel and Ellie sprawled on the attic floor, on their bellies over an area rug, elbows levered. A camera, likely set on a self-timer, captured the scene.

Ian angled another 5x7 into the light and Agnes moved to his side for a look. In the tightly-framed, from-the-shoulder-up picture, Ellie's cheek rested on Daniel's left shoulder while he leaned the side of his face to the top of her head. The pose looked restful, and the expression in their eyes, soft and dreamy. The lovers wore clothes different from the previous picture, although the backdrop definitely was the same.

"That must be why I felt warmth in certain areas on the attic floor," Agnes said.

"You frequently sat where they used to hang out. You got it spot on. I had to hand it to you."

He picked up two 3x4 pictures taken in the still sparsely furnished kitchen. Here, Ellie stood where the upright refrigerator was, facing it, hands to her waist. Daniel, right behind her, fixed a ribbon tied to her hair. She wore a flowing gown similar in color and style to dancing attires common in ballroom dancing.

In the other picture, Ellie leaned back on a cupboard, arms at ease, while Daniel sat on a chair right in front of her, as if regarding her.

Agnes bit her lips. She hollered in the direction of the south-end staircase. "Chris, over here!"

In an instant, a heavy scamper came from the kitchen-side staircase. A wild-eyed Christopher emerged. He came running across the dance floor. Ian kept the discomfited groan to himself. It took a lot to convince him to remain in the kitchen for the duration of the next séance.

"Over here. Look at this picture." She replaced the right-side-up pictures where they originally laid. She stepped back, waved Christopher in, and directed his attention at the young lover's photographs in the kitchen.

Christopher's eyes bulged. "No way."

Agnes awned her arms to her sides and grinned at Christopher. This once, the gleam in her eyes perfectly matched her full smile.

"Oh my god, her hair... like yours. She even stood where..."

Ian picked up on Christopher's hesitation. Beyond doubt, something happened between his two companions down there. The doppelganger conundrum didn't seem to astonish the two. They stood close together as they checked out the pictures. They seemed caught up in an uppity mood a looming séance session didn't even seem to bother them. He couldn't believe he would ever put the disparate meanings of "something's not right" and "heartening development" in the same context.

Christopher reached for the upside-down pictures.

She intercepted his attempt through a lightning-fast slap at his hand. She flashed a mischievous grin. "We're not sure if we're supposed to look at them yet."

"I say we turn them over." Ian declared. "Guys, the picture layout is obviously his attempt to compartmentalize the presentation. He wanted us to see the next photographs last. Chris, do us the honor. Flip them over."

⸺

DANCE FLOOR PICTURES, all four of them. The missing link to the mystery laid out on the table by Daniel himself.

In all of them, Ellie wore the same white, shin-length gown. Her various tresses marked the different occasions the pictures were taken. Daniel also appeared in different outfits, always formal. In one of them, he wore a tuxedo.

The lovers had two, similar-themed full-body, formal portraits. In one, they faced the camera, as people would in a pre-wedding studio portrait.

In the second colored 5x8, Daniel took on a professional dance pose at the dance floor center, a leg and arm extended, eyes where his hand pointed, demonstrating grace, balance, and flexibility. Not far behind him, her face to the camera, Ellie mimicked his pose with what appeared to be a scene of wild, awkward abandon. Ellie's self-mocking antics further convinced him only Daniel wore the dance shoes.

He noticed the south-end log posts in the background, both of them still straight and light in color.

Agnes pulled herself a chair and examined another 5x8 wherein the lovers took in an intimate dance pose, their feet high off the ground.

"He's a dancer, no doubt," Ian said. "This studio must be his."

"She's got to be a dancer, too." She passed another photograph to him.

He shook his head. "I don't think so."

The Ellie solo showed her in an elegant ballet dancer-like riposte to music. Here, she appeared to have leaped off the ground, and the camera caught her at the top of the action.

"A non-dancer couldn't leap that high and look that relaxed and that intense at the same time."

"You have a point there. However, extensions typical to dancers are suspiciously missing. Another thing. Look at her shoes. They're faux ballet shoes, whereas Daniel wore ballroom dancing shoes each time. He even used tap dancing shoes in one picture."

"How can you tell?"

"My wife and I took ballroom dancing classes. Don't ask. Long story."

"I'm not convinced," she snatched a 5x8 from Christopher's hand. "Here. Look at Ellie's backward limp, whatever that dance pose is called. She must have some dance training to lean back that far."

"I agree with Agnes, sir. The way he held her, the way they both froze in the air, looked real. Their feet, too, all pointed down, as if they jumped at the same time."

"And they struck that pose," Ian said, "after taking to air at the same time?"

"You tell me. They could be that good," Agnes said. "Do they even have good digital photo editing then? The image didn't strike me as photoshopped."

Ian tipped his glasses and turned the photograph to the light.

In the dramatically choreographed portrait, the two lovers' bodies fused together, as Daniel's arms wrapped tight at the arch in Ellie's back. Her upper body dropped back. Her head, arms, and hair hang limp. Daniel buried his face in her bosom in a sensuous, classic fashion. Her eyes were closed, her lips slightly parted, the overall expression in her face, pure serenity.

Ian took a closer look at the picture, reviewing details one at a time.

The creases in and around her waistline looked too exaggerated for a ground shot manipulated to appear otherwise. He took into account a detail that Christopher mentioned earlier—the lovers' feet pointed downward like they both took a concerted leap. He re-examined the lover's end position in relation to the height of the wall-set hand holds at the right side of the frame. He calculated the wall mirrors and the ceiling heights as corroborating references.

Confirmation bias. They all assumed the couple jumped together for the pose and it appeared in their collective heads as such, despite the fact the picture presented a totally different reality. He estimated that the lovers' feet should be anywhere from four to six feet in the air. Not possible, unless they were super athletes, and only if they had a good head-start. Even then, they should have pivoted as they completed the mid-air pose. He also found no tell-tale photo editing fingerprints where the people and the backdrop merged. The shadows looked self-consistent. Again, he scrutinized the way the couple's feet hung in the air. They were key to resolving the enigma.

He ushered his two stupefied companions into an open area on the dance floor. He motioned them to face each other and showed them the intriguing reference picture. "Re-create this pose for me, please."

Agnes laughed. "Are you serious? You want me to lean back and have Chris bury his nose in my chest?"

"I'll have no problem with that."

She took a jocular swing at Christopher's face. He staggered back, laughing.

He placed Christopher's arms around her, at her lower back. "You lock it in hard, plant your legs on the floor this way." Ian demonstrated a fencer-like riposte.

Christopher stepped forward and copied his pose.

He pointed at Agnes. "You lean back as far as you can."

The two did exactly as told. Agnes even dropped her arms to her sides and allowed her head to droop back.

"Doable, is it not?"

She nodded. Christopher looked confused and non-committal.

He snapped his fingers. "As you were."

The two carefully recovered their old positions and stood together, while Ian slipped between them and showed them the dance portrait photograph that they had just re-created.

"Both of you remember your form when you mimicked the Ellie-Daniel dance pose, right?"

The two nodded.

"Recall how your feet were, all flat on the floor, resisting gravity as they should. Now how do you explain this." He pointed at the lovers' legs and feet dangling. "Imagine yourself close together and jumping at the same time and then at the top of the leap, striking that pose. You think your legs would end up in a relaxed dangle like that? Maybe they got themselves to hook up and hang by invisible lines anchored at the ceiling. Perhaps, at a later time, they had commissioned a pro lab to erase the Marionette lines. I don't think so."

"I'm not into dance," Agnes said. "Though I've seen enough dance posters where pros leap into the air to strike a pose. You're right. She even looked too relaxed. Like she was about to fall asleep."

"Now that you pointed it out," Christopher said. "I think something's weird in that picture."

"They could have…" Agnes hesitated. A second later, her eyes glared at Ian. "You think…"

"Look at Daniel's eyes and the grimace he made as he ducked to her bosom. Look at how his jaws clenched. Was he expressing passion or was he concentrating, holding on to a force he had set to motion?"

"You've got to be kidding me."

"He held hard on her lower back because he supported her weight. There was no joint leaping action."

Agnes cupped her mouth as she gasped. Her eyes bulged. "He was levitating, for both of them. Oh my god. How did we miss that? In Ellie's mid-air solo, he was the one who levitated her, too. It all makes sense now."

"Agnes, in your trade, did you ever hear of anyone levitating people through mind power?"

"No. Not even of someone who had levitated himself."

"Let me play devil's advocate. Here's another possibility: Daniel, obsessed with fantasies of having telekinetic powers, had manufactured the scene. How he did it, beats me. Of course, we'd never know for sure, the same way we'd never know for sure if Chris's latent telekinetic abilities had helped magnify Daniel's ability to manipulate the environment."

Agnes glanced at her wristwatch and shook her head wearily. She beckoned everyone back to the séance table. "We're getting too far into the night. Let's get to it, guys. Clear the table, and put the pictures back into the box."

"I'm staying, right?" Christopher said.

"Fine with me. Ian?"

"All right. It's our last night. We'll stick together."

Christopher gave a sigh of relief so emphatic he nearly puffed out a whistle.

"You sure you're up to it, young man?"

"I'm all in."

"You sure you can rein it in."

"I do, sir."

Agnes patted her pocket notepad that she had left at the table first thing when they got there. "Ian, don't forget to leave them here, her obituary and your notebook." She eyed the two men. "When we're done, everything connected to the séance should be left on this table. No souvenirs."

The two men nodded. Ian emptied his back pockets. Christopher checked his wallet. He set the automatic writing materials on the table and then reached down the floor for the candle lighters. He handed one to Agnes who promptly marched away to light up the east-side floor candles. Christopher covered the floor's west side.

Agnes turned back and pointed to the north-end staircase. "Where's the firewood bundle?"

The two men traded blank stares. Christopher shrugged. "I didn't put it away."

"Same here, unless I picked it up while sleepwalking," Ian said.

"Chris, can you hop down the living room. Give it one look around."

Christopher bolted off and scurried down the north staircase.

"When was the last time you saw that yule log?"

"I don't remember," Ian said.

She wandered about aimlessly around the north-end landing before she stopped on the very spot where she had originally set the séance furniture on. Ian followed close. She surveyed the ceiling above it. "Is it just me, or do you also feel this space is so much colder."

"Yeah, it's a meat locker right here," Ian said. He backed away and paced an imaginary circle beyond the cold zone. He felt goosebumps rising. He returned to where Agnes stood. "No drafts anywhere and yet it's really cold here."

"Somewhere in your interrogatories, ask him about what happened on this spot."

"You know he doesn't like this place. I don't like this place, either. Let's just leave this one out."

"Please, I insist. I have to know."

Christopher reappeared with the yule-log bundle. He dropped it in the same spot they had seen it last.

A deep thud; a familiar thud.

Christopher's eyes widened. He chafed his arms and joined them immediately. Ian turned to Agnes and he could swear the expression on her face was a copy of Christopher's. No one bothered to ask him where he found the yule log.

She double-stepped towards the dance floor center. The men followed. "Séance commences in a few." She stopped suddenly as she neared the séance zone.

Something new graced the table: a discolored, age-worn greeting card. No doubt, the memorabilia was procured and presented to them by Daniel. It seemed the paranormal drop-in elicited little reaction from any of them. Magic. It was starting to become disarmingly commonplace.

She gave it a good read before she handed the card to Ian. She seated.

Ian read the familiar handwriting alongside Christopher:

To my dear Ellie:
Next year, we'll be together, forever. Daniel.
November 7, 1995.

Ian left the card with Christopher. He snatched his pocket notebook from the table and riffled through its pages. The date in the card had more than tangential significance to the six numbers eerily etched, like burn marks, at the wood cladding near the main door's entryway. He picked a pen and placed slash marks in between the numbers in his notebook:

12/12/96

He poised for the reveal but Agnes, looking over his shoulder, beat him to it.

"I also noted that same number at the door. Twelve-

twelve-ninety-six. It wasn't a street number." Agnes backed into her seat. "It was right there, all this time."

"Twelve-twelve-ninety-six. Should be the year and day they were set to meet, here."

Christopher compared the date on the card with the numbers encircled in Ian's notebook. His eyes glowered. He made a hasty sign of the cross. "Holy shit. Today's December twelve."

Agnes said, "She would have turned eighteen, that day, that year."

23

Forestalled Blessings

"Daniel, how did you die?"

Her writing hand remained limp. At the séance's outset, he had asked him where and when he died. Then as now, no response.

Ian had shrunk the séance table's operational space to accommodate new references. This included the local newspaper Christopher had picked up during his party's stopover at Bakersfield. The first day in, he said he tossed the paper under his bed and forgot about it. That information might have been useful two nights ago.

They were more prepared this night than on any other. He vowed to no longer allow himself to be caught in a circular back and forth with a confused and capricious spirit that may not even be remotely aware his visitors would be gone from his realm by daylight.

First off, he opened his notepad into the candlelight for illumination. Then he displayed it in three random directions. At each instance, he pointed at the encircled and annotated date:

12/12/96

Right below it, he scribbled the numbers as it was written in front of the house. He displayed the notepad again into the light and in several directions:

121296

"Daniel, we know you wrote these numbers by the front door. For the one on top, I added the slash marks. You have to know this was the day you and Ellie promised each other that you would meet."

Agnes' slowly gyrating head rose from its slump. She wrote:

"Yes."

Heartened, Ian reiterated: "You and Ellie agreed to meet in this house on December twelve nineteen-ninety-six, correct?"

"Yes."

"Where in this house did you agree to meet?"

"Here... here."

"On the dance floor, right?"

"Here..."

"Were you here, in this house, on that day?"

"Yes."

"Did you and Ellie meet here on that day?"

"Ellie, my Ellie, here... there, right there."

"Did Ellie meet you here on that day?"

Murky scribbles on the pad.

"Did you and Ellie meet anywhere else after December twelve nineteen-ninety-six?"

The pen rolled off her fingers. Christopher quickly replaced them.

"You wrote twelve-twelve-ninety-six in front of this house." This time, he flashed to three different directions a contemporary calendar, with the present day, and the date circled in red.

He dropped the calendar on the table and with his other

hand he raised the folded newspaper, headline up front, in different directions. He pointed his forefinger at the publication date under the banner. "This is the newspaper from three days ago."

On the table, he lined up the calendar and the newspaper side by side. "The month is December, the day is the twelfth, but in the year twenty-twenty-six. The calendar date in the newspaper is exactly three days old. The newspaper date and the calendar serve as proof that this is our time, not yours. Your father, Caleb Pershing, told us you had passed away thirty years ago. Do you understand me, Daniel? Today is December twelve twenty-twenty-six. You and Ellie were gone from this world a long time ago." He pointed at Agnes. "You and that psychic medium whose name is Agnes Haskell, couldn't have met in your lifetime."

"Ellie, Ellie, my Ellie... there, there..."

"No, Daniel, no. The day you should have met Ellie was December twelve, nineteen-ninety-six, the day she had turned eighteen. Look..."

He unraveled Ellie's obituary and fronted it at the candle lights for a second. Then to three directions. "This is proof that Ellie passed away on October seven, twenty-twelve. Ellie can no longer meet you here because she's waiting for you on the other side. There's only one way you two can meet again —that is for you to cross over, to the afterlife."

"Waiting."

"You will wait forever for Ellie unless you depart from the world of the living."

"Ellie there... Ellie there."

Ian sought a break from the circular argument. "Everything in this house, the pictures, your memorabilia, Ellie's obituary, they were all a memorial to your soul by your family who loved you and who continues to love you. They want you to cross over and be in peace. The three of us here were all hired by your father, Caleb Pershing, to help you cross over. Your father is getting old. Someday he will stop sending people like us to communicate with you. Then you'd be stuck here, waiting, for nothing, forever."

Ian paused and glanced at his notes. He sought a less direct way of fulfilling Agnes' request as to why he refused to accommodate a séance on the medium's chosen spot. He had an inkling why. But it should come from him.

He noticed that although Agnes had started to perspire, her clothes remained undisturbed. "Daniel, can you please tell us, for the record, when you passed away?"

Agnes' pen hand remained down. He wasn't buying into redundancies anymore.

"Where did you die?"

No response.

"What is the day and the date that you died?"

The pen slipped off Agnes' fingers. Christopher replaced them immediately.

"What did you do when Ellie did not arrive on that day you were supposed to meet?"

Nothing. Everything on the table, even the candle flames, appeared so still as if they, too, were listening in to the conversation and anticipating a long-deferred outcome. Ian decided that it wouldn't hurt to bluff. "December twelve, nineteen-ninety-six. You died that day, did you not?"

Agnes grabbed the pen hard. Her hand trembled.

That close. He wouldn't let the opportunity slip away. "You died on that day. You know that as a fact. Your photo album collection ended in the year nineteen-ninety-six. You won't answer me even when you know that on this day, thirty years ago, you passed away, in this house."

He waited. Agnes' hand relaxed on the table, the pen cradled between her fingers. "Agnes is getting tired. Really tired. Maybe you feel likewise. We should probably call it a night, now." Agnes straightened. The pen flipped around her fingers and landed squarely in writing position. He went for it. As forcefully as he could: "Did you die on this very day—"

"*Yes.*"

Ian locked stares at Christopher. He wiped the sweat from his brows. "How did you die?"

The pen fell on the table. Christopher promptly replaced it.

From his diaphragm, he bellowed: "Where did you die in this house? Where?"

The table vibrated. Agnes scribbled nonsense on the sheet.

Ian pushed back against his chair and stood up. He braced for his last major question that night, confident the hidden cameras would capture the moment, a capstone to a job well done. He pointed to the spot on the floor where Agnes originally wanted to hold the séance. "Daniel, that was the place where you died, am I right?"

The table shook as if in a low-intensity temblor, followed by a rumbling disturbance from under the floor. Ian grabbed the table corners. It wasn't the time to lose heart, he told himself. "Daniel, the three of us took risks to help you cross to the other side. Please, tell us how we can help you cross over."

The steady vibrations continued. Agnes leaned back on her chair, with her right arm hooked to the chair's ladder back. Her head movements assured him she was still in a trance state.

"Daniel, for the last time, talk to us. I'm sorry if something I said offended you. This is the last night the three of us would be communing with you. If you do not cooperate with us, you would lose your chance to cross over. You have no reason to continue waiting for Ellie in this house because she is on the other side, the afterlife, where you two can be together, forever. Tell us how we can help you cross over, tell us."

Christopher pulled his seat closer to an exhausted-looking

Agnes who just slumped limply on her seat. Upon closer observation, Ian realized she had sweated profusely and that much of her gown's fabric clung to her skin. Add to that the constant tremors in the entire vicinity. He had the perfect pretext to end the session.

"This is it, Daniel. Agnes is beyond tired. She can't continue with the séance any longer. We have tried to help you cross over and it appeared like we have failed. You have to find a way yourself, to cross to the other side where the soul of Ellie is waiting for you. I'm bringing this séance to a close, a final close. I bid you goodbye and good night."

The tremors escalated. The windows started to rattle. Agnes sank deeper in her seat.

"Wake her up, now."

Christopher pounced on Agnes and shook her frantic.

Ian raced north for the light switch.

The creaks radiated to the walls, then to the ceiling. Ian had lived in Southern California much of his life and any hint of a temblor terrified him. The shaking—more like a vibrating murmur than a steady throbbing—went on.

The lights turned on, flickering.

No let up on the shaking. He wobbled his way back to the séance table. He saw Christopher pouring bottled water fluid into his cupped hand. He whisked it into Agnes' face and she immediately stirred. She got to her feet and tried to stand. Her body quivered, and her eyes reflected panic that one would expect from anyone wakened by ground shaking. Christopher helped her sit.

The smell of snuffed candle wicks reeked.

The shaking stopped.

The overhead lights started to behave. The candle wicks continued to emit wispy smoke.

In a blip, the place turned into a quiet, sheltered night.

Agnes, fully awake, reached for the automatic writing pad.

Ian pushed it aside. "Leave everything as is. Your words. We're talking about this downstairs."

Agnes grabbed the artist pad. "Where are your notes?"

"We're done here, my call."

"I say when we're done."

He pushed his notebook in her direction. "Review the notes. Every conceivable question I can throw at him I did. He's no longer cooperating. Maybe he's tired, too. Regardless, our job is done, period."

Agnes grabbed the artist pad and the other stationaries before she stormed off towards the south-end staircase. "Let's go talk about this in the kitchen."

She paused and canted her head to the left as if she heard something. She returned to the séance table, dropped the pads and stationaries on it, and took back her seat.

"We're done here," Ian slammed both his palms on the table.

By then, Agnes' attention was elsewhere. She tilted her head as if she was trying to trace the sound of a barely audible voice.

"You want to read the notes, read them downstairs. Let's all head down. Now."

"You two may go. I'd like to stay here awhile."

"You stay, we stay. We're not leaving you alone anywhere."

"I know you two did the best you could and it can go without saying our project has come to a close." She started to gather the séance paraphernalia towards the center of the table. "Can you two hang out with me here awhile?"

Ian lets out a sigh of resignation. He sat and folded his arms. Christopher took his old spot.

"It doesn't matter what our religious affiliations are," Agnes said in a solemn tone. "Some of us may not even have any. As people, we can confer blessings on others. Even to the long gone. Five minutes of silence, guys. That should be time enough for us to confer blessings to each other and to everyone else with us the last few days and nights."

Ian nodded agreeably. So did Christopher. It was a request any reasonable person can concede to. Agnes straightened, placed her hands on the table, and closed her eyes. He did likewise.

24

Nocturne in E-flat

Ian and Christopher were a step down the second-floor south-side staircase when they looked back and saw Agnes, whom they assumed was behind them, parting a west-side window curtain. She rolled down the shutters and peeped. Nothing to see outside that time of night. Ian didn't even bother to ask. Nothing he would say or do would hasten their extended leave-taking ceremony.

Minutes ago, all three of them, as per Agnes' request, had taken turns wishing Daniel well and waving goodbye every which way. If it was up to him, the whole-house temblor would have served as a parting shot to their supernatural weekend adventure. The calm and quiet that followed the shaker should have served as Daniel's sendoff to them. They should have been gone from that infernal floor, never to return to it. They were still there because she deliberately lingered. He couldn't read her because she almost always faced away from them, as if she was still trying to reach out. Ian couldn't wait for them to hit the ground floor where he would officially call it a night. After that declaration, he also intended to ask that no one speaks about Daniel, until daylight.

1:27 in the morning.

Relief came when Agnes headed straight for them, grinning. Her sad eyes still betrayed her feelings. She smacked her hands. "That's it, guys."

An abrupt crackle came from the CD player unit by the second, west-side window.

Agnes halted. A few more tinkling notes and Ian recognized a mellifluous, piano intro rendering of Chopin's Nocturne in E-flat Major, arguably the composer's most famous romantic masterpiece. The volume turned up.

A little later, a full orchestra joined the piano music. Agnes' face lit up. She spun around. He thought she actually whirled.

Ian woke up from the stupor ahead of everyone else. He stomped impatiently. "C'mon, people, we have to go."

"I know this music." Agnes pivoted clockwise, then the other way around. Her captivated eyes roamed the bright spaces around her. She motioned Christopher to come over and the young man joined her without as much as a conferring glance at him.

"Chris, dance with me."

"I don't know how."

"Neither do I."

Too late. Just like that. The mood set up was masterful and seductive. Daniel had sucked them all back to his realm.

Reluctantly, Ian motioned his two companions to step forward, his way. "To the dance floor, please." He pulled the unlikely couple together, the woman much taller than the man, to a dance partner position. He opted for the simplest slow dance configuration. He placed Agnes' left hand on Christopher's top right shoulder. He positioned her partner's opposite hand to the rise in her waist. Then he brought the dance partner's parallel arms to shoulder height where he joined their hands to a snug clasp. Agnes lets out a bashful snicker. Ian adjusted the couple's outstretched arms to a lower height. "Shoulder and waist hands, steady. The man leads. Now watch me."

He stepped away and took on a dance form with an imaginary partner. "Feel the music. Let its cadence tell you how to move." He stepped about in a slow swirl, picking up on the music's medium tempo as it headed to its final movement. "Hit it, guys, in a circle, like this."

A few seconds into awkward rocking and sashaying, the couple started to move in a circular fashion. He could relate the tell-tale shuffles and clops on the floor to the couples' tensed-up legs and flat feet.

"Sorry, Chris," Agnes said. "Your partner is already sweaty."

"I didn't even notice."

"Really?"

"I don't mind. Even if you sweat more."

"Chris," Ian said, as he reversed his direction of travel. "Just mind your steps. Agnes, keep it steady. The man can swirl in the opposite direction anytime."

Christopher, his eyes on Ian's footwork, accidentally stepped on Agnes' foot. They both faltered. Laughter followed as if to cap the music as it reached its end.

It restarted seamlessly, the piano tune picking up from the slow beginning.

Ian stopped to watch with amusement, the two ungainly dancer's performances. "You two are doing great, for first-timers, really."

The couple giggled, as they traded coy glances at each other.

"Keep your backs and your shoulders straight but relaxed, ease the tension in your legs, eyes steady on each other." Ian shadow danced again, his eyes on the amateurs. "Agnes, lean your head and shoulders further back, like this. "Turn your face to one side, like a snobbish high-lifer."

Agnes heeded, flung her hair to one side, and straightened before she leaned back. Christopher struggled with his footwork.

Ian felt woozy. He backed into a séance chair, sat, and crossed his legs. "C'mon, young people, give it some spice."

The music intensified even as it slowed down to herald the finale. The finale, subdued and sentimental, winded down.

The dancers stalled as the music ended.

Ian waited a few seconds before he jumped to his feet. He clapped his hands above his head. "Whooo! Bravo! Bravo!"

The couple joined him in boisterous applause. They linked hands and bowed once. They hugged. He waited.

The music did not restart.

He took the lead to the south-side exit.

The couple, hands together, backed away, as if waving to an unseen audience.

"Dance."

Ian felt a shudder in his chest. It was the first time he heard, what he only heard in horror films—a cold whisper through a tunnel; a disembodied voice. Agnes and Christopher, likewise stopped, their eyes alarmed. He couldn't place where the voice came from. "Everyone heard that?"

"Dance... with me."

He motioned the petrified couple to head for the staircase. They both held on to each other and looked around in great trepidation. Agnes braced against herself as if a window near her popped open and wintry air blew in.

"Please... dance with..."

"Daniel... Agnes and Christopher had already danced for you. What more do you want?"

Agnes gestured for Ian to stop as she tipped her head to the right as if attempting to trace the source of the hollow, cold-sounding voice.

"Dance... with me... please."

At that moment, Ian couldn't even tell where the goose-bumps were coming from. Agnes, holding on to Christopher stepped back. Ian pounced and motioned his companions frantic, for a full retreat.

"Don't go... don't go. Please, don't go."

25

Ghost Dance

A three-hundred-sixty-degree turnabout. They were back at it again, seated around a séance table, dependent on points of candle flames to make out anything in the dark. He didn't even try to mount a second appeal. He still felt drained from choreographing the dance and his nerves remained frayed from Daniel's unexpected haunting. He wasn't willing to restart an argument with the certifiably bullheaded woman. At least she agreed to send Christopher downstairs, earlier, to bring up a fresh change of clothes. Clearly, she intended to seize the moment and put their contractual obligations to a close, and on a high note at that. It was still night, after all.

As he watched Agnes slip into a trance, pangs of regret caught up to him. He should have convened a pre-séance rehearsal before they opened a door wide open to Daniel's caprice. The new arrangement practically reduced his role and that of Christopher's to mere spectators. Far too late to convince Agnes that they were treading new grounds in giving consent to have her body used for purposes other than as a communication medium.

He tucked bottled water between his thighs, ready to squirt its contents to her face should the situation call for it.

Agnes' head stopped gyrating and her head drooped. She lurched forward and her face came to light before her head flung back with sensuous grace uncharacteristic of the normally prim and unaffectionate woman. She dropped back to her seat, her shoulders stooped, arms limped, like someone who had passed out from exhaustion. She continued to lean back along with the chair, until the chair teetered on its two back legs. Christopher reached for her to avert a fall. He stopped mid-stroke when her seat lurched forward. Sitter and chair regained balance, an unseen force surely behind the feat.

A crackle from the CD player.

Its volume turned up. The same gentle piano intro played. Agnes lifted her face at the same time she straightened. Then both her arms raised to shoulder height as if her extremities were tied to strings and lifted by helium-filled balloons. She took on a hands-on-partner's-shoulders arm position. A familiar, toothless, ecstatic smile broke from her face. She canted her head to the left like she acknowledged the presence of a partner who had just swung around behind her and pressed himself against her back.

She rose from her seat. Christopher's eyes bugged out. From his angle, he must have observed the anomaly earlier than he did. Because she kept rising until her limp legs and feet cleared the top of her seat's back. She hovered to a complete stop. If Ian had a dollop of doubt on the integrity of the whole spectral affair, Agnes' levitation had totally dispelled it. No money in the world could create a technology that would bring about the spectacle that was unraveling before them.

Her loafers fell on the floor. Her body clung to the air as if she got trapped in a different universe where the laws of physics had broken down. He had seen space station footage where people were napping unrestrained. They float about, spin slowly from every axis, hair radiating about, appendages every which way. Yet Agnes remained suspended mid-air as if encased in a zero-gravity bubble unaffected by physical realities inside a man-made structure in space. Her smile reflected both serenity and sweetness as he could imagine a human face could possibly express.

At the top of the music's second movement, she spun from her axis once, an unseen partner apparently with her. Very slowly at first, she started to orbit the séance table zone. The edges of her fluttering skirt grazed his hair and that of Christopher's as she spun on her axis and orbited around the séance zone. She floated further outward as her orbital flight widened and her spin axis accelerated. Her legs and bare feet gracefully stepped about in the void, fluidly synced with the music, a ballerina on tiptoes, a fairy in white.

He might as well be dreaming. Agnes danced about in the void, basked in faint candlelight, in and out of shadowy zones and at times nearly disappearing in the hazy darkness induced by the weak candle lights at the dance floor flanks.

The candle flames on the table and around the dance floor grew in size, or so it seemed in his eyes, as the CD player volume increased. The music waned toward the finale at the same time her spin-and-orbit trajectory reversed and she turned counter-clockwise, still waltzing about with an invisible partner.

Christopher followed the spectacle in helpless awe, the expression in his eyes more mesmerized than terrified. His mouth and chin quivered.

Agnes drifted in complete ease, her eyes closed, her smile consistently sweet, her hair flinging as freely as her skirt.

The split second after the music ceased, her body fell limp, like someone who had passed out and was held up in the air by someone holding her by the armpits. A jumble of hair covered her face. She hung on one spot, as an inanimate object in orbital space would.

Music restarted and she reanimated in a heartbeat. She swiftly reacquired a dance position. Her head and shoulders leaned back this time, as her spin-and-orbit movement caught up with the changing cadences in the romantic music.

During Agnes' southward swing, Ian didn't bother to look back behind him since he expected her to re-emerge from across a flank. His stiffened neck prevented him from swiveling in his seat to follow her entire orbital movement. When Agnes failed to show up at a point where he expected her, he stood up and pivoted a one-hundred-eighty. When she reappeared, he realized that the lag was due to a more elongated, elliptical trajectory that she had taken. At the long end of the elliptic, she vanished for a second or so into the void. For a moment, he thought the disorienting effect of the place's unusual lighting were playing tricks on his eyes. A cursory perimeter ocular check revealed total darkness had fallen elsewhere outside the immediate vicinity. The air reeked again of snuffed out candle wicks.

All the perimeter candle lights had died.

Something about the new orbit was also amiss. He turned on his necklaced flashlight and raised his hands high. "Daniel, Agnes is very tired. Sit her back in her chair and let her rest."

Her coasting speed slowed. As she neared the narrower west side of the new orbital path, Ian thought Daniel had conceded. But her movements sped up as she swung at the farther side of the elliptic. She disappeared from sight. When she re-emerged into the light, she was hurtling from the other way, at a faster clip.

This time, Agnes zoomed up in a horizontal body position, as if the invisible force cradled her limp body, unseen arms under her knees and back. He motioned his partner to stand guard. The music continued. Daniel's interest had shifted.

He went for the CD player and turned it off.

Christopher, on his feet, flashlight on, blocked the east side of the dance floor, ready to intercept.

Ian mustered a commanding voice, as loud as he could:

"Daniel, I want you to put her back to her seat, right here, right now."

Again, Agnes, still unconscious and in reclined body position, floated past them the other way. Christopher advanced and waved both his hands in the air to block her turnaround. In front of him, the unconscious woman hovered a few seconds, before it scooted around him and headed back north.

The delay gave Ian time to grab bottled water and to place himself in intercept position on the west side. As Agnes came hurtling, he doused her body with water. Missed.

Following his lead, Christopher grabbed bottled water from under the séance table and gave chase. He crossed the dance floor laterally, to the east side, poised to intercept. As Agnes sped by, he squirted water straight into her face. A bullseye. She disappeared into the far end of the elliptic again. He couldn't tell if she had wakened. Ian had a hunch where the run around would end up.

"Chris, turn on the lights."

He saw the nimble young man race to the floor's north end before he disappeared in the darkness. From the emerging shadows on the wall to his left flank, Ian knew Agnes neared for another swing.

Overhead lights flickered.

The entire floor lit up.

Then a blackout.

The rest of the candles died at once. The place smelled of freshly-extinguished candle-wick smoke. At the same time, he heard the familiar disembodied voice:

"Room... room, where..."

He looked back at Christopher who seemed to have heard and comprehended the spirit's voice. He knew that it was just a matter of time before the apparently confused and conflicted spirit would find its way. "Chris, when she's farther up north, head down the south staircase. Lock all the ground floor rooms from the inside. Take the keys with you."

"I'm on it, sir."

When Agnes drifted north, Christopher took off at full tilt, towards the south.

Ian found Agnes to his left, still unconscious, in the same reclined position, hovering with her knees bent, her upper torso limp, unseen arms cradling her. He approached cautiously. "Daniel, you are a good man. You did not take advantage of Ellie in your time. You will not take advantage of Agnes Haskell, the unconscious woman in your arms. Please, put her down slowly. Let me wake her up."

He shone a light to Agnes whose body slowly lowered to the floor. She stirred and groaned.

A door banged from downstairs.

The lights flickered.

Then it was completely out again.

Someone scampered up the wooden staircase. Christopher.

Weak light beams, his and Christopher's, crisscrossed through wisps of smoke in the pitch black. Nothing but the void.

"Chris, where's Agnes?"

"I don't see her. I don't see her."

Ian surveyed the dance floor's length. "He must have taken her downstairs. I'm heading down this way. Take the south staircase, go." Ian scurried down the wooden staircase. Christopher run the other way, his stilted voice hollering for Agnes.

Down in the living room, Ian slowed down to recover his bearings. His flashlight arcing in every direction, his footings unsure, he hobbled his way toward the hallway. Whenever a flashlight beam crossed in front of his face, he gleaned vapor coming out of his mouth. It must be that cold down there. Yet he didn't feel it.

Making his way to the hallway, Ian heard Christopher, as

if rummaging somewhere in the kitchen area's far end. Then followed the sound of water rushing out of a faucet.

A heavy thud, like someone ramming a door with his shoulders.

Across the narrow hallway, his light beam found its mark. Agnes levitated body hovered by the master bedroom door. Thumps on the door continued at quick intervals.

"Daniel, put her down, right now."

Christopher, flashlight necklaced, light beams bobbing about in every direction, rounded the kitchen-dining corner.

A low whoosh and a stream of water sloshed into Agnes.

A plastic pail clattered on the floor.

"Agnes, you have to wake up," Christopher said, rocking hard her reclined, still floating body. Not a sign she even stirred on her own.

The door banged even more violently.

By the time Ian had reached Agnes, Christopher was gone.

He nearly slipped from a puddle. He slapped one side of Agnes' face. No response. She was completely out. The door kept banging. He knew it was just a matter of time before the door would give. "Daniel, put her down, now!"

The door banged another time. He expected another one when Agnes' body slowly lowered to the floor.

He heard a whimper, as that of someone in pain, coming from the kitchen. Was it Daniel or Christopher?

The lights, from one end of the room to the other, returned.

The bright hallway down-lighters revealed the watery mess on the floor.

Dazed and disoriented, Agnes went on all fours and struggled to stand. She dropped to the floor and backed into the bedroom door. Water from her clothes dripped into a large puddle where she sat. She started shivering. "What happened? Why am I here?"

AGNES, surgical gloves on both hands, held Christopher's left hand over a towel laid atop the dining table. She applied burn gel carefully on several areas in the three middle digits of his left hand, in and around ugly blisters and burned skin. Ian couldn't tell where the first-degree burns melded with the second-degree ones. He must have held his hand on the stove flames for a good while.

Ian looked back on their first-night fright-fest in the master bedroom. The rippling action in Agnes' clothes then pointed to the likelihood Daniel could manifest his telekinetic powers independent of Christopher's consciousness. The young man was asleep then. Although he couldn't be one hundred percent sure on that. From then on, the progression of events related to poltergeist activities in the place eventually convinced him that compulsions shared by Christopher and Daniel, despite the gulf between their realms, must be shuttling in and out of each's psychic fields, a phenomenon that must be akin to electricity in a transference loop, or of psychics tapping into the cosmic ether to harvest useable links. If legal and scientific standards were the same, Ian would embrace his theory on the principles of the preponderance of evidence alone. He couldn't think of an alternative explanation. Then a curveball from nowhere struck.

The abduction attempt had not only raised the threat to Agnes' safety to another level. It also presented a new set of contradictions. It was unlikely Christopher had engaged in kidnapping fantasies during Agnes' ghost dance. At will, Daniel also found a way to deepen Agnes' trance state to the point attempts to wake her up had failed.

Christopher's presence of mind also pumped fresh air into their post-project alliance. No doubt the poor man's crude attempt to short-circuit elements of his sexual fantasies lodged deep in his subconscious by inflicting intense pain on himself had worked. Ian wondered how he figured out that such drastic action would derail Daniel's spell over her. The timing was indisputable. That one audacious act had wakened her.

The worst should be over. He'd make sure of that. He vowed to take full command of the team and declare their job done. They couldn't gamble on Agnes' safety anymore.

"Next time, stick your hand into the freezer or something," Agnes said. "This is so brutal."

"I had to do something fast." Christopher grimaced as Agnes stuffed cotton balls in between the afflicted fingers, to keep them apart. Ian once again ran a hot-set electric blow drier in and around her still moist hair. Earlier, she toweled down and suited up fast so she could promptly attend to Christopher's burns.

"Let the gel work for a while. I'll gauze up your fingers later." Agnes gently lowered his hand, back first, into the towel. "Thank you, anyway. Your quick thinking saved me from... whatever."

Ian coiled up the hair drier, left his companions, and started pacing about the far west end of the kitchen floor, ruminating on strategy. Taking over the reins while they were still in the psychic medium's domain required a plan. Daniel was pretty much still around, too. A fresh gown from nowhere laid on top of the dining table by the time they had regrouped there. He could still pull a surprise. Even with another séance completely out of the question, he knew he needed to wrest control over how they should spend the last few hours before daylight.

A good three hours remained.

"He stopped at about the same time you burned yourself," Agnes said. "Putting together your account and that of Ian's, you couldn't possibly be having fantasies about me while you two were running around, trying to help me. Why did you think you needed to hurt yourself?"

"Nothing worked. He's still at it. It just popped into my head, that it might help."

"Whatever impure thoughts about you that Chris had once taken liberties at," Ian said, "there should still be remnants of them in his subconscious."

"I should have known better," Agnes said. "There are mechanisms of the mind that can't be shut off completely. Not your fault, Chris."

"Our brain records everything we heard, saw, or experienced since early childhood. We can't recall them but the records are all there. Just as in a disabled computer hard drive. A skilled hypnotist can make your mind retrieve them while you're under the influence of hypnosis. The more unscrupulous ones can even add false memories and make you recall them as if they had happened. The human mind, especially the subconscious aspects of it, is much more fragile, and more vulnerable than we imagine. Think about it. If hypnotists can directly manipulate the subconscious to suit their interest, it is plausible that the departed can tap into some cosmic ether that crisscrosses the realm of both the living and the dead and use a connecting portal to get into the deepest recesses of our mind and manipulate it to impose their will on us. I think Chris did the right thing. Agonizing pain might have interrupted his brain's neural networks, cutting off any connection, tenuous as they might be, between the two engaged telekinetic agents."

Christopher said, "What should I do to keep Daniel from taking Agnes again?"

"Nobody needs to do anything on that matter from here on," Agnes said. "I'm no longer in a trance state and I have no more plans on getting onboard again."

The words Ian has been pining to hear from her. "Nice to hear that, finally."

"Thank you again, Chris."

"What you did," Ian said, "something I wouldn't even consider."

Agnes laughed as she rubbed the top of Christopher's undamaged hand. "You could have just slapped your face hard."

"I did that, twice. Didn't work."

"You're incorrigible. If I didn't know you, I'd be creeped out. Now I'm really curious what those fantasies look like, if only I can see them."

"I hope you never do."

He reminded himself constantly not to glance at the ceiling trims where he knew cameras had recorded the end of their journey. Regardless of what they had actually accomplished, Ian celebrated in his heart his conviction that they had prevailed. He believed the upbeat conversation they were having only validated beyond doubt the fact their job is done. No more arguments with the self-willed Agnes. He need not play father protector to an uncouth, immature man anymore. As for the resident ghost, may he eventually rest in peace. The sense of relief he felt could never have been better. As he watched his two companions engage in small talk and observe Agnes attend to Christopher's burns with motherly care, he also felt certain his two associates would part on good terms.

As he continued to pace around the kitchen-dining zone, Ian allowed his mind to wander where it may find comfort. He found himself ruminating again on Christopher's avowed infatuation with their snotty, condescending associate. Maybe because he had been a hormone-driven young man himself once, the sexual energy dynamics that factored into the entire affair continued to astound him. He considered another angle to the extraordinary series of psychic phenomena that had overshadowed their entire project. Human biology, not solely the young man's concupiscence, might be an accessory culprit.

Agnes might be ovulating.

Women in mid-cycle emit pheromones that ramp up

testosterone in men throughout the subject's vicinity, making them more aggressive. He himself had witnessed how men brazenly hit on women in bars, dance places, and other closed public spaces where the odds are high that one or more nubile women are ovulating. A two-way street in the human species' evolutionary drive to reproduce and pass on their genes. Daniel could have exploited the incidental alignment of two sexually vulnerable young people during their hormonal peaks.

Her biological timing, he conceded, was likely accidental. No way Dr. Pershing's people could have anticipated their hireling's biological cycles and incorporated it into a master plan. Certain aspects of the project had to be unique and unforeseen.

"When was the last time," Agnes said, her eyes still on Christopher, "the last time you were thinking about me that way?"

"That was very early in your ghost dance. You were swirling around us, your skirt flying about. I didn't look under or anything like that. I may have seen stuff. I don't know."

Agnes nearly bawled. She slapped him on his right shoulder. "Really? You saw stuff, with just the candle lights on?"

"It may just be my imagination."

Ian grabbed a seat. Time was on their side. For so long as Agnes doesn't consent to fall into a trance, the two people's occasional forays into carnal talk should now be moot. They could flirt all they want for all he cared.

Everyone deserved a furlough. He would devote no more brain cells to the unwritten protocols about their project's last hours. He'd let the clock run out on its own sweet time. He smacked his hand, "All right. We're all tired and we could use some quality shut-eye before pick-up time. Three-thirty on the clock. We retire in the living room. To be sure we don't get blindsided, each of us would take turns, on the night watch, one hour each, or up until daylight's in. Chris, you take the first watch. Agnes, you take the second. The old man would do the last."

His companions displayed him a thumbs up.

"I'd set the alarm clock to seven-thirty. That would give us a two-and-a-half-hour lead time before pick-up. No one wanders around without waking someone. If someone observes something unusual or disturbing during his watch, please wake the others up. Did I make myself clear?"

His two companions nodded.

"People, do not over-think the situation. Past is past. I bet we did more work than any psychic under Pershing's employ had ever done. Agnes, most especially. Let's ease our minds into that—the mindset that we did more than what was required of us." Ian eyed Agnes and emphatically pointed to the living room. Then to Christopher. "Nightwatchman, wake up Agnes in an hour."

26

The Wee Hours

Ian wakened to someone shaking him. In the quiet and the dim light, it took a while before he realized it was Christopher, on his knees, behind him. He whispered close to his right ear, "Sir, look." He pointed towards the hallway, at Agnes, slouched on the floor, her back against the wall. It was a familiar spot, marked by the bathroom door directly across. She looked small, swaddled with a blanket, and her head scrunched to her upright knees. Ian kept seated, as he waited for his spirit to catch up. His right eye felt heavier than his left such that when he lined up his wristwatch dial to the downlighter, he still couldn't read the time. Christopher helped him get up. He reached for his eyeglass case and grabbed a blanket.

He whispered to Christopher, "Go get yourself a blanket. Let's join her."

"I got this, sir. You can go back to sleep."

"Nice try, kid."

Ian shrouded himself with a thick one, collar to ankles. He shuffled to the hallway and sat beside Agnes. Like the night before, Christopher bookended her from her left side. Ian felt he had no energy reserves in him left to persuade the straggler to return to base. Soft whistle caused by winds drifting about outside all came from the hallway window vents. It felt beastly cold, but not in the abrupt spectral presence sense.

4:15 a.m.

He slept just a little over an hour. He leaned on her and tried to resume his sleep. He felt pushback from her side. Of course, Christopher snuggled against her. Discomfort in his tortured neck and back swiftly caught on. He would have laid down on the floor if it wasn't that icy cold.

Agnes raised her head. Her weary eyes wandered her flanks before she dipped into her knees again. "Sorry, guys. I can't sleep."

Ian couldn't even muster a lazy response. Besides, it just wafted through his mind, the dreams that had visited him during a deep-sleep phase in his slumber. He needed to review and re-archive in his mind his most vivid dreamwork, along with all the others he must dredge up to some point of organization and clarity, so he can make sense of them. Ian rubbed his cheeks as he felt woozy again. He struggled to keep awake. He nudged at Agnes. "You sure you don't want to go back to bed?"

"The wee hours," Agnes said, desultorily, while she shook her head.

"The wee hours," Christopher said. "What hours are those, exactly?"

"The small hours of the morning, like now," Ian said, "when most people are asleep and the world is darkest and most quiet."

"Does it make you sad?" Christopher asked Agnes. "You looked very sad when you said wee hours."

"When I was a child, I once woke up at about this time, in my own room. I was scared. Maybe I just wanted to hang out. I went to my foster parent's room and the door was locked. I didn't knock because I didn't want to bother them in their sleep. I sat across their doorstep, just like this, hoping someone would wake up to use the restroom in the hallway and see me there, maybe invite me in. It didn't happen. The thought just came. The answer is no, Chris. I don't feel sad right now. Because you guys are here, hanging out with me."

"Next time, wake us up," Ian said.

"There's not much time left before dawn. I thought it wasn't worth the bother."

Christopher leaned forward, as if trying to get her attention, his widening eyes gleaming with delight. "I'll give you my number. Someday, if you wake up in the wee hours and needed to talk with someone, you can call me."

Agnes gushed.

"I'm serious. I keep promises."

Agnes elbowed him and laughed. From his camp, Ian felt Christopher's affectionate hard lean on her.

"I'm so glad I woke mister Bishop up," Christopher said. "Or I would never know what it felt like."

"Felt like what?"

"To sit beside Agnes, in the wee hours."

"Oh my god, Chris. This is not a good time to get anything started. You want me to tear those bandages off your fingers?"

"That's it," Ian said as he wriggled out of his cocoon. That close to daylight, he would not take any chances. He turned aside to stand. "Discipline is starting to break down. Back to our old campsite. I'll be in between you two."

Christopher groaned. Ian barely got to his feet when Christopher gave Agnes another hard lean and she nearly tipped over to her side. The two laughed.

They followed Ian and marched back to the living room. Ian and Christopher replaced the comforters to their former makeshift-bed configuration.

As she poised to join them in bed, Ian noticed that Agnes' upbeat demeanor abruptly dropped. She turned her face away from the down-lighters and half her face disappeared in the shadows. She relieved herself of her blanket, put on her slippers, and without as much as a shoulder covering walked back to the hallway.

Ian thought she had urgent business in the bathroom. Yet she walked past it and wandered about the narrow space, her eyes all over, like someone wanting to savor the last vestiges of a cherished event that was about to close.

Ian struggled to get out of his comfy cocoon. He went on all fours. Christopher helped him up. On his feet, he held back the young man, poised to follow Agnes. He thought it was only fitting to accord Agnes the last word, the last blessing, whatever it was she sought to achieve as she wandered the hallway. This was her show all along. He'd let her be.

"This is it, Daniel," she spoke. "We did our best. It would be dawn soon. Take care now."

Familiar shuffling steps hurried towards the master bedroom.

An echoey, disembodied whimper of a man, followed.

Ian and Christopher double-stepped into the hallway.

A globe-eyed, open-mouthed Agnes turned to them. "Guys, did you hear that?"

Ian decided to pretend he did not. He tugged at her sleeve and stage whispered, "Agnes, c'mon, this project had already wrapped up."

Another whimper. This time it emanated from inside one of the rooms. The whimper sounded weaker but more plaintive, almost like a suppressed lamentation.

"It's coming from the master bedroom," Christopher said.

"Listen to me, both of you."

"Shsssh," Agnes warned. "There it goes again."

Droplets of water trickled down Ian's right arm. He caught some of it. Warm water. From Agnes and Christopher's reaction, water had dribbled through them, too. Droplets scattered on the floor. He gazed at the ceiling.

Agnes turned to the two men, her eyes coruscating like she

just solved a long-sought solution to a puzzle. She showed them a cupped hand, holding some of the fluid. "Warm. They're tears."

"Or condensation. Maybe there's a leak upstairs."

"There's no plumbing upstairs, sir."

Ian glanced at his wristwatch. Five a.m. He shook his head. It hit him, a strong presentiment that she sought to regain the initiative, one last time.

"I know how to end this."

"You've got to be kidding me."

"I have already decided. It's still night."

"I know the night is your domain. I've given you a lot of passes on that accord. Not this time." He pointed repeatedly at their campsite. "Everyone, back to bed."

She stood her ground and smiled, faintly. "Trust me, guys. I know how to end this."

"You know shit. Nobody does. Not him, not any of us. It's nearly daylight. Our job is done."

Agnes shook her head. The wan smile on her face didn't match the in-the-driver's-seat look in her eyes. "Chris, get the keys. Open the master bedroom."

27

The Promise

Everything in the master bedroom appeared in hotel room condition, exactly as the first time she had walked in there. Early morning cold had crept in, even after Ian had Christopher reset the thermostat to fifty-eight degrees on all floors. Nothing unusual occurred in the surroundings since she had started pacing the floor, a blanket piece shawled over her shoulders. All she heard were the occasional creaking from the kitchen floorboards, made by someone a wall across, who carefully shifted his weight as he eavesdropped. Christopher, most likely.

Agnes knew Daniel was there with her in the room. Three days on the job and she could sense his presence. Though his energy signature seemed to be weaker now than the last time, he was still there for sure.

All those years summoning spirits and allowing them to temporarily possess her, she knew when the spirit's energy fields no longer lingered. She expected the sense of dread to escalate as the end game neared. Yet to her surprise, even as Daniel continued to make his presence felt, her confidence grew. Indeed, she felt a big surge in her sense of control over the whole affair. Her hands and feet were clammy but they weren't shaky. She had no problems locking the door, even as she understood no one could help her if Daniel had found a way to induce in her a trance state. No camera would even record the events in there.

She wasn't afraid. Not at all.

Time, above all, was on her side. One more hour, more likely less, and her world and that of Daniel's would be completely separated. Could the spirit even have a notion of how the financial windfall from the project would change her life? Would he recall a single memory from the entire affair or would he be totally unaware of what happened that weekend when another trance medium, in a future time, makes another attempt to conjure his spirit? For all she knew, their whole effort, like the others before them, had failed to nudge him one bit to the direction of the afterlife. She had to try one last time.

She continued to pace the floor, arms folded tight, her eyes roaming. "Daniel, if you are here, please show me a sign."

The drinking glass by the nightstand tinkled.

She smiled. "Daniel, I know that you would never force yourself on me if I don't give you my consent. If that is true, let me hear a tap on the floor, once. If you believe you cannot control yourself, then tap twice."

A light tap on the floor ahead of her.

"I was once attacked by bad people and I couldn't defend myself. I was too young. Alone. The hurt never healed. Here, now, I won't be able to defend myself against you if you choose to force yourself on me. But I don't expect bad things would happen to me or I wouldn't be here, alone, talking to you. Still, I ask you. Please, treat me like you had treated Ellie when she wasn't ready yet."

She sat beside the bed and placed her hands on her knees. She allowed the blanket to slip off her shoulders. It turned cold quickly. For a moment she got distracted by the luxurious feel of the satin on the quilted bedcovers and the cozy feel of the room, a far cry from the lumpy floor bed she and her companions had used the past two nights. She wished she could slip under the covers that very moment. "I would let you touch me, if that is what you want, this one last time, but only if you promise me that you'd find a way to cross the other side. If you understand my condition, tap once. Tap twice if you didn't."

A tap on the floor, close to where her right foot was.

Cold air swept in and chills corkscrewed around her body. She braced for it. Hair from the back of her neck rose. She was too far in to take a step back. "I ask again. Would you cross to the other side—find a way to get there, where Ellie is, if I consent to you touching me? Do not make a promise you can't keep. Daniel, do we understand each other?"

Another tap, to the left of her feet.

"From here on, I will no longer accept taps for an answer. Use your gift to give me a clear answer. A tap won't do. I want a very clear confirmation of your promise. I must remind you that you need to promise me, first. You can touch Agnes only if you promise that before dawn comes, you would find a way to cross to the other side."

The door unlocked. The latches popped. The hinges creaked as the door opened halfway. Warmer air streamed in. She heard shuffling on the floor heading out towards the living room. The door quietly closed.

28

Dark Dreams

Ian knew from the creaking sound of un-oiled hinges and from the fleeting shadow in the hallway, that the master bedroom door had opened. Agnes wouldn't open a door that steadily, slowly. It closed. A precise click.

Christopher, who has been pacing like a cooped-up dog thereabout the kitchen wall, halted in his tracks. He glared at him.

"Yes, that's him." Ian, at the dining table, took a larger bite of the pineapple strudels. "Quit pacing around. She knows what she's doing. Let them run out the shot clock."

Christopher went to the kitchen island where the first aid kit was. "I'm changing the bandage."

"Let her do that for you. The gauze had already bonded with your skin. It's going to hurt."

"That's the idea, sir."

"You did it once. Don't do it again without my permission or hers." Ian sipped his espresso.

Christopher backed into a chair. He chafed his palms on his lap. "I'm worried, sir. I'm really worried."

"Worry no more. You'd just be sending negative energy

into the cosmos. Bad energy that might interfere with what-ever Agnes is trying to accomplish." Thoughts about the young man's persistent fantasies drifted in. "On second thought, I'd rather that you worry as much as you want." He glanced at the east-side kitchen window. "The sun would be up, soon, anyway."

Fifteen past five. In time, it would be a new day. They would have ample time to shower, to luggage up, and maybe even have a hot breakfast where they could also share a light chat. While killing time, they'd also take turns congratulating each other for a job well done. He could hardly wait to clean out his rack and stuff everything and the hangers in the luggage bag.

He understood he was just distracting himself from the old doldrums that has been gnawing inside him as the night drew to a close.

Ian resumed his meal, eyes intermittently at the wall clock. In the lull, as the whole house heater hummed after a long break, he found himself in a rut again, his thoughts slipping inexorably into the past. He wondered if spirits do experience it, too—that two-sided tradeoff for the benefit of having human consciousness. He wondered what it was like to wake up one morning to a clean slate, like a pre-homo sapiens being that lacked self-awareness and totally incapable of remem-bering the past. He'd be immune from recollecting what might have been. The self-flagellating issue of forgiving and forget-ting would bedevil him no more. He'd be like a faithful dog bereft of faculties that would enable it to understand that his deceased master would never come back. The dog would go about his day, waiting for his master's return at an appointed time. The dog's anticipation doesn't lead to despair—just to another day of anticipation. The next day, the whole cycle goes again. Dinosaurs came to mind, too. They ruled the Earth for hundreds of millions of years and yet not one of them had lived a second of time. They only existed. Nothing in the universe mattered until human consciousness came to be. The dark price for the evolutionary gift of consciousness, of course, was suffering. Even a lifetime of it for an unfortunate turn of events. He decided it should be time to make a pact with himself, to force himself to accept he was simply too old to continue hoping time would heal it. He must find a way to let it go.

Christopher fretted uneasily about his chair. "I really hope she knows what she's doing. She's not above making stupid mistakes."

"On the contrary, I believe she's much wiser now than when we first started."

"I can't wait for her to come out."

"Oh, she will."

The notion of the light streaming through the kitchen windows brought in an unexpected upward mood swing. Until unbidden thoughts about Trent intruded again. This time, he tried to see it, from another perspective, from the vantage point of the new day he and his companions would face in a matter of minutes. They would part ways but in the future meet again, even regularly, as lifelong friends. A second later, it went again, the pull of the downward spiral.

As a practicing psychologist, he had lectured people on the world of difference between forgiving and letting go, on the complexity of the former and the simplicity of the latter, and the need for understanding the netherworld between the two. Someday, he told himself, he had to own up to his old stock-in-trade advice to strangers. He imagined Agnes, at a future time, conjuring his son in a séance so that he could go ask him if he had at least hinted, at a subtle plea for forgiveness from him buried in the subtext of small talk during their fishing trip in Colorado. Perhaps he'd find another way to make a pact with himself to bring the ceaseless cycle of suffering to a final close.

Not a creak or a scraping sound from the master bedroom.

He resolved to devote the last quiet moments before daylight to dwell on concerns about his remaining obligation to Dr. Pershing. When they go their separate ways, his companions may never know about the most important retro-cognitive dream clairvoyant assignment he had been commissioned in his lifetime. As it is, all he had to show for it were visions filched from someone who had an entirely different gift. He had no plans to admit to his sponsor that save for the last one, his dim-lit dreamwork were mere clones of Agnes' clear-as-day visions on Daniel and Ellie's romps in the house. While Dr. Pershing was mum on his motives for his dreamwork assignment, Ian believed the old man needed reassurance his son's wonderful memories in the old house far outweighed the bleak ones that followed after Ellie's departure.

In his recent, hour-long or so foray into a deep sleep cycle, dream segments had surprisingly cascaded in a sensible order. Ironically, a considerable part of the dreamwork was of the sort that he knew Dr. Pershing would rather never know. Just how could he tell his sponsor that he himself was a key part of the dark, dream chain that had coalesced into a story, about what led to the tragic event in the house, a tragedy that Dr. Pershing surely knew. It was clear to him now why Dr. Pershing had prohibited him from sleeping over on any floor in the house but the first.

He saw the teen-aged Ellie, looking out from the rear window of a car packed with belongings. The car navigated a winding road that leads out of the estate. Her face streamed with tears and an older woman, probably her mom, consoled her. Dovetailed to the same scene was a younger Dr. Pershing, on a baronial mansion balcony, his despondent eyes watching the car disappear beyond the gates.

In another dream fragment, inside the relocated house, he saw a distraught Daniel, in formal ballroom attire, wandering the emptied-out attic. He also saw him in the master bedroom, roaming about restless, a transparent plastic garment bag with a white gown in it, clutched in his arm. He unzipped the bag, pulled out a white gown from it, and laid it out neatly on a bed.

That scene jumped into the living room fireplace where he picked up a yule log bunch and carried it up the wooden staircase. The log bunch dropped upright at the second-level landing. A heavy thud. Daniel peeped out from the first west-side window, into the setting sun.

A rope swung up and looped around one of the exposed wooden joists in the ceiling. The log bunch dropped the second time on the floor, perhaps at the part of the dance floor that Agnes had originally chosen as their séance spot. Daniel, silhouetted in the dream's dimming light, stepped into the upright log bundle.

In another dream scene jump, Ian recalled two consequent images: the first one, a man's leg, presumably Daniel's, as it kicked the upright wood bundle under his feet. The wood toppled. The last image showed two legs, in ballroom pants and in formal shoes, hanging limp.

"I smell candle smoke," Christopher said as he started for the hallway.

Ian grabbed him and pulled him back to his seat.

A minute ago, he caught a glimpse of a floating lit-up candle coming from the hallway and veering quickly into Agnes' room. The door was slightly ajar and its opening and closing escaped Christopher's attention. Daniel. For sure, he wanted no interference from Agnes' companions.

"Let them be," Ian told Christopher. "It would be dawn soon, anyway."

Ian flipped open the sash window shutters near the back-exit door. "Look."

Christopher peeped. "The skies, they're a bit lighter. Is it still the wee hours?"

"Maybe. Maybe not."

"When the sun goes up, what happens to…"

"It's no longer our concern." Ian led the way back to the kitchen proper. "Try the strudels. Come, I'll also make you a proper cup of coffee."

29

Warm Kisses

It took over a minute for the soot from the candle flames hovering a handspan from the ceiling to draw three squiggly letters:

P...R... O...

Agnes checked the time. "Daniel, that's enough. I get it."

The flames die. The candlestick fell on the floor.

"Daniel, I'd let you touch me, now. Then you cross to the other side, as you promised. Make it come true, for you and for Ellie." Agnes slipped into the covers and reclined. This time her heart throbbed so violently she could hear it. She closed her eyes and willed herself to relax.

Seconds pass.

The satin quilted blanket slipped away from her in one smooth, gentle yank.

The early morning cold again pervaded. She had changed into the gown from the plastic garment bag and regretted the switch too late. The gown didn't fit her well, unlike the others. The neckline pulled up uncomfortably and the hem fell short, like it was tailored for a small person. The thin, cotton fabric also offered little protection from the cold.

She felt her lips squish—one long, gentle, sweet-tasting

kiss. She once heard that first kisses taste sweet. Maybe it was just her imagination. She didn't recall Christopher kissing her in the mouth. Maybe he did but the sensation of it got scrambled in the many things he was trying to do amid a flurry of pushbacks from her. She knew then and there Christopher's influence had gone. Her clothes behaved. No unseen hands went loose in a fondling frenzy. It was Daniel, on her, she was sure. The moment she gasped, he departed from her lips.

Another warm kiss came, this time it pressed to her left breast, right where her heart was. It stayed in the same place as Agnes counted the seconds. She stiffened. She recalled bombarding Christopher with conflicted consent affirmations that when he cut himself loose, she had found herself in a situation where she could no longer backtrack nor bargain. She didn't regret it but she realized by now that the two men couldn't be any more different.

She couldn't interpret the awkward pressure in her chest whether it caused a tingling or a tickling sensation. She started to get fidgety. The pressure eased.

The pattern in the kisses made Agnes anticipate where the next event would take place. Nothing happened as she continued counting seconds. She opened her eyes. Nothing in the room had changed. She searched for any clue he had gone. She realized he was still there when he felt her legs slowly parting. She sensed an onset of warmth probing between her thighs, awkwardly, hesitantly, until the warmth settled on her crotch. Her heart raced again. She closed her eyes and commanded herself to relax. *You can be touched now.* She reminder herself that, knowing full well that despite the fact Christopher delivered more than what she had bargained for, she didn't regret a moment of it. Despite his rough awkwardness, he made her feel what it was like to be made love to for the first time. The men who once abused her no longer held sway.

She could do nothing more than count the seconds. He

stayed there awhile, longer than in the previous ones, providing her a tiny oasis of warmth as the cold swept through her bare thighs and legs. She started to shiver.

The coldness became overwhelming. The warmth in her crotched eased. She had no way to know if he had departed or not. Instinctively, she rose, pivoted to her feet and she reached for the blanket on the floor. She nearly yelped when she felt a burning sensation on both her thighs, right about the level of her clothes' hemline. Static? She rubbed the hemline region above her knees. Nothing unusual turned up.

The bedroom door opened. The candle on the floor was gone. The door remained open, wide open.

Agnes swaddled herself with the blanket, picked up her slippers, and stepped out.

30

Let it Go

"I thought you knew when sunrise would be," Agnes told Ian, while she snipped off surgical tape ends from Christopher's third-digit finger bandage. She had two ends of a blanket tied over her neck, and the floor-length fabric draped like a cape on her back. He understood why the young man struggled to keep his attention elsewhere. Cape notwithstanding, she wore a nightgown much shorter and tighter than the ones she had on before. Even from his distance, he could make out the outline of her underwear. He thought stirring up modesty issues should be the last item in his to-discuss list as the much-anticipated dawn neared.

Ian peeped through the kitchen window shutters. He replied, after a lag, "Unless you want to get the souvenir calendar upstairs, your guess is as good as mine. The fog is drifting away. Relax. The skies are getting much lighter now."

Six a.m.

He could hardly wait for sunlight to shine through the shutters, either. He struggled to keep his eyes open. The makeshift bed in the living room had never looked that inviting. Two hours of shut-eye would do it. More opportunities for a productive dreamwork.

He assumed Dr. Pershing and company would arrive on the dot. In the back of his mind, he would keep an extra half hour or so, in reserve. He could skip the shower and a sumptuous breakfast. Not the wardrobe loot. Since day one, it wafted in and out of his mind—the pristine big brand name clothes on designer hangers. If he could only swap loot with Agnes. What a pleasant surprise would it be for his wife.

He rejoined the others at the dinner table.

Agnes finished up on Christopher's burn dressings. "Hope they'd give you something extra for that." She pointed at the bandaged spot on his head. "And for that."

"Yeah, a grand would be nice. Just kidding."

"Anyway, thanks again for the—"

A solid click. It had to be the kitchen exit door deadbolt.

An acrid scent blew in from the hallway. "That's not candle smoke," Ian said.

He took off and surveyed the hallway. The lights flickered. The smoke detectors would have wailed if there was a fire.

He rushed into the living room, Christopher and Agnes right behind him. He stopped and spread his arms apart. His companions behind him halted. A thick cloud of white smoke formed a plume that descended the wooden stairwell.

"Oh my god," Agnes cried. "Fire."

Ian motioned for the kitchen door. "Go, run, run."

Agnes took the lead, taking off with a dead man's sprint that the agile Christopher trailed way behind her.

From his position at the rear of the panic-stricken party, Ian saw the exit door swing inward, like someone opened the way for them. He didn't bother to look back.

His companions cleared the exit, with him close behind. "Go left, to the trucks."

As soon as the three of them had hit the dirt, the smoke alarms from inside the house blared in concert. Christopher held the lead this time, beelining film truck row. He slowed down and turned to check on them. Ian, panting, proceeded in jog-trot pace, careful with his footings. He paused to look back at the house.

Openings at the ground floor's windows and the back door billowed smoke. Tongues of flame licked out of windows on the second floor.

Ian's companions sheltered under a film truck. Their terrified eyes shot at him when he ran past them. He urged them to move into the white Chevy work van, parked in between the trucks, its nose aligned to the east-side gate. "Over here. I know what I'm doing."

The van doors were unlocked, as one of Pershing's people, when Ian arrived at the site three days ago, had assured him it would be. Interior lights lit up. He jumped in the driver's seat. He found the key under the sun visor.

In the side mirror, he saw his companions, closing in. "Who remembers the gate lock code?"

Agnes raised her hand. "Both of you, open the gate and wait there. The propane tanks could blow up anytime." Agnes and Christopher raced for the gate.

The starter cranked. The engine sputtered. Cold weather ignition. "C'mon."

The engine rumbled. He turned on the headlights to bright and geared into drive. His companions held the door open. The van tires dug into the gravel. He drove half the van's length into the gate before he slammed the brakes. He waved them in. "Get in, quick."

From the passenger side door, Christopher helped Agnes up and into the bench seat. The van doors closed and Ian drove out of the compound. He turned into a narrow dirt road and followed the fence line, his eyes on the main road that crossed the front of the lot.

As he merged into the main road, he swung right, into a wider, flatter, earth-packed road. "Both of you okay?"

His two shaken companions nodded.

"Where are we going?" Agnes said, as she removed the blanket from her back.

"Anywhere far enough, wherever that is."

Christopher looked out of the window, back to the house. "Sir, the way out of this place is the other way."

"Too late for that now." Ian noticed Agnes' leery eyes, fixed on him.

"You knew about this van, all along."

"Use of this van as an emergency vehicle was left at my discretion. What else can I say."

He spotted, too late, the open ground that marked the end of the packed-earth road. The van bucked as he floored the brakes. Ian reversed gears. Too late. The tires spun on soft ground.

"Sir, ease down. We're not going anywhere."

"We're far and safe enough, I think."

"Chris, step out," Agnes said. "I want to see it."

The engine sputtered and died. Before he could open his mouth, the two had already slipped out. They headed in the direction of the compound.

Ian stepped into the cargo hold. He turned on the interior lights. Utility compartments lined both sides of the van interior. The floor was padded and he saw three rolled blankets by the wayside. What looked like a monitor screen stared down into the interior from the top left corner. The green LED dot on its base suggested to him it might be an activated computer screen that was hibernating. He monkey-walked towards the van's double doors which had windows apiece, both of them quickly defogging. He unlatched the doors and threw them open.

Oven-like heat radiated into the cavernous interior. The van's open back framed the burning house a distance off.

Ian took a moment to observe Agnes and Christopher standing close together by the roadside dirt, her arm locked on his, as they watched the giant bonfire. The heat the house fire generated had squelched what would have been a frosty pre-dawn cold spell.

They couldn't have gone a quarter mile out into the wilderness. From their vantage point, it was clear the fire had already engulfed the house.

The inferno lit up landscapes for miles around. Plumes of white smoke blew windward, to the east, away from them. The horizon line and much of the skies disappeared. Window glasses from the doomed house shattered; collapsing wood frames popped and crackled. Ashes and embers drifted everywhere. "You two, get in here, now."

Agnes and Christopher backed away towards the van, their eyes intermittently on the conflagration. "I said get in here, quick. We get any of those embers in here, the van might catch fire."

The two climbed aboard and closed the twin doors. Agnes turned back and pressed close against the van's rear glass window. She put her right hand on the glass. Ian saw it coming, an uncalled-for blessing about to issue from her lips. He grabbed a rolled blanket.

"Rest in peace, Dan—"

She squealed as the rolled blanket landed square on her rear. "What the…"

"Let the man go. Don't say anything that might hold him back. He no longer needs our blessings or our goodwill. Think no more of him. Let him go."

The smolder in Agnes' eyes diminished. She sat on the floor and lowered her head. Ian knew his point had sunk in.

"He self-immolated," Agnes said in a small voice as if she was talking to herself. She closed her eyes. "You're right. He made this happen. We should think of him no more."

"What do we do now, sir?"

A swoosh came from the direction of the fire, like broken fire hydrants releasing pressurized water. Ian and his companions crowded the rear windows. Water jets, apparently from the water trucks, converged into the fire. Sensors rigged on the trucks probably activated the automated fire-control system.

Darkening smoke clouds, along with seething water vapor, enveloped the entire compound. No explosions. The fire must have spared the propane tanks on the mobile platform.

"They know what happened," Ian said, as he slipped back to the driver's seat. "We'd get an earlier pickup, that's for sure. This is it, our accommodations, for the time being. Gather any sleeping gear you can use and take whatever shut-eye you can get." He rolled up the cockpit windows up and left a crack, for ventilation.

Ashes and embers swirled outside. Daylight crept in through whatever part of the sky that the fire-borne smoke hadn't obscured. He yawned. He reclined the backseat.

Utility compartment doors on the cargo hold's sides banged and clattered. "There are pillows here," Christopher said. "Oh, a porta potty."

"Guys, we all step out for number one and number two."

"No problem here," Christopher said.

Agnes laid out a blanket on the floor. "Join us. There's space for the three of us here."

"I'm good here. For the umpteenth time, everybody, night-night."

Blue light flickered from the back of the van.

Someone cleared her throat, through a microphone.

From a computer screen at the left corner of the cargo hold, popped up the clear, well-put-together face of Dorothy Soon Smalls, solo in the back of a luxury vehicle, staring down on what must be a laptop lens. She bucked occasionally from her seat, indicating a bumpy ride.

She said in a complaisant tone:

"The three of you okay over there?"

"We could have gotten killed back there," Agnes shot back, almost to a growl.

Dorothy was taken aback, flustered, though she quickly recovered her professional composure.

Ian joined the two at the back of the van. Blindsided by the ferocity of Agnes' retort, Ian held fire and pondered on the situation. He could either join the fracas and possibly antagonize their employers, or he could mollify Agnes' defiance and risk a backlash from her. He contemplated a middle way.

"Agnes, please listen to me."

"How dare you people put us out there without warning us about the dangers we might face."

"We could have broken out earlier and sounded the alarm," Ian said, with intentional sarcasm. "But that would have whittled down our bonuses, wouldn't it? Ah, we're ordinary people. You wouldn't understand."

Dorothy's staid facial expression didn't hide the motherly empathy reflected in her eyes. A good sign. It might work, in case his hunch on the true source of Agnes' antagonism was true. After all, she had played them before.

Christopher raised his bandaged hand to the screen and pointed a finger to the side of his head. "I don't even have insurance for this."

Still at it, Agnes snarled at the screen. "I bet doctor Pershing is sleeping like a baby in some comfy far-away place."

"He's in Sacramento, boarding a helicopter. He would be here with us very soon. Agnes, Ian, Christopher. Please, listen to me. We've been monitoring you over the weekend from a base not far from here. We have emergency response teams on standby all the time. Right now, we're not far from the BLM road, with the fire department a half hour behind us. Whatever grievance you people have with us, and understandably so, let's deal with that later, privately. The most important thing is that all three of you are safe. All video records of the events that took place in the house were transmitted to us in real time. The hardware evidence, needless to say, was destroyed by the fire. The fire incident was an eventuality we had

prepared for but have never expected to happen. Please, we ask that you would honor your cover as film set house-sitters, should investigators ever talk with you."

"You have no contingencies for a fire?" Ian said. "Please, don't put us on a spot. Lying to investigators was never part of the deal."

"I know. We can make this right. It would be best for all of us if we get your cooperation. I'll tell you what you need to know in case you get asked. But first, my personal apologies. I am not Doctor Pershing's secretary. Like you, Agnes, I'm a psychic. I headed this project and many others like it for the last twenty-two years. Doctor Pershing trusted me to keep him updated on the events in the house. Every hour, every day, I saw your group come closer to drawing Daniel in, better than any other group had in the past. I took the risk. I did not recommend to my boss that he terminate the job when I should have."

"You mean Doctor Pershing is hearing about our horrifying weekend for the first time, right now?" Agnes said.

"Yes and No. Hours before the fire, I had already told him everything. I assumed then the project was about to end and that he needed to know. Doctor Pershing didn't need to be in the field monitoring station all the time. Keeping him updated was my responsibility. We discussed developments in your project. But I held back a lot on the goings on there. He wouldn't be able to interpret the video images anyway because it is our project policy to keep the monitoring devices in the public areas of the house mute. Privacy. Anyway, we can talk more about the many instances when I kept him in the dark, later. Can I talk to you people about your backstory, as a film set house-sitters, now?"

Ian moved closer to his companions, sought their eyes, and quietly communicated to them his position on Dorothy Small's request. He believed they both assented. He gazed up the screen and said, "Go ahead."

31

Windfall and Ashes

The dying embers inside the compound had all turned into ash heaps. An army of clean-up crew worked on them. Bulldozer and dump truck engines riled up what would have been a quiet morning in the valley. Nine a.m. No investigator dropped by to interview them. The fire brigade and the BLM reps had gone and the ground crew that remained were completely oblivious to Pershing's people and their fleet of luxury sports utility vehicles parked along the dirt road, not far from the gutted house. Dr. Pershing's helicopter had already landed a mile down east of the road. They could be his people, the ones working on the clean-up.

All freshened up and changed from the previous night's outfit, Ian and company sat inside a Toyota Land Cruiser parked on the packed-earth road. Several other sports utility vehicles lined the road in front of them. Christopher occupied the passenger's front seat. Agnes and Ian shared the backseat with Dorothy, who occupied the far end of the bench. Her eyes were on a laptop screen, fingers tapping at the keyboard.

It was coming down in real-time, an unbelievable windfall of a bonus, such that one wish had preoccupied Ian since Dorothy had started moving funds for direct deposit into their respective bank accounts: that no contrarian surprises would turn up to reverse their good fortune. Seated by the door side, he distracted himself from the onset of end-game anxiety by looking out the window, all the time hoping that Agnes would just shut the hell up. Christopher may not even be aware of it —the quiet back and forth between Dorothy and Dr. Pershing by radio, and how the old man's trusted associate had lobbied to up the team's bonus profile.

"What I get, they get. Has that been clear?" Agnes said, in the same cold tone that he presumed would have changed when Dorothy had announced Dr. Pershing had finally increased their final bonuses to a round million, each.

"Of course. As I said, Doctor Pershing had honored your wish. No hesitation, believe me. He also said that should you need financial planners to help you manage your money, he would provide each of you with one, for free. The title of the van would be given to Christopher, as you people agreed. Our company is also footing any medical expenses associated with the events that happened in the house. Please note that it may take a day for the bank funds to clear."

Not a sigh from Agnes. She sat straight, her arms folded.

By the window side, Ian took a deep breath and gazed up at the skies. He could have been an atheist and he would have learned to pray then and there.

"One last thing. Doctor Pershing would like to talk with all of you. He said he wanted to personally express his remorse for your ordeal. Of course, above all, he wanted to convey his gratitude, for the incalculable gift of peace the three of you have given him and his family. He had lived for this day, to know for sure his son's soul was set free. He told me to tell you in advance that it would take a while, for him to tell you stories about who Daniel was as a person. I do ask that you keep your minds open. Looking back crushes him. Please, also bear with the old man and his repetitiveness and his senti-mentalities. For sure, he would ask everyone about how

Daniel was. I just need to give you people a heads up on that."

A buzz on her walkie-talkie and she swiftly took the call. "Yes, sir... send Doctor Pershing over. I'm just about done here."

In the steely quiet in between idle talk—in the tension-filled process by which their final emoluments were negotiated —in the ever-looming threat that Agnes might talk out of turn —Ian knew any of those eventualities would have set off a panic attack if he hadn't been familiar with relaxation techniques that he had prescribed to hundreds of his clients in the past. Take deep breaths; have a handy safe-place imagery ready whenever anxiety sets in. Above all, nothing beats the firm reminder to oneself about the one recurring truth in life —that most of people's worst fears do not come true.

He could fill his lungs with fresh air now. The team had survived Agnes' meticulous once-over of the additional non-disclosure agreements and the liability escape clauses on the paperwork that they needed to sign prior to the funds' transfer. Among them, Christopher appeared coolest—if not detached —slouched as he were against the window glass, seemingly disinterested.

"There you go," Dorothy said, gaily, as she made an emphatic tap on the keyboard. "Like I said it would take a day for the funds to clear."

Steely silence from Agnes' camp. Great.

Ian has been itching for the opportunity to check his account. Dorothy had already returned all pre-assignment personal stuff that she had confiscated, including electronic gear. In better circumstances, he would have used his cell phone to peep at his treasure. He needed to step back, relax, and consider the deal ironclad closed.

Dorothy turned off her laptop and exited the car. "Doctor Pershing would be here any minute now." She smiled, reached out, and shook Agnes' hand and that of Ian's. Then Christopher's. "You people might meet Doctor Pershing further down the road. Not me. All the previous teams' attempts to get Daniel to cross over had failed. Those failures kept me employed all those years. Off the record, it did cross my mind, when you were in trouble over the weekend, to call off the project. Had I done so, I'm sure I'd still be working for the doctor, for many years to come."

"Why," Agnes said. "Why did you hold back?"

"I'm still processing the answer to that."

"I have a question," Christopher said. "You sure he's gone?"

From the car mirror, Ian saw Dr. Pershing, a man assisting him, cane-walking his way from a two-car length distance. Dorothy took notice. She moved closer and spoke low:

"Daniel did set the fire. We saw via micro-cam CCTV transmissions, a lone candle wandering around the dance floor. Its wick ignited and flamed up. It lit up several curtains before it traveled to the attic, where it made kindling out of paper there. After twenty-two years managing paranormal projects, I've never witnessed anything remotely close to what had happened in that house over the weekend. For us, there are still loose ends that we needed to tie up. Not for you. You may have heard about that old Chinese saying—when you reach the last page, close the book. For the three of you, this project is done."

"For what it's worth, we wish you people well," Ian said. He saw Agnes nod and smile at her.

"I'll see you again, Agnes, Ian, Christopher. In the afterlife, maybe."

32

The Hallway with High Windows

Into the wilderness road, the van brought up the convoy's rear. Christopher had volunteered to drive, despite three of his fingers being out of commission. A dead-tired Ian opted to sack out at the cargo hold, having pledged to foot any ticket should they be stopped down the road by the highway patrol for having neither seatbelt nor seat to show for his ride.

Agnes couldn't care less at that point. Whatever time of the day it was, and regardless of the legal integrity of their ride, her awareness that she was looking out to a world that in her entire life had never been that bright continued to grow.

They followed Dr. Pershing's Land Rover close enough that Agnes could see the old man reflected in the passenger-side mirror, occasionally smiling at them.

The old man had a hearty conversation with the team that lasted an interminable hour. It would have been much longer if Dorothy hadn't reminded him of their twice-changed lunch reservation in a restaurant down the way. Dr. Pershing insisted that the weekend team join them. They'd get another ear-bender session with him, for sure. It really mattered little at that point.

Agnes checked on the driver whom she caught the third

time smiling silly at her, whenever his eyes leave the road. Once, she saw him in her peripherals, casting a downward glance, ostensibly, at the van's passenger side knee well. The petite-size spare white blouse that Dorothy had provided her fitted well. But the gray skirt fell short at the low end, laying bare a good part of her thighs. His good fortune has to be enough distraction and she pushed the skirt's hem as far forward as she could.

"I can't believe we did it," Agnes said.

"You feel kind of light, huh?"

Agnes nodded.

"He's really gone, for good."

"For sure."

"Ellie's gone, too."

Agnes suspected innuendo as she observed Christopher's sticky grin. She looked away. It wasn't a good time to start a coquettish conversation with a driver who might be imagining, among other good things, a house blessing with his clan. Besides, Daniel still clung to her mind. She always considered her slumber dreams a bottomless trash bin where meaningless and chaotic imageries of the unconscious mind go. Yet over the weekend, her dreams about the innocent-looking young lovers came in perfect order and clarity. She heard their distinct voices and saw them in full color. On the dance floor, Daniel demonstrated dance movement techniques before a big, tripod-mounted camera, while Ellie, in the background, sabotaged his choreography with cartoonish mimicry. She heard Daniel groan and Ellie's high-pitched, mocking laugh as her partner patiently re-sets the scene.

At the attic, she witnessed the dying afternoon light streaming from the dormer windows and casting ghostly lights on the couple, as they roll on the floor and passionately kiss. In another scene, at a location she didn't recognize, she saw Ellie rub the top of Daniel's hand as if reassuring him things would be all right.

One scene set on the ground floor showed the lovers crab-crawl their way through the living room and into the hallway before they sneaked into the master bedroom. She heard the unmistakable slow creak in the hinges and the barely audible click in the lock.

Inside a room, threadbare of draperies and bed linens, the young lovers, muffled giggles in their throats, tiptoed their way into the bathroom. Thereupon, Daniel and Ellie fell on each other and bounced from one tile wall to another. She saw Daniel's hand go under her skirt and at the same moment flinch back as if he realized the limits.

She wished she had the chance to tell her weekend companions the intimate moments between the lovers, on the bare hallway floor in front of the restroom. She saw them there, several times, wearing different clothes, in various stages of undress, in that one spot that had always struck her as the darkest, dreariest part of the house. They were hiding from everyone else in the estate. The hallway, with its high windows, and its oblique position in relation to the other windows on the ground floor, would have been impervious to prying eyes. That spot was their subterfuge; their favorite haunt.

From the psychic community, she had met only two dream clairvoyants. From them she had a peek into their unique ability to relive in their dreams events that happened on specific locations where the psychic had slept on. Agnes never had that particular gift. Somehow, Daniel found a way to channel in her mind insights on the beautiful little world inside the empty house that became his and Ellie's playground. As if Daniel knew her enough to care to send her memories that he might not be able to take with him in the afterlife. It also gladdened her to think she'd be heading home with two new friends along with memories of one liberated spirit who had gifted her on their final night in his house, the three kisses that he laid on her very gently, very carefully.

"He healed me," Agnes said.

"You're saying something to me?"

"I said he healed me."

"Oh, I see."

She saw a tinge of disappointment on Christopher's face, as he turned his eyes back to the road ahead. She could almost hear his repartee, *"Do I get some credit?"* or something like it. She would have laughed at such comeback as a form of acknowledgment. Christopher kept to himself.

She glanced over her left shoulder. Ian curled in a jumble of blankets, dozing. She edged closer to the middle of the bench. She took Christopher's right hand and placed it on the top of her left knee. His hand was coarse and warm, like that of the men who once assaulted her. Yet she didn't shudder. Not at all. She looked out of the window and let her hand go. She felt his grip immediately tighten. In a moment, his hand started to slide further up. Agnes caught it and pressed on it a second or so before she lifted them away.

"Pay attention to the road." She spotted a bend down the road that sliced in between two tall rock outcroppings and pointed at it. Then she reached back for the paper bag that contained the used ill-fitting nightgown. It could be Daniel's gift to Ellie that day. She regretted putting it on. It should have been consumed by the fire.

She rolled the window down. "Slow down when I tell you. I'm tossing something out."

"Wait. This is public land. I don't think that's a good idea."

"I'll pay the fine."

"I really think you should burn it, in a kind of ritual, you know. Let's do it in your backyard or someplace private."

"I don't have a backyard."

"Maybe we can drive up to a desert place like this one time, make a bonfire, and—"

Agnes swung at him. "Okay."

"That's a yes, right?"

"Yeah, yeah, yeah. We're doing it."

"I'm really happy we're cool now."

"Can we forget the part when we weren't cool to each other?"

"Yeah. But first, I need to get something off my chest."

"Forget it, Chris. You get something off your chest, then I need to get something off mine, too. Between your drama and my drama, we get melodrama. Get my drift? I'm not in the mood for one right now."

"I really need to say something to you."

"All right, go ahead."

"You were once mean to me and I reacted by having fantasies about you in a bad way. I regretted them… my point is, some of Daniel's worst actions might not be entirely his." He raised his bandaged hand. "I deserved this."

Agnes pressed at his right arm gently. "When we get to the restaurant, remind me to change the dressing, okay?"

It turned gloomy as they drove in between the rock outcroppings. The van shimmied. Agnes still wanted to jettison the nightgown. She'll just raincheck a future meet-up with Christopher. She intended to link up with him anyway to thank him personally, another time. On second thought, she decided to keep the gown, for now. The gown is the last existing relic from Daniel's affair with Ellie. She either had to burn it soon or she must turn it over to Doctor Pershing.

Sunlight returned, and when she looked down at the white sleepwear in her lap, she noticed dark, squiggly markings at the hem of the skirt. Upon closer look, the marks were clearly burns seared into the cotton fabric's surface. She felt goosebumps rising from her shoulders and nape while she unraveled the ruffled fabric. She recognized the individual letters. They resembled the doorway number scrawls and the candle soot writing on the master bedroom ceiling that Daniel's spirit had tried to finish. She straightened the hem fabric. The burn marks read:

Thank you, Agnes.

She stuffed the nightgown back into the shopping bag and dropped them on the floor. She rolled up the window and leaned her head on it. She tried to distract her mind with the beautiful scenery. None worked. She closed her eyes and tried to hold it in.

"What's wrong?"

She held it until she realized holding it up only made it worse. She let it go.

THE END

Author's Notes

You've reached the end of the book and I'd like to thank you for the journey you took with me across the pages of this novel. If you had enjoyed the read, I'd truly appreciate it if you'd leave a review on Amazon.

The author-reader journey is a shared experience and at the end of the road the reader is the final arbiter on what the work's true value is. Only through reviews and ratings, however, that you complete the feedback loop.

For our part, we read feedbacks and take them to heart. We deem criticism—the positive, the negative, and those in between—as a means to improve our storytelling craft. Over time, insights we glean from reviews also help enhance our literary sensibilities. Your review posting efforts, in fact, makes you an active participant in an indie author's writing and publishing evolution.

If for any reason you didn't find time to leave a review, this author is grateful enough that you had taken this one journey with him to the last pages of the book.

Best wishes to you and I hope to meet you again down the road for another shared literary experience.

Acknowledgments

I'd like to thank family and friends for their generous support through the years. Again, to those who cared, thank you.

About the Author

Ursus Ariston writes in various speculative fiction genres. He also pens thrillers, contemporary/mainstream fiction, short stories, and dabbles in screenwriting. The former Philippine journalist immigrated to the United States in 1993. When he isn't scrunched in his desk, the author hangs out with his kin, all of them located within a square-mile radius in Los Angeles. He likes to walk and jog in the backyard or at the beach, always ruminating on his next projects and daydreaming on his bucket list.

Made in the USA
Columbia, SC
03 March 2023

13192957R00157